PENGUIN BOOKS
BLASPHEAR

Sohail Ahmed, who writes under the pen name of Sohail Rauf, has a PhD in electrical engineering and works for an engineering firm. Originally from Pakistan, he lives near Houston, Texas, with his wife and two children. *Blasphear* is his first novel.

'Sacred and scary games in Punjab. This is an earnest warning of a novel about perils of too much religion and too little humanity'—Mohammed Hanif, author of *The Case of Exploding Mangoes* and *Our Lady of Alice Bhatti*.

'A journey into the labyrinth of Pakistan, where a routine suicide investigation takes us into the world of religious parties, the blasphemy laws, a lynching and ordinary lives getting intertwined with forces that they cannot control. A deft and fast-paced work about very contemporary trends in South Asia'—Saba Naqvi, journalist and author of *The Saffron Storm: From Vajpayee to Modi*.

'With a Chekhovian eye for select details and a remarkable insight into the culture and habitat within which his novel *Blasphear* is placed, Sohail Rauf tells an extraordinary tale of happenings—lynching, murder, betrayal and despair—that would have been considered unusually tragic. However, the perpetual recurrence of a tragedy—as is the case in Pakistan—turns it into a commonplace incident. Rauf does not allow that to happen. Through a combination of his deep courage as a writer and formidable artistic ability, he poses a challenge to the spectres of bigotry, fanaticism, trickery and violence that hover above our heads'—Harris Khalique, poet and author

BLASPHEAR

A novel

S O H A I L   R A U F

PENGUIN BOOKS
An imprint of Penguin Random House

PENGUIN BOOKS

Penguin Books is an imprint of the Penguin Random House group of companies whose addresses can be found at global.penguinrandomhouse.com

Published by Penguin Random House India Pvt. Ltd
4th Floor, Capital Tower 1, MG Road,
Gurugram 122 002, Haryana, India

First published in Penguin Books by Penguin Random House India 2024

ISBN 9780143466833

Typeset in Adobe Caslon Pro by Manipal Technologies Limited, Manipal

www.penguin.co.in

Dedicated to all those who are wrongfully
accused of blasphemy

Mein darta hoon musarrat se
Kahin ye meri hasti ko
Bhula kar talkhiyan saari
Bana de dewataon saa.

[I'm scared of ecstasy
Lest it should make me forget all bitterness
And transform my existence
Into something like gods'.]

In the memory of
Ammi and Abba Jaan
And for
Tallat, Saalaar and Soha

1

Waqas

Present day

'Waqas, they found the body of a boy hanging from a ceiling fan.'

It was the early hours, and the police station was slowly stirring to life. Lights were being switched on and people were getting their desks ready for the day. Station house officer (SHO) Inspector Shakir Qazi gathered the files still scattered across his table from the day before and threw them with a thud into the 'Out' tray, which grated and almost slipped off the table.

Standing with my hands crossed behind my back, I watched him. *You're a fool if you think I'll steady the tray, Shakir.*

Shakir cursed the tray and dragged it back to its position. 'In Shanti Nagar. Find out what happened,' he added.

'Shanti Nagar, sir?'

Shakir tore some papers into pieces and hurled them into a dustbin behind the table. 'That's where the blasphemy riots took place a few months ago. Don't you know?' Shakir spoke in

1

his usual hurried tone of disbelief and irritability. He was a tall, thin man—except for a pot belly—and appeared to channel the energy of his frail frame into his anger. 'It happened before you were posted here. But you must have heard about it—on the news?' he asked.

'I have,' I replied. I remembered the gory incident vaguely, having followed it through newspapers. Fareeha would switch to another TV channel each time the riots were covered. She knew I'd be upset.

'If they insist it's a suicide, find out if an autopsy is needed. Also, see if we can arm-twist the family. If they're well off—Shakir finally looked up at me, but did he see the disgust on my face?—'they might pay under the table to hush up the case. Now hurry up. I've got other things to take care of.'

Shakir opened the table drawers and slammed them back, one by one, without looking inside. '*Behan chod*!' he cursed.

Did he call me a sister-fucker? No, he almost certainly said that to the stubborn drawer.

A suicide investigation was the last thing on my mind. All morning, I'd been thinking over Fareeha's concerns about the new house we had moved into two days ago: no running water, two bulbs missing, one power outlet that gave her a shock, giant rats roaming around in the kitchen, my second uniform which she forgot to pack before we moved . . . But wasn't I glad to leave the police station and its awful ventilation! If it was hot outside, the inside was a boiler. Even the location impeded office work. We sat in the middle of a bazaar, listening all day to the screech of blacksmiths at work and the quibbles of shopkeepers, tonga wallahs, rickshaw drivers and cyclists.

Before leaving the station, I called Fareeha. 'Do not worry about unpacking; just focus on making the kitchen functional,'

I told her. She said she would and sighed. An unorganized home always did that to her. I imagined her sitting on a carton and wondering where to start while the kids ran amok around her.

Accompanied by my small team, I drove to the boy's house in a noisy, clunky, tank-like jeep, which I parked outside the double-storey coffee-brown building standing out among the crop of smaller houses in the neighbourhood. Dust clouds rose as the jeep pulled in. The crowd gathered near the entrance made way for us.

Did people notice my short stature and wrinkled black shirt, or did the police jeep and dark glasses pack a punch? Taking a deep breath, I exhaled, then issued instructions to my subordinates before stepping towards the door. A man in his early thirties emerged from the small crowd.

'You want to come inside, Inspector Sahib?' he asked.

'And you are?' I asked, relieved that someone had volunteered to come forward.

'I'm his—Hasan's—brother.'

The man wore a brown shalwar-kameez and looked a mess, with unkempt hair and a tear blotched unshaven face. He glanced uneasily past me at the dispersing crowd.

Talking to mourners constricted my throat. Should one be nice or formal? Which was the right way? 'I'm sorry about the demise of your brother,' I finally blurted out.

He led me through a small parking space in which a white Suzuki Cultus appeared to have been force-fitted, its rear end touching the closed gate. We entered through the narrow passage past the car into a drawing-cum-dining room. A dining table dominated one corner of the large room, and two sofa sets stood against opposing walls. Leftover utensils, a dupatta and books were strewn across the room which, smelling of what was probably last night's chicken curry, needed air and light.

'Please have a seat,' the man said, motioning towards the sofas.

As I sat down, I removed my glasses and tucked them into my shirt pocket. After an awkward pause, he sat down on the sofa opposite me.

'What's your name?' I asked, as I reached into my pocket for my diary.

'Jawad, sir.' He wiped the sweat on his forehead with the front of his kameez, revealing a large belly, and then dropped it promptly.

'Okay, Jawad. What happened?'

Jawad took some time to gather his thoughts. The soft whir of the fan blades came to a halt with a melancholic grind. It became hotter and more suffocating in the room—and silent. Sweating, I unbuttoned the top of my black shirt. Summer was not a good season for people to die.

An older man inched into the room warily and sat beside Jawad. 'This is my father,' Jawad said, with a glance at the older man.

The man nodded as a gesture of salaam. I nodded back. Through the open door, I could see women and children moving around the house, some of them peeking at me every so often.

'What happened? Who will tell me?'

Father and son looked at each other awkwardly. Then the son spoke jerkily, 'When we woke up this morning, we found Hasan hanging from the ceiling fan. We brought him down.' He paused and licked his parched lips, as if recalling something. 'I mean we cut the bed-sheet he hanged himself with . . . And laid him on the bed. He was dead . . . Then we informed the police.'

'How old was he?'

'Seventeen.' Jawad looked at his father, who blinked his eyes. I took that as an agreement.

'Islam. It's all about Islam.' An old woman, perhaps in her late seventies, uttered these words. She seemed to have appeared out of nowhere. She trudged forward until she stood close to me. Putting her hand on my shoulder for support, she gathered her breath and resumed. 'He was a gem, my boy. Until he got into . . .'

When she paused for breath, I wondered if I should stand up. I didn't.

'Amma, please go inside,' Jawad's father said, rising to his feet, looking embarrassed.

He held her shoulders and turned her towards himself. With tears flowing down her wrinkled face and a stooping posture, she looked miserable. The older man helped her out of the room. Had she wanted to say something more?

'She's my grandmother,' Jawad said. A mournful wail came from somewhere in the house.

'No backup power?' I asked, fanning my neck with the collar of my shirt.

'No. Yes—no. We have one, but the battery has failed.'

'Well, that's . . .' I trailed off. How could I complain about the electricity when these people were mourning their dead?

'Where's the body?' I asked.

'Upstairs. In the room where Hasan was sleeping.'

'After I finish, we will send him—the body—to a cold room. No burial until I let you know.'

Jawad nodded. His father returned, wringing his hands.

I continued, 'Who found him?'

'Ammi. I mean, my mother. She went to his room to wake him up. He goes—went—to college.'

'I want to see the room.'

We stood up and both men waited for me to follow. My entry into the inner house, which smelled of cinnamon, mint and sweat, caused a stir. Women and children made way for me as Jawad led me through a small lounge and up a staircase. A commotion resulted from the many shoes on the tiled stairs.

On the upper floor, a terrace faced the street and two rooms sat at the rear. The heat was unbearable, and I stopped at the door as I surveyed the smaller, almost square room. I motioned to Jawad, who pulled the curtains on the window, finally affording us some light. The body lay on the bed, covered by a flowery yellow and blue bed-sheet. Even in the dim light, it looked fresh, perhaps recently bought. Fareeha would have been quick to notice the irony of fate. As I slid aside the bed-sheet, my heartbeat quickened. Thanks to a beard, the boy looked older than his age. I touched the side of his neck near the windpipe. There was no pulse.

'Who moved the bed?' I asked.

It looked disoriented. Someone had dragged its foot to position it below the ceiling fan.

'It was like this when we—Ammi—entered,' Jawad said. 'We haven't touched anything.'

'Call your mother.'

Helped by Jawad, a woman, perhaps in her late fifties, entered the room. She had red eyes, puffy and wet. She first wiped her tears and then the sweat on her brow with the dupatta on her head.

'What did you see?' I asked.

Damn! That was callous. I restarted, 'Take it easy, Amma Ji. Take your time.'

'I knocked on the door this morning. It was locked from inside,' she said slowly.

'How did you enter, Amma Ji?'

'Through the balcony door, over there.' She pointed at a screen door made of wire gauze and a wooden frame. The adjoining door, all wooden, stood wide open.

I walked to the screen door and pushed it. It opened with a mournful creak to a balcony.

Jawad said, 'The balcony can also be accessed through the other room, which is next to this one.'

'Do you keep the balcony door open? Anyone can climb up the balcony and enter the room?' I asked.

Below me, I saw an empty plot of land, littered with old furniture and trash. The smell of garbage and rotten fruit assailed my nostrils. But the cooler air was a relief.

'We only keep the screen door closed to let the air in,' Jawad said. He then turned to his mother and said, 'Ammi Ji, please speak.'

She said, 'I thought the screen door would be latched, but . . .'—she steadied herself against the door frame, taking in a shaky breath—'I could at least look inside and see what was up with Hasan. I found it open.'

'Could someone have come in during the night?' I asked as I re-entered the room and pointed towards the balcony.

The family members looked at each other, before the mother whispered, looking away from the bed, 'Hasan is— was—careless. He often forgot to latch the door.'

'What did you see when you entered?'

'He was . . . hanging from . . .' The woman burst into tears. Jawad put his arms around her.

I looked away and surveyed the room. A grey, plastic stool lay toppled in the middle of the floor. Jawad said, 'Looks like he stood on this stool and then kicked it away after putting his neck in the noose.'

'You don't need to do the police's work. Leave that to me. Just answer my questions,' I said.

The mother was still in tears. Another woman entered and helped her out of the room. An uneasy silence prevailed, adding to the suffocation in the room. A child cried in another part of the house.

Ashraf, an assistant sub-inspector, entered the room and gestured with his right forefinger that he wanted to talk. I took him to the balcony.

'What is it?'

'Sir,' ASI Ashraf said, 'The boy may have had links with the religious party, Deen-e-Kamil. Many of its followers have been seen near the house. This looks like a sectarian issue. Maybe you can confirm it with the family.'

Ashraf was a sensible chap, although his rustic mannerisms belied it. When I reported to this police station a few days ago, I learnt from my superiors that Ashraf was one of the few officers who knew their job.

Back inside the room, I asked the anxious looking Jawad and his father to return to the drawing room. I also instructed Ashraf to send the corpse to the morgue before sealing the room. I added, 'I need statements from all the members of the family, including the women. Get one or two lady constables here. Ask them to talk to the women one by one, in isolation and to record their statements.'

I resumed my questions once we entered the drawing room.
'Was Hasan into drugs or something?'

'No, I'm sure he wasn't,' Jawad's father replied. He looked
like a penitent convict in a courtroom.

'Had he joined any political or religious party?'

'I don't think so,' the old man whispered and cleared
his throat.

'Really? Then what are those mullahs doing outside
your house?'

It was Jawad who answered. 'We don't know, sir. He had
some religious friends. If he'd become active in a party, he
didn't tell anyone in the family.'

'Any family feuds? Money matters? Anyone you think
might have wanted to kill him?'

Both men stared, like schoolkids who knew that anything
they said would be a wrong answer. Then Jawad said, 'No.
None at all.'

'Alright. This investigation is not over. I'll call you two to
the police station soon.'

As I left the house, I noticed the men Ashraf had spoken
about. With their shalwars tucked up above their ankles and
their heads covered by white caps or turbans, these bearded men
certainly belonged to a religious outfit. Most of them stood apart
against different walls, seeking protection from the scorching sun.

Jawad's grandmother's words reverberated in my head again.
What were these men doing here? Were they just curious about
a boy's death or did they want to do what they had managed
to . . . to scare the people? Wouldn't the Hindu families living
in this town feel alienated in this milieu of men whose Islam
consisted of little more than threats against disobedience? Why
did something as sacred as a beard and the way they dressed

become symbols of fear? Muhammad, our Prophet, loved a beard. Abba's beard made his face so angelic, the almost black colour lent a luminous halo to his face. Why did these beards appear so scary? Had she seen those men, Fareeha would have begged me to walk away, to have nothing to do with this case.

As I opened the jeep door, I saw a piece of paper lying on the front seat. Before I could read it, I heard a familiar voice behind me.

'Hello, Inspector Waqas.'

My heart missed a few beats. It was Amber, my university classmate, now a seasoned journalist. I turned around to face her. Thanks to her almost see-through, off-white kurta and dark glasses, she looked, amid the dust and heat, like a UFO in the desert.

'Sub-inspector, not inspector. At least this time around, the police have come before the media,' I said, trying not to look overawed by her height—she was half an inch taller than me— and allure.

Oh, God! I had invited trouble. She wouldn't let go of this opportunity to mock my English accent.

'Men always come earlier than they should. That's why I never married.' I had no answer to her retort. 'However, I appreciate your willpower as you try to peel your eyes off places where they shouldn't be; you are certainly doing better than a maulana I spoke to a minute ago. Anyway, what have you found out about the murder?'

'Murder? It looks like a suicide. But we're digging out the facts.'

'That's the reply I'd get from any policeman,' she said, looking around. 'You should do better as you've benefited from a university education and my company.'

'I'm serious. That's all I know.'

'Any connection to the blasphemy riots that took place two months ago?'

'Can't say yet, but I don't think so. You say this because both occurrences happened in the same town?' I tried to sound as if I had all the angles covered.

'My gut feeling says they're related. The maulana I talked to disclosed, in passing, that the boy was a member of their party, the Deen-e-Kamil, which was behind the blasphemy riots. Revenge could've been a motive.'

'Possibly,' I said, trying to wrap up the conversation. I was aware that people might see Amber as an ultra-modern journalist; her presence somehow made me uneasy.

A vegetable seller, a young man in jeans and T-shirt, a garb that didn't fit his profession—was I seeing dividing lines everywhere?—had parked his cart right behind the jeep. I gestured to him to move aside, which he did smartly, steering the cart like a stroller.

'I need to talk to you. Later, maybe. About something else. I have to go now,' I said, as Amber turned away. Sitting in the jeep, I noticed the piece of paper again. It read, 'Sir, I have some information about Hasan, the boy who died. Please call me. Furqan.' There was a mobile number at the end. I glanced around to see if the writer of the note was nearby, but I couldn't guess who it might be.

Back at the police station, I called Ashraf to my office as soon as he returned. He stroked his thick moustache, ordered Rooh Afza drinks for us, and said, 'Hasan's household consisted of the parents, a grandmother and four siblings, including him. The eldest is Jawad, the one you spoke to. He's married and has a kid. The next oldest is a sister, twenty-something, who goes to an evening institute.'

A clang from the blacksmith's forge behind the police station jolted us. It sounded like the collapse of a metal tower.

'Yaar, how do you guys work here? This tun tun is maddening!' I griped.

My office, a cubicle in a corner of a large hall, with a window opening into the bazaar, offered no respite from the noise.

I added, 'By the way, who chose this site for the police station?'

'Here, enjoy this Rooh Afza, sir.' He took a glass from the tray brought in by the canteen wallah and placed it in front of me. 'It will refresh you. We've gotten used to the din; you will too.'

I gulped the drink down in one go. Oh, the comfort! But it was as short-lived as it was welcome.

'Not happening. Anyway, go on.'

'Hasan, who was in his late teens, used to go to college. Then there's another sister, a few years younger.'

Ashraf read from a diary, a small pocketbook with black binding and a rubber band around it. Well-organized people impressed me.

'Learnt anything about their income?'

'Jawad and his father run a garment shop somewhere near the Rungreza bazaar a few kilometers from here. The shop does well. Now a little bit about Shanti Nagar, since you're new here, sir; it's a lower middle-class locality with a sizeable Hindu population, a fact that counted in the recent blasphemy case.'

Sizeable. Really? My knowledge of the region's demography told me the Hindu population all over Punjab was scant. But before I could comment, Shakir called me to his office.

'What took you so long?' He jumped up from his chair as soon as I walked in. 'I like to go prepared when I brief Deputy Superintendent of Police (DSP) Sahib. You've left me no time. You'll answer all the questions.'

DSP Abdul Khaliq was a soft-spoken man who seemed likeable despite—or perhaps because of—his paunch. A few minutes with him and you'd feel he wouldn't harm you, although that wasn't always the case, I had heard. He could be harsh, especially when he filed his subordinates' annual evaluation reports. His air-conditioned office, which was close to our police station, was not a bad place to be in while at work.

Once Shakir and I sat down, Khaliq asked me to brief him. I narrated my observations to him. 'Without an autopsy, it's difficult to say if it is a case of suicide or not. One noteworthy piece of information is that he had recently joined Deen-e-Kamil, which means it could be a sectarian issue. And that means trouble.'

'Sir, I would stay away and accept the obvious, which is suicide. The religious parties will pounce on anything to stir up trouble. The dust of their previous mischief has not yet settled,' Shakir said.

Gone was his eagerness to blackmail the family. So wary of the mullahs? A Faiz couplet leapt to my mind:

Kher, dozakh mein meh milay na milay.
Sheikh sahib se jaan tau chootey gi.

[Well, I may or may not find wine in hell.
But at least I'll be rid of the mullah.]

'Wait a minute,' Khaliq said. 'Waqas, you said someone might have climbed up the rear wall, entered his room and hanged him, making it look like a suicide. A rival sectarian group— which one is that?'

'Millat-e-Islam, sir,' Shakir chipped in.

'Yes, the Millat-e-Islam. Don't they crop up like sham housing schemes? The rival party wouldn't kill like that. They like to make a statement, create an impact.'

Khaliq had a point, which sounded ironic in his shrill voice and apologetic tone. 'Besides,' he said, sounding scholarly as he leaned back in his swivel chair, 'during the recent blasphemy riots, these two parties supported each other.'

'Good point, sir.' Shakir looked at me for a riposte. Bloody bootlicker!

I said, 'Sir, these religious parties have strange ways. Their belief justifies anything to them. I'm not really suggesting sectarian rivalry. What I mean is that because of the Deen connection, we will face stiff resistance, especially on the autopsy issue. What's your advice? If you say it's important, we'll go for an autopsy.'

'Let's see who wants an autopsy. His family? His party? If no one does, what blessings do we gain from carrying out an autopsy?' Khaliq was delivering one gem after another, all the while reclining in his enormous chair, as if discussing a cricket match rather than a death.

He continued, 'Meet the boy's party. The Deen-e-Kamil. Find out what they're up to. But be tactful. Don't sound like you're offering them the option. I'm sure Islam doesn't obstruct the path to justice, but most of the people tutored by the mullahs think autopsy is un-Islamic. If they point a finger at the other party—Millat, I mean—then meet them and get to know their story.'

He instructed his PA on the intercom about what his wife needed for dinner, indicating that the meeting was over.

Back in my office, I asked Ashraf to call Jawad and his father. 'Tell them to be here by noon. Also, find out where we can meet the Deen people.'

'Sir, they have an office in Shanti Nagar. If you want, we can go there right away.'

In a few minutes, Ashraf and I sat in the office of the Deen-e-Kamil. It was perhaps the living room of a large but poorly constructed house turned into a madrasah. From the outside, the madrasah could have been a warehouse. There was no signboard on the wall. The man behind a small desk had a long, nicely combed beard. He introduced himself as Maulana Saleem Ur Rehman. I recalled seeing his face on giant posters, several feet long, tied to poles on the rooftops. With Deen-e-Kamil flags, buntings and pamphlets all over town and loudspeakers bellowing out his lectures on repeat, he was a ubiquitous presence in the town. A bit like an Orwellian Big Brother— Amber introduced me to *1984*, one of the few English novels I read with her help. I wanted to ask Saleem if Islam permitted the portrayal of the human face but decided it was unwise to trigger a debate. Instead, I went straight to the point.

'This boy Hasan, whose dead body was found in his home, had links with your group, Maulana Sahib,' I began slowly while surveying the small office, which was a vestibule to the madrasah.

With one desk and a few chairs placed against the wall, there was little room for walking. Ashraf and I, and another member of the madrasah, a quiet looking young man, took the chairs. Behind Saleem, a wall-mounted bookshelf stuffed with religious books, files and loose papers looked disorderly. *The Clash of Civilizations* by Samuel P. Huntington and a few other English works caught my attention. More surprising was the slim volume of Meeraji published by Oxford University Press. The poet's sketch on the front page showed long hair neatly combed back. What was a bohemian poet doing on a mullah's bookshelf?

Before the maulana could speak, I said, 'It's interesting that you have books by Western authors in your collection.'

The maulana smiled and leaned forward, placing his elbows on the small table. He had a long face with a beautiful, chiselled nose and almond-shaped dark eyes. 'Contrary to the general perception, we try to understand our rivals' point of view. We read their books. That also helps us prepare our counterarguments.'

Judging by his assured mannerisms and sonorous voice, he appeared educated. However, from the dust on the books and the bookshelf, it didn't look like anyone had recently read a book from that bookshelf.

'I never expected to see Meeraji in your collection. Anyway, going back to Hasan . . .'

'Yes, Inspector Sahib. He was a good boy, learning the *deen*. But he hadn't formally joined us.'

'Which deen do you mean? Deen, the party or deen, the religion?'

I leaned back in my chair and shook my right foot, which rested on my left knee. This posture somehow gave me confidence. Leaning forward slightly, Ashraf sat quietly like an obedient boy.

'They're the same. As you know, *kamil* means perfect. Deen-e-Kamil means the perfect religion, the perfect way of life.'

Inside the madrasah, a child swore loudly as he played with his cohorts. I couldn't help smiling at the irony. Saleem acted as if he hadn't heard anything.

I asked, 'Do you think the Millat people may be involved?'

'You're suggesting it's a murder. But that's not how religious parties operate.'

The maulana paused as he realized he had almost confessed that the two parties targeted their opponents. I suppressed my laughter again.

He continued, 'I mean, why would Millat kill our member? We're trying to forget our differences. You know, Inspector Sahib, Islam is very simple. All of us, whatever the school of thought, have faith in one Allah. Millat supported us in our campaign against those trying to commit sacrilege against our deen. You know about that.'

The maulana was alluding to the blasphemy riots. I listened patiently.

'With the blessings of Allah, we remained united and brought the blasphemers to the end that Allah has decreed. That's why I'm sure Millat wouldn't do anything like that.'

'Any thoughts on what may have prompted him to take his own life? After all, he was on the path to strengthening his faith. Someone like him isn't expected to commit suicide. It's forbidden in Islam.'

'Yes, the boy sinned. But then, this world is an evil place. We don't know what went on within the four walls of that house.'

'What do you mean? Do you suspect anyone from the family?'

Leaning back again, he took ages to respond. 'I hardly know them,' he said finally. 'What I mean is that a family conflict or quarrel might have triggered the events that led to Hasan's suicide. You know how emotional youngsters can be.'

'What are your views—I mean, Islam's take—on carrying out an autopsy? What if we go for a post-mortem to ascertain the cause of death?'

'You make it sound like the police would listen to us,' the maulana said with a smile—he could kill someone with it—cloaking sarcasm. Faiz must have had the maulana in mind when he coined the epithet *waayiz-e-chabak zuban*—a preacher with a whip-like tongue.

'But because you asked, here's my humble viewpoint. Islam forbids mutilation of the deceased. It doesn't matter if it's expected to help in fact finding. As it's against Islam, it will eventually lead to chaos rather than wisdom. It's time our society realizes that in everything—and I mean everything—we must seek guidance from Allah. Make everything subservient to Allah and see how society prospers, Inspector Sahib.'

I thanked the maulana for his time—for his pearls of wisdom too, I wished to add but didn't—and left.

When I returned to the police station, I found Jawad and his father sitting on a bench in the veranda under a noticeboard and staring at the floor. I called them to my cubicle and asked them to sit down.

'Do you want to press charges against anyone? My investigation tells me it might be a suicide case.' I paused—did the work of the last few hours count as an investigation? 'But if the victim's family thinks it was a murder, we'll go for an autopsy.'

Father and son looked at each other. They were in more presentable shalwar-kameezes now but appeared to have returned from a long journey, their brows creased with worry.

I said, 'You can go back to the veranda and discuss it in private if you want.'

They nodded and left the room but returned after a while with tentative footsteps and furrowed brows.

'We're not interested in an autopsy,' Jawad said. Both remained standing.

'We might ask you to sign a few documents.' I analysed their faces. 'You two can go now.'

I asked Ashraf to draft a report before we closed the case. As I reached inside my khaki trouser pocket for my phone, I discovered the note I had found in the jeep in the morning. I nearly threw it in the bin, but on second thoughts, I dialled the number written on it.

'Hello.' He immediately took the call, as if he had been waiting for it. The voice sounded gruff, like that of a boy who had recently reached the age of adolescence.

'I'm Sub-inspector Waqas Mahmood. Who is this? You left your number in my jeep.'

'Yes, sir. My name is Furqan.' The voice lowered to a whisper. 'I have some information about Hasan, the boy who died. He is . . . was my friend. It might be helpful for the police.'

I was in two minds. Should I listen to him or should I forget about it? Finally, I asked, 'Where can we meet?'

'Sir, there is a small hotel near Hasan's house. I will text you the address.'

'Okay. Let's meet at seven. Does that work for you?'

'Yes, I'll be there.'

2

Furqan

Six years ago

I first met Hasan when I moved to a new school in grade five.

Abba had managed to get me admitted to an expensive school. I discovered, though, that it wasn't half as good as it claimed to be. It was one of those pseudo-English medium schools that attracted parents with fancy labs, colourful Parents' Days and festive events. One thing the school did was accentuate my inferiority complex. My dreams of our bungalow and a shiny car became more frequent.

Another annoying thing about the new school was the mandatory summer camp, which spoiled my holidays. Ammi said it was one more way of fleecing the parents and making them pay for something the children didn't need. The school allowed us to wear informal clothes, rather than the school uniform, during the summer camp to make us think we were at a funfair. For boys like me, that was an additional worry because I didn't have enough clothes to wear to school. Ammi said I could wear the school uniform, her one-dress-for-all-occasions solution. I had even gone to a wedding reception in my grey-and-white school dress. All I did there was hide from people's mocking eyes.

'This boy always wears his school uniform. Doesn't he have any other clothes?' was something I had heard a few times at school.

My approach was to pretend I had not heard it until one day another voice said, 'Furqan, he wants to outsmart you with his expensive clothes because he knows he can't beat your grades.'

Surprised, I lifted my gaze from the pavement and discovered that the words had come from Hasan. I knew little about him then, though we were in the same class. The plump boy with the expensive clothes had slipped away.

'Why do you let them talk that way to you?' Hasan asked, as he walked in step with me. 'Hit them back.'

'Okay.' This utterance must have told him how hard I could hit back.

'You're pretty good in your studies. Don't be afraid of them. Let me know if someone bothers you.'

'You read a lot?' He found me sitting in the classroom another day, using the lunch break to read an Urdu novella on Tarzan. Most of the other boys were running around, screaming and throwing chalk at each other. 'If you have some books to share, we can do an exchange. I have some too.'

Hasan and I became good friends because of our book exchange. From that first meeting until a few months before his death, I held him in awe. He was smarter, cooler, wiser, richer and better mannered—better than me in every way.

I even thought he was good-looking, although he was slightly hefty.

He usually rode his bicycle to school, but sometimes we walked together. I visited Hasan's home occasionally. It was nicely furnished and bigger than mine but by no means the mansion my eyes saw it to be. He had his own room, which was always untidy. I thought to myself, if I ever owned a separate room, I'd keep it sparkling like a car showroom. We studied together, read and discussed books, and watched movies. Sometimes, his grandmother, whom he called Dadu, trudged in, prayer beads in hand, and kissed him on the cheek. He pretended to be angry and asked her to make up for it by telling us a story. She made a few starts, only to be reminded by Hasan, 'We've heard that one.'

'You've heard all my stories. I've nothing new, Bandar.'

Often, Hasan agreed to listen to one of her favorite stories about Prophet Muhammad, Alif Laila, Ameer Hamza or one about his grandfather. She spoke slowly, with frequent interruptions, coughing and conversing with Hasan's mother about one thing or another. These disruptions irritated Hasan, but I enjoyed even the breaks. They added to the story's suspense.

We also flew kites. Lubna, his older sister, joined us sometimes. I never learnt to fly kites but Hasan and Lubna were champions. I held the kite until they were ready and gave it the initial push upward, or held the ball of string while they flew the kites. Once, her long, flowing dupatta obstructed her view. Hasan laughed, and I joined him. 'Why don't you take it off?' he asked.

'Can't you see those men ogling at me from their rooftops? And that aunt over there? She will squeal on me to Ammi.'

Lubna adjusted her dupatta with one hand and handled the kite expertly with the other. '*Tauba*, look at this audacious girl!' She mimicked the aunt, sending Hasan and me into peals of laughter.

'Don't worry about Ammi or any aunt,' Hasan said, eyeing the kite in the sky. 'Dadu is there to take care of them. Watch out for that male chauvinist kite swooping in to cut your flying string off.'

'Don't worry, Brother. I'm up to the challenge.'

* * *

A year later, when I met Ram and Mohan, I didn't know it would be the start of a beautiful friendship. How it would end was even less foreseeable.

'Boys and girls, come to my place and get some toffees!' I shouted, not exactly at the top of my lungs, as I should have. Customarily, these words had to be shouted loudly with the right pauses, almost in a sing-song fashion, to let everyone know that a certain family was distributing eatables. This ritual of calling children always made me self-conscious because it drew everyone's attention towards me. So when I saw a boy eyeing me inquisitively, I felt myself sweating.

'You want to grab a sweet?' I asked him.

'Are you selling them?' The boy looked unsure. He was thin, with a brown complexion. He was obviously new to the neighbourhood, else he would not have asked this question.

'No. They're free. My Ammi asked for something from Allah. I don't know what it was, but she got what she wanted so she's giving out these sweets as a token of gratitude. I'm supposed to call the neighbourhood kids to come and grab one. You want one?'

'I'm a Hindu. Am I allowed?' He looked funny, with his legs sticking out of his short shorts—he must have outgrown them a long time back—like two sticks.

It was my turn to be unsure. 'Wait, I'll check with Ammi.'

Ammi sat just beside the door, holding a bag of sweets from which she handed out one sweet to each child.

'Can I give one to a Hindu boy?' I asked.

Ammi was too busy to think about it. Without much consideration, she said yes. I picked up a candy and gave it to the boy. He thanked me.

'You want to try calling the other kids?' I asked.

'Yes, sure. What do you want me to say?'

I told him the words. Rapt, he listened as if I were teaching him a mantra, and with the same diligence, he put his hands on either side of his mouth and shouted.

'Good job,' I said, relieved to be out of the spotlight. Kids kept coming, and soon we ran out of sweets.

'What's your name?' I asked him as we stood aimlessly in front of my home.

'Ram. I know you. We're in the same class. You and Hasan, right?'

'Yes.' His face looked familiar now. He smiled self-consciously as I stared at him.

'So how does it work?' he asked presently. 'I mean, how do you ask God for a favour? Do you promise something in return? Did your mother say, "Oh, God, if you do such and such thing for me, I'll distribute sweets to the kids"?'

'Well, kind of, I guess.' Before that day, I hadn't thought about what Ram said. 'Except you don't have to promise. You ask for something and if Allah gives it to you, you thank Him by offering something. Do you guys do the same?'

'Yes, except that Ma spends more time in front of the god at the small temple we have in our home. And she promises to visit Jagannath, a bigger temple. We usually distribute homemade sweets. Ma's a great cook. You should come to my place one day. She'll let you taste what she cooks.'

'Thanks! My mother offers extra prayers too. We call them *nafals*. I wonder why all mothers are like that.'

'Women more than men, I guess.'

'But why?' I asked as we walked together up and down the street.

'Hmm . . . maybe we should ask my brother, Mohan. He reads a lot of books and is very wise.'

'Where are you from? Has your family only recently moved to Shanti Nagar?'

'Yes. We used to live near Faisalabad.'

'Why did you move? Because of your father's new posting?'

Ram thought for some time and a playful smile appeared on his face, making me wonder if he was thinking about something funny. I later learnt that whenever he faced a challenge—on that occasion, it was how to explain to me the reason for their move—he would look excited and amused. 'Papa said the people in that town were not happy with Hindu festivals. So, most of the Hindu families migrated to other cities. When Mohan, my brother, finished his intermediate exam, we thought it was a good time for us to move out.'

I didn't understand how a community's festivals could offend other people. I wanted to ask if Ram's family made a lot of noise, but I decided against it. 'We also moved here two years ago,' I said to show solidarity with him. 'Abba Ji is in the telephone department, where people often get transferred to new stations.'

We met again the following morning in the classroom. I introduced Ram to Hasan. 'He's Ram, a new student in our class. He's a Hindu,' I said.

Ram and Hasan shook hands and then looked at each other, not knowing what to say.

I said to Hasan, 'We discussed the other day why women offer to appease Allah. I mean, why women are more into asking Allah for things and then returning the favour, more than men?'

Hasan pursed his lips and stroked his chin, his way of making himself look important. He thought a long time about this, although what he eventually said was hardly impressive. 'I believe women have more time. Men are busy with their jobs. They don't have time for this. My grandma prays a lot. She does that nearly all day because she has nothing else to do.'

'You didn't have to tell me he's Hindu,' Hasan reprimanded me as soon as Ram was out of earshot.

Wondering where I went wrong, I said nothing.

Hasan continued, 'Anyone can tell Ram is a Hindu name. I'm not an idiot. And you don't have to point out when somebody's different. That's bad manners. It's like someone limps and you introduce him as lame.'

'Being a Hindu is different from being lame. I mentioned it for no particular reason.' I guess I did because I wanted to present Ram as somebody special so Hasan would be impressed that I had made a good friend. But knowing that there was no way I could win an argument with Hasan, I said nothing more.

Ram and I talked often and exchanged notes. He was good at most subjects, especially Mathematics, and did well in class tests. He was crazy about sudokus and crossword puzzles. Whenever he saw an English newspaper, fresh or old, he would grab it, his intelligent eyes shining with excitement, and look for the games page. During a free period, he often pulled out an old, neatly folded newspaper from his bag, placed it on his desk and solved the puzzles on it. I sometimes joined him, and although I wasn't a great help, he appreciated it whenever I suggested a word.

Hasan was lukewarm towards Ram. I guess it wasn't because he was a Hindu but because Hasan didn't want to show he was impressed by my new friend. He was like that in most things. As I couldn't do anything about it, I stopped worrying and forgot about it.

Once Ram's family was hosting a party because his brother had bought a motorcycle. When I asked Hasan if he wanted to go to Ram's, he smirked. 'Who throws a party for buying a motorcycle?'

Maybe it was a big event for their family, or maybe Ram just wanted to be nice to us. Why did Hasan have to be so analytical? But I couldn't present my arguments. Just then, Ram turned up to ask me if I was coming. When I confirmed I was, he said to Hasan, 'I'll be glad if you also come. It would mean a lot to me.' Ram's statement showed me that sometimes you don't need many arguments to convince someone, because it made Hasan say yes.

* * *

Ram's drawing-cum-sitting room was so narrow it was almost a passage. With chairs alongside opposite walls and a rickety table between them, there was hardly any space to move around. Ram's whole family—his father, mother and his brother Mohan, who was eight years his senior—was thin to the point of emaciation. We ate samosas, barfi slices and laddoos, which Ram's mother had cooked, while the family watched with sheepish grins on their faces.

'It's not really a party,' Hasan whispered to me as Ram left the room. Why should we care if it's not a full-fledged party when we could feast on the delicious treats, I wanted to say, but I remained quiet as Ram's mother was looking at us, perhaps thinking we needed something. When we had eaten, Ram invited us to the rooftop where, in a corner, was his brother's room.

'We play cricket here, Mohan and I. Complete eleven-a-side, Twenty20,' Ram said. 'The bowling side sets imaginary fielders, and if the ball goes from the bat in the air to where a fielder is, one wicket goes down. And of course, the batsman can be bowled out, or leg before wicket.'

'Interesting! Must be fun,' I said, wondering how much fun it was to have a brother who played with you. Mine was nearly as old as Mohan but didn't play with me.

Ever the critic, Hasan said, 'But sometimes fielders drop catches. It would be *real* fun if you could put that in your match.'

'Of course, you can't do that in this game, but pretty much everything else can be included.'

'Which side do you cheer for when you watch a Pakistan–India match?' Hasan asked.

Ram pondered for a while, perhaps wondering for the first time in his life why he should not cheer for Pakistan.

'Pakistan, of course. We're Pakistani, aren't we?' Mohan appeared from his room. There was silence as I watched Hasan's reaction. He looked away, his broad jaw set and his large eyes sullen.

Ram broke the uneasy silence. 'Bhai, Furqan asked why women are more—how do we say it?—religious. Hasan said it's because they have more time as they don't have a job. See what I mean?'

Mohan had intelligent eyes like Ram's, a big forehead and an even bigger smile. 'Interesting. And I guess Hasan is right in some way. The more idle one is, the more one worries and therefore thinks about gods. But I guess it has more to do with being worried. About being insecure. Most women in our society are weaker. More insecure, dependent on men. The one who's in control is less likely to be religious.'

He paused and smiled, enjoying the discussion. Then, leaning against the brick parapet, he added, 'For example, a farmer is very religious. He needs the mercy of the gods to have good crops, to have the right weather, rain, sunshine, etc. He doesn't have any control over these. Before he goes to sleep every night, he lies awake, worrying about them. Do you know that even an early monsoon can wreak havoc with the wheat crops in our country? So he prays to the gods for the right conditions for farming.'

'Along came industrialization,' said Ram, who had obviously heard this lecture before.

'Yes,' Mohan continued. 'With industrialization, man became less dependent on nature and the gods. Machines were like gods, in fact—powerful, almost magical. There's an interesting story by Wells about how a man becomes captivated by a machine. So man started drifting away from religion. You see, the people in the villages are more religious than those in the cities.'

He strolled away from the wall and sat on a monolith of bricks. 'I better stay away from this wall; a few of its bricks fell—was it a month ago?' He looked at Ram who nodded. 'When Ma came to collect her washed laundry. Fortunately, no one was hurt.'

Ram giggled as he recalled something funny about the episode. The two brothers were perfectly at ease with their humble living.

Hasan appeared to be fascinated but bewildered. He said, 'Does man think he is too big for nature? What about earthquakes and floods and other disasters?'

'Another good point. Now and then, nature keeps reminding man that he's still at its mercy. Such a disaster jolts him back to reality. But you see, man's evolution—his struggle to gain control over nature—is a continuous process. With advanced technology, earthquakes and floods will pose fewer problems. We will be forewarned and thus forearmed. But then other challenges may crop up, such as new diseases, new social problems. Challenges continue as long as life does. But they're not to be feared. Interesting, isn't it?'

Hasan said, this time less belligerent and more inquisitive, 'That means technology is taking us away from Allah? That means it's bad?'

'The answer to the first question is yes. As for the second question, I'm not sure. When I was your age, I was more obedient to my parents. I was a good boy—went to bed on time, spent time on my studies. Now I know more things, I earn some money for my parents, I have become more useful to them and I can protect them. But now, I often stay away from home till late at night, smoke and play cards with my friends. Does that mean I've been corrupted? Which version of me would my parents prefer, the present one or the one from eight years ago?'

'The best of both,' Ram said, with a mischievous glint in his eye. We all laughed.

As we talked, we followed Mohan into his room. It was inappropriate to call it a room, though. Two new walls and a rooftop made from tin combined with two existing walls to make a small, rectangular room. The brick structure stood out like an unfinished project. The walls had no paint or whitewash on them—only the redness of the brick and the silver–grey of the cement was visible. Ram later told us that with the money they had, this was the best they could do. Inside the room, books were on the floor, stacked one above the other, because there were no shelves. The only furniture was a charpoy, a table and a chair. As we entered, a few lizards scrambled to their safe havens, startling me. Ram and Hasan laughed. Mohan said with a smile, 'Looks like you and lizards aren't friends.'

'Yes, I don't particularly like them. I can't say anything about their feelings towards me.' Every time I stepped into that room, I remained wary of lizards. But my herpetophobia was more than neutralized by the magnetic pull of Mohan's books.

'Looks like an interesting man, this brother of Ram, don't you think?' Hasan asked, as we left their home. Hasan rarely admitted to being impressed by someone. 'We should visit him often. Did you see his book collection? He had the book on the Arabian Nights and one on Ameer Hamza, not just Hindi books. But look, Furqan. I'm not sure how my family's going to react to this, to our friendship with a Hindu. You see what I mean?'

I didn't, but I nodded. He continued, 'I have an idea. We can tell our parents that Ram's brother helps him with his studies and that he wouldn't mind if we sat in the coaching session once or twice a week. I don't think Ammi will object to that. What do you think?'

'Yes, that sounds good.'

The next day over dinner, I brought up the matter. Ammi and Abba readily consented to my going to Ram's place to attend the coaching sessions. They would have agreed even if I had told them the truth. Ammi had a minor objection, though: 'Don't eat there,' she said while sitting on her kitchen stool, looking sweet in her concern. She always entertained worrying thoughts while sitting there, in the small world of her kitchen, which was nothing more than a corner of the veranda.

Sitting on the other stool in front of her and eating spinach, I wondered how I could say no to the mithai from Ram's household. Luckily, Abba intervened from his world—his bed, where he did almost everything, from sleeping to reading, office work, watching TV and talking to Ammi—and said, 'It doesn't matter. Hindus use the same ingredients that we do. They won't poison their food with things smuggled from across the border.'

Hasan's family, especially his Ammi, was conservative. He told me the following day in school that he got his plan approved by his Dadu, who was more liberal. She said there was no problem if Hasan ate at a Hindu household.

We visited Ram's place a few days later, taking along eatables from our homes. Ammi made carrot halvah at my request, and Lubna cooked biryani for Hasan. We needed these dishes to appease our would-be teacher, we told the ladies. Ram's parents couldn't believe their eyes when we presented our delicacies to them. Act casual, Hasan had tutored me. But lying and acting were not my forte. Hasan did a good job, though, which impressed Ram's family.

'We want you to tutor us, Mohan Bhai,' Hasan said, when we were in his room after we had amazed them with our gifts.

'But Ram tells me you two do well in academics. What do you need the tuition for?'

Hasan and I looked at each other as we sat on two wooden stools. It would have been rude to say that our parents did not allow us to visit our Hindu friends. Mohan sat on his charpoy, looking perplexed. Ram was amused, as if we were playing riddles with him. He wiped his running nose with the back of his hand, something he often did especially when he was self-conscious.

'Look, we didn't know what our parents would say if we told them we're friends with you—Hindus, I mean. So we said you're offering us tuition. Astonishingly, they didn't mind. But the thing is, now we cannot back out of that lie. We're sorry for this.' Hasan did a smart job of blurting out the truth while making it less unpleasant.

Mohan laughed. I realized years later the magnanimity he had shown by hiding his chagrin behind the laughter.

'Don't worry. I'll play along, and you can come over. But what will you need help with?'

'These,' Hasan said, pointing at the piles of books. 'Tell us stories, would you?'

'Oh, these. With pleasure.'

'Where do you get all these books from?' I asked Mohan as he picked up one hardcover and shook the dust off it.

He smiled. 'A wonderland of books has cropped up in a place in our colony. I get them from there. I'll show you one day.'

* * *

A few days later, Mohan took us a few streets away to a homoeopathy shop run by a man named Karamat Ali. He appeared to be in his fifties. When he first eyed you over his glasses, you'd think he didn't like you. He limped slightly and the limp, combined with his reticence, lent him an aloofness. He had recently moved in from Islampura, where Mohan's family had lived previously, so they knew each other well.

Karamat had a nice little library in his shop, which initiated us on our journey into the world of books. We started visiting Ram's place often to finish our homework and spent an extra hour or two listening to Mohan's stories. Sometimes we sat inside or in front of Karamat Ali's shop-cum-library. Mohan was a storehouse of stories. He could talk about any topic and make it as interesting as a story. He talked about history, adding occasional light doses of philosophy, mainly Marxism and Communism. One thing Mohan's stories did was to change my heroes—and perhaps Ram's and Hasan's too—from princes and warriors to men of learning and wisdom. We listened to him and dreamt of how we could become agents of change.

Being with Mohan was like walking behind him through a museum. He didn't hold our hands. He walked a few feet in front of us, looking back now and then to make sure we were following. And we were so enthralled by what he showed us. Never could I have imagined then that a few years later, things would turn out to be as ugly as they did.

3

Waqas

Present day

Before meeting Furqan, I decided to go home and change into a shalwar and kurta, as I was itching to get out of my sweat-drenched uniform.

Fareeha looked pitiable when I reached home. Her shalwar and kameez were drenched in sweat, her sweet face was blotted and her hair was hanging loose. Opened and unopened cartons stood all around the compound and in the two bedrooms beyond it.

'How's our new home doing, Fari? Does it meet your expectations?' I asked.

'Don't ask . . .' She pushed a loose strand of hair behind her right ear and pulled out the kitchen utensils from a carton standing in the middle of the compound. I tried to give her a hand. 'You must be tired. I'll handle it.'

'Not half as tired as you are. I understand there are some repairs needed. I'll talk to the landlord first thing in the morning. You know there are teething problems in every place.'

My mind drifted from short-circuited electric sockets, fused bulbs and rusty sink pipes to Amber, the boy who had died and the boy I was going to meet.

I said with a wink of my eye, 'Let's have a shower together. We need one—and each other—badly.'

'Oh, please. The kids are home. And if you need company in the bathroom, there are plenty of roaches in there.'

'Oh, my unromantic wife!' I walked into the kids' room. Sitting on the bed, they were absorbed in a ludo game. I hugged and kissed them before I stepped into the bathroom.

'Fari, consider it closed,' I said when she asked about the suicide case as I emerged from the bathroom after a quick shower. I wanted to put her mind to rest. Amber's pointed questions continued to echo in my mind though, until my thoughts skipped to her kurta. Amber had always been like that. In the university, the registrar requested her to mind her dress. When I first saw her, I never thought we would ever consider marriage. She wasn't my type at all. But I hated it whenever Rehan, a classmate of ours, reminded me of that.

'Where are you going then?' Fareeha asked, handing me a glass of salty lassi. She moved in and out of the minuscule kitchen, arranging the utensils on the shelves.

'You know why I love lassi?' I eyed her over the glass as I gulped it down in one go while sitting on a carton. 'Because it's like you: white, creamy on the top, and tasty underneath, both in its sweet and salty forms.' Fareeha feigned anger—I loved it when she did that—forcing me to answer. 'I've got to see another man. It's about another case. Don't worry, my lassi.'

But there was no smile of contentment on her face. Whenever I showed exaggerated affection, she could sense I was hiding something. I had better stop using that trick.

As I kick-started my motorcycle and set off, my mind went several years back . . .

'Now that the master's is over, what next? Marriage for ladies, jobs for men, I guess.' Someone says . . . in a loud voice. We're sitting around a large table, eating.

'How chauvinistic! Men start with the assumption that women are not meant for practical life.' Amber is her usual belligerent self.

'You might be an exception, Amber. But the truth is, that's the fate of most women. I'm not insulting women, just commenting on the ways of society.'

'By the way, our exceptional woman is also thinking marriage,' another guy chimes in.

'Oh!' Several voices . . .

'Who's the unlucky guy?' Laughter . . . 'Let me guess . . .'

Everyone looks at me. I try not to blush and say, 'I have to find a job before I can think of marriage, like everyone else.'

'Amber will be a working woman. She'll earn and you'll have fun, man.'

Another guffaw.

'Oh please, guys. Don't jump to conclusions.' Amber gets irritated.

'So there's nothing cooking, Amber? Waqas hasn't denied it.'

'There's nothing, honestly.' I'm hardly audible.

'Actually, there is—was, in fact.' Rehan finally speaks—I dread it when he does. 'Waqas's and Amber's families met but couldn't reach a decision. Well, it happens. Isn't it, guys? Their families' lifestyles are poles apart.'

Many people nod.

Behan chod! Why is everyone always licking his balls?

Amber glances at me and looks away. She's pissed off.

A while later . . .

Everyone's leaving . . . Rehan emerges from the restroom. 'You didn't have to mention our break-up in front of everyone,' I whisper.

'Whose break-up? Do you mean Amber's and yours? You can hardly call it that.'

He wipes his hands with a napkin.

'I think she didn't like it.'

'In fact, she might be happy, no offence to you. After all, girls drool over army men.'

What? Does he mean Amber was considering him? She never mentioned that to me.

'All set for the army, then. Congratulations!' I can recover. No big deal.

'Yes. I start training next month. And by the way, if I had to embarrass you, I could have mentioned your police job in front of everyone. It's final, right? You know the police cannot stand up to the army. But I didn't mention it, did I? After all, you and Amber have been my best pals here. Without you, I might not have passed a few courses, I acknowledge that.'

* * *

'Did your wife permit you to see me?' Sarcasm was Amber's forte. I ignored it. I had learnt to do so when we were in the university together.

'We meet again after three years.' I took a seat. 'I thought your anger might have subsided.'

'Anger?'

'At not having married me, of course.' I fought fire with fire.

'Very funny! Get to the point. What did you want to see me about?' she asked, when I settled into a chair. The evening was a few hours away, and the restaurant, which was near her office, wasn't busy. The place was small but stylish with vinyl flooring and abstract art on the walls. The air conditioner was not working though, as the generator couldn't take the load. The languid air from a humming pedestal fan made me sleepy.

'Tea, coffee or cold drink? It's on me because I requested this meeting,' I clarified, because Amber had big issues with men displaying chivalry through their wallets.

'Coffee, please.'

I ordered a cup of coffee and a cold drink and said, 'I'm looking for a job. This will be my last posting in the police force.'

'So?'

'What are my chances in journalism? What are the prospects?'

'Why do you policemen think you can barge in anywhere, anytime, without any warrant? Even into journalism?'

'You know what? Your retorts can be very annoying. Of course, I will come with the necessary qualifications. I want your advice on whether I should go for it or not, which journalism school is good, which papers I can apply to—those kinds of things.'

'If you ask me, your present job is as good as any. If you're a misfit in this one, you'll be a misfit in journalism.'

A bored looking waiter placed a cup of coffee—a heart made from coffee powder sailed on its surface—and a Coca Cola bottle on the table between us. Amber had changed into blue jeans and a green kurta—not tasteful but more socially acceptable.

'Indeed, fit men go into the army and misfits keep changing professions.'

'What's that supposed to mean? If you're taking a swipe at Rehan, why would that bother me?'

She always had a look in her eyes that suggested she hated looking vulnerable because of a display of sentiments. When she was angry, the steeliness in her eyes increased.

'I thought you might be pleased. The army guy called off his commitment to you. What did he say? That his family wouldn't like your lifestyle and that you wouldn't be able to pursue a career in journalism while he's posted up north, in Swat or Federally Administered Tribal Area (FATA).'

'He was never my choice, and you know it, Waqas. Dad just kept pushing him my way. I thank Allah that Rehan saw I didn't love him . . . But why are we discussing this? You want to go over it again?'

'You started on the wrong foot. I reciprocated.'

'I'll leave if we're going to talk about this bullshit . . .' She rose to her feet.

Waqas, you called off the marriage plans after Ammi raised her eyebrows at Amber's liberal clothing and lifestyle. Also because you knew that with no job in sight you stood nowhere before Rehan, who was her dad's choice. So why act like a crybaby now? You've gotten over the parting, but you've got to do something about the ghost of your failure to stand up for what you wanted.

'Alright, please sit down. I'm sorry. I mentioned him to find out where he is these days.'

'Not far. In Pindi, with the military intelligence.'

'Right. Any word of advice on a career change?'

She sipped her coffee. 'This coffee's the best in town. Try it.'

'I will, but not in this heat.'

'To answer your question, I have only two suggestions. One, be prepared to tough it out. Two, take along some pride from your present job, which you're not prepared to do.'

'What do you mean?'

'It's simple, Waqas. You need to walk away with a sense of achievement. I know you haven't had a great career in the police force.'

I opened my mouth, but Amber raised her voice in her typical peremptory way.

'I know you have differences with the way the police force works—you told me all that. But the thing is, Waqas, every place has its problems and flaws. What makes you think there are angels in journalism? You must find your way around the obstacles you come across and succeed, whatever success means to you. At least show you're good. Earn respect, I mean. Only then can you walk into your new job with self-respect.'

For once, Amber made some sense. I pondered over it but didn't have much to say. Outside the restaurant, rickshaws, cars and motorcycles sped up and down the road which was lined by trees—mostly rosewood and figs. Shadows had lengthened and the heat had abated but the traffic was noisier. This locality was not posh but less dusty and religion-infested than Shanti Nagar and Ferozepur where I lived and worked.

Amber continued, 'You don't seem to be interested in the Shanti Nagar case, evidently because your mind is on your resignation and the next job. My hunch is this is an important case. I thought you would literally dive into it.'

Amber paused, but I didn't comment. She knew I had a good reason to be interested in it, but how could I tell her that the same reason scared me; that if I unravelled this case, it might loosen some threads that had remained knotted for three decades?

She continued, 'I don't want to tell you how to do your job—you know that well enough—but an autopsy can reveal some facts. Who knows, an autopsy on this boy's body might be a post-mortem on our society. It may afford us a peek into whether we're killing ourselves or someone else is doing it.'

'Well said.'

She might be bossy in personal matters, but in professional ones, she was respectful.

'Dig into it well and you can resign from the police force with pride. Who knows, after this, you might want to continue with your current job.'

'Yes, that makes sense. Thanks, Amber. I appreciate your advice, 'I paused and rose to my feet. 'I've got to meet someone else. Will catch you later.'

That short conversation felt different from the ones we had had in the last few years, but it was too early to tell her I was convinced. She didn't know I had run into problems in every police case assigned to me.

* * *

The small hotel looked as if it offered cheap food to local workers and residents. It was nearing dinner time, and with customers coming in, the electric fans running at full speed and the wall-mounted LCD TV blaring ads, the place was noisy. I surveyed the main hall of the hotel, looking for the boy. He sat at a table and raised a schoolboy hand to indicate he was the guy. He had obviously seen me that morning and recognized me.

'You're Furqan?' He nodded. 'What have you got, young man?' I asked as I sat on a monobloc chair in front of him.

'Sir, I don't think Hasan killed himself.' He began slowly, paused, looked around and leaned forward. He added, 'In fact I'm sure he didn't.'

In his late teens, the boy was of average height and slight build. He had probably recently begun to shave his chin but left his upper lip unshaved to grow an ambitious moustache. Restless eyes behind large plastic-framed glasses, though, suggested an insecure child.

'What makes you so sure? How well did you know him?'

The TV was so loud I couldn't focus on the conversation. I wanted to shout to the burly man in a dhoti and vest on the counter to lower the sound, but that would have attracted unnecessary attention. Something about the boy told me he had braved great danger to offer something valuable.

'Sir, I'm his best friend, perhaps. I've known him for over six years.' The boy was sweating profusely. Now and then he would adjust his glasses or lift them to wipe his perspiring nose.

'Are you alright? What are you worried about?'

'Sir, this is a blasphemy-related matter—Hasan's death, I mean. The riots that happened in March, I'm sure Hasan's death is connected to them. And I'm afraid that . . .'

'Nothing's going to happen to you,' I put a consoling hand on the boy's hand. 'Calm down and tell me everything in detail.'

I hailed a waiter and asked him to bring us two Coca Colas, which he quickly placed on the plastic table between us. The ice-cold bottles with beads of moisture sliding down them cooled me down. I hoped they would placate the boy too.

'Go on, drink it and chill.'

'Sir, you're not like other police officers,' the boy said, as he sipped from the bottle. His smile looked forced, but there was something sincere about him. With a fair complexion and dark eyes, he looked cherubic, despite a big nose.

'How many police officers do you know?' I smiled to put him at ease but failed. 'Anyway, go on about Hasan.'

'Sir, he was very depressed in the few weeks before he died. He felt guilty about the lynching incident after the blasphemy case.'

'Why is that? What did he have to do with it?'

'Sir, he was part of the lynching mob. He was one of those who rioted. The police rounded up several of them. Hasan was one of them. I thought his name must be in the police records.'

'Yeah. I wasn't here when it happened, but I know of the Hindu boy's death.' I regretted not having done my homework. But how was I supposed to know that?

'The Hindu man was blamed for insulting Islam and our holy prophet. You know all about that, I guess.'

I recalled that the police arrested the Hindu guy and released him before he was lynched. 'I do, but tell me what else you know.'

Suddenly, the electricity was shut down. In the ensuing darkness and heat, the hotel staff shouted at each other. Someone was supposed to switch on a generator but couldn't. A great deal of cursing and swearing in Punjabi began soon after. Someone shouted that the generator had developed a fault. A hotel attendant started lighting candles on each table, but the heat was unbearable.

'Let's go for a walk.' I got up and paid at the counter. The burly man's vest was soaked in sweat. Furqan followed me.

'There's a park around the corner. We can sit there,' Furqan said as he tried to walk in step with me.

'Okay, go on,' I said, once we reached and sat side by side on a bench. It was a small, unclean park which people visited to get some respite from the heat.

'It was all very horrible. The blasphemy charges were disturbing enough. Then the rallies, the arrests, the people's ire. It was so frightening. No one knew what was going on. A mob is a dangerous creature.'

Dangerous. That word sent me decades into the past.

I turn and look behind me repeatedly as I run, wiping away my tears to see more clearly. There's a crowd, seething, surging, changing shape, growing limbs . . . now here, then there . . . like a slithering, crawling prehistoric protozoa in a sci-fi film, approaching him. He stands firm, dressed in white. He does not budge, and the organism absorbs him . . . eats him up. I run and run . . .

The electric power returned and the lights in and around the park came alive, blinking. The kids in the nearby houses roared in a single chorus. Some families started leaving, but a few youngsters and children were whooping and running around. With the mosquitoes and children's screams, I was finding it difficult to focus on what Furqan was saying.

Furqan continued, 'The Deen men marched towards his house and gathered outside it, chanting slogans.'

'The Hindu guy's house, you mean? Did you witness this?'

'No. Unless one wanted to be part of the rally, one knew it wasn't safe to be out there. I heard it from people. But this was what happened. You may find out about it in the police reports.'

'So you said Hasan was part of the lynchers?'

'Yes, Hasan was there.'

'How do you know that? He told you?'

'Yes, he told me later. The police arrested him after the incident. Him and a few others. Everyone knew.'

'How was he released?'

'No one knew. But he came back. He wouldn't talk much after that, not even to his family. He didn't meet me for many days after his return. It was weeks before he talked about it. I could see he felt guilty about it. He was very troubled. I think even his family didn't know how to deal with someone who had been part of a mob that killed a close friend.'

'The Hindu guy was a friend?'

'A friend like no other.'

Furqan's voice mellowed, as he seemed to drift into the past. The boy who appeared meek and childish at first now looked like a sensitive and sagacious man. His choice of words and his measured manner of speech impressed me.

Furqan continued, 'In a way, I compounded the situation for him because I tried to convince him that lynching was not the right thing to do. He refuted my arguments, but I knew he felt guilty.'

There was a long pause. I tried to brush aside the platoon of invading mosquitoes while Furqan gazed at the starry sky.

'With so much guilt and depression, Hasan might have killed himself,' I said.

Furqan gathered his thoughts before he spoke. 'I don't think so. If he considered suicide, he would've done that earlier, when the police released him. That was when he was severely depressed. In fact, nearer his death, he seemed to have found some optimism. It seemed he was getting out of the quandary he was in.'

'What do you mean?'

'I felt he looked for answers and perhaps got them. There was more optimism in him. He was even willing to discuss things with me. He wanted to. Unfortunately, I was away for a few days.'

'Was he consulting someone? He might've sought spiritual guidance, something that gave him solace.'

'I don't know. But he also saw the Deen people quite often. Maybe some of them—the maulanas—were able to put his mind at rest.'

'So, do you think someone killed him? Who might've wanted to do that?'

'I don't know, sir, but I don't believe he could've taken his own life. So, I decided to share this information with you.'

The park was nearly empty now. A few children scampered near and far. I continued as he looked around, 'By the way, what made you think I might listen to you? Most people fear the police.'

When Furqan didn't speak for a while, I thought he had no answer. Then he said slowly, 'I feel I've been silent too long. I've lost two friends, and silence doesn't do justice to their deaths.'

That was relatable.

He continued, 'Sir, I saw you on a TV programme. You sounded very well read. My whole family said you resembled Humayun Saeed, the TV star, you know. I thought you might be different when I saw you on Hasan's street this morning. I thought I could speak to you—or speak through you.'

The boy had struck a chord. 'Oh, that. Yes, they did the talk show to discuss public–police cooperation. What did I say that appealed to you?'

'You quoted a line from Faiz: *hum jinhay rasm-e-dua yaad nahi* [We who have forgotten how to pray].'

'Oh, really? Don't let poetry-quoting people fool you, though. Some politicians and generals do it merely to impress their audience.' I laughed.

'You sounded sincere.' The boy smiled—his was a shy smile that seemed to hide itself, but when revealed, it looked reassuring.

'Back to the case. I need more details, young man. If you have time, please tell me everything. Start from the beginning.'

'Beginning, sir? Beginning of what?'

'Good question. Let's start with how you came to know Hasan,' I said.

4

Furqan

Three years ago

Mohan earned a Bachelor's degree in Science with flying colours. We asked him about his career plans, as we knew we too would need to make such a choice soon.

'You'll pursue a Master's degree now?' Hasan asked him as we made ourselves comfortable in his room. 'Physics or Mathematics?'

'The answer to your first question is yes. To the second question, no. I won't pursue either of the two. I'll do Fine Arts. Maybe another Bachelor's—a four-year programme—in Fine Arts.'

We looked at Mohan as if he had told us the silliest joke. Ram intervened to explain, 'You know he loves drawing and painting. Haven't you seen his artwork?'

We had seen his sketchpads but hadn't thought much of them.

'You can't be serious about the Arts. After all, the good jobs are in the Sciences, right?' Hasan paused and asked, 'And if you love Arts so much, why did you waste two years pursuing a Bachelor's degree in Science?'

'Both are valid points. You already answered the second question. Arts don't fetch money. Papa wanted me to study Science. But now I realize it's not for me. I won't be able to do much in that field.'

'But you got good marks,' I said.

Mohan, who sat on the charpoy, now rested his back against the craggy wall. 'Marks. They don't mean much. With some effort, even without interest, you can do well in an examination, the sort of system we have. That's what I did.'

'So you'll start another Bachelor's?' Hasan asked.

'He quarrelled with Papa,' Ram said, looking as amused as he always did.

Mohan went on. 'My parents want me to start a job soon. I'll enrol in a Master's programme and look for a job as a lecturer. Alongside that, I'll offer home coaching to children to earn something.'

We returned from that interview with Mohan feeling no wiser about our career prospects. Mohan executed the plan he had shared with us. He did admirably well during his Master's studies, immediately after which he got a teaching job at the same institute. A couple of years later, Ram announced that Mohan had won a scholarship in the USA.

Amazed, Hasan and I went to congratulate Mohan. He was excited in his humble way while we envied him for going to America. In the next few months, we seldom saw him as he was busy with his passport and visa formalities. Ram told us about Mohan's departure and how later he sent home some money that he earned in America through his scholarship and odd jobs.

Mohan often emailed the three of us and told us about his life in America. About his university, and the places he visited. We read his emails wide eyed and discussed them later as if we were talking about a fairyland. He returned in about two years, during which time Ram, Hasan and I had finished school, besides having read many more books Karamat lent to us. When we went to meet him, Mohan enthralled us with more stories about his stay in America. As we had to choose majors in college, we also sought his advice on career choices.

'I guess you guys can choose one of three options: Engineering, Medicine or IT. These fields promise good earnings.'

We sat in his room, which now looked in better shape, with a proper roof and whitewash.

'But earning was not your consideration when you chose your career. Double standards!' Hasan put in.

Mohan laughed. 'Agreed. But I had a clear passion. Do you have any? If you had one, you wouldn't be sitting here asking for my two bits.'

In response to our blank faces, he added, 'If you hear a particular profession calling you, as I heard a call from the Arts, you hear it loud and clear. As in the poem "Sea Fever", it's a loud and clear call that cannot be denied. Do you guys hear one?'

Hasan and I looked at each other as if asking, 'Do you hear a call?' I didn't hear any and apparently neither did Hasan. But what we wanted was to emulate Mohan in making bold, unorthodox decisions and prove people wrong, people like those who laughed when Mohan chose Arts over Science.

'I know I love Maths, but all I can hear is the neighbor's rooster crowing,' Ram said.

Abba wanted me to be an engineer in the telephone department where he had worked as a technician all his life and where he also managed to get a job for my brother. Once, when I talked to Abba about taking up Fine Arts, he looked disappointed but said he couldn't force me into a profession I didn't like. That meant I couldn't break his heart. Abba and I knew how to convince each other.

Mohan said, 'Look. If you're undecided, Engineering's a safe bet. See, even if you can't make up your minds now, with a background in pre-Engineering, you can choose almost any field later.'

Mohan could make things pleasantly simple. The three of us decided to take up pre-Engineering. Choosing a college was simpler. There was only one national-level college in the city, Islamia College. It was famous, and everyone wanted to study there. With our good marks in the matriculation exam, admission to the college was easy. Little did we know that going to this college would lead to the undoing of this blissful friendship the four of us enjoyed.

The college was huge. The buildings that stood on either side of a narrow road—there was one multi-storied block for each department—looked intimidating in contrast to the single-storey structure of our school.

On the day the admissions opened, the three of us went along with the crowd. We were clueless about where to find the application forms and how to submit them. We didn't ask for guidance from anyone who could have been a senior because we knew he would either pull our legs or intentionally misguide us. We decided that each one of us would join one of the many queues in front of the blue admission office and, while in the queue, talk to people to find out if it was the right one. We found the right queue in this way, but after a two-hour crawl, it dispersed. Someone revealed that the admissions office had run out of application forms and that the students should come again the following day.

As we were returning—Hasan and I disappointed and Ram amazed at the college's architecture—a young man with a neat beard approached us. 'You're first-year boys and you're looking for application forms, right?' None of us answered, but we stopped as he approached us. He had a comely face, which looked saccharine thanks to the smile on his lips. He pulled out three forms from the bag he was carrying on his right shoulder.

'Where did you get these? Are you a student?' Hasan's tone betrayed suspicion.

'Yes, my name is Faisal. I'm a student, a year senior, and with the help of some colleagues, I try to help newcomers, so they don't face any problems. Heard of those days when seniors used to rag the juniors? Those days are over. Here, fill them out quickly.'

The boy sounded like a vendor marketing a product. We took seats on a nearby bench and shared the pen the bearded boy had lent us. While he was away talking to a few guys—he was a busy man who knew everyone—we filled out the forms and attached to them copies of our certificates, photos and other documents. He returned quickly to ensure that we had completed the forms. We thanked him and our stars for this God-sent help.

Faisal was ever-present on the college campus. We saw him again a few days later seated on a lawn surrounded by several boys. He greeted us with a loud *Assalam-o-Alaikum* and asked us to join the gathering. Wondering what it was about and knowing we had no immediate commitment, we sat on the grass at the outer fringes of the circle of boys around him.

Faisal said, '. . . Now you're in college. You're adult Muslims, *Alhamdulillah*. We, all of us, must worry about other things besides our studies. We have a responsibility towards our nation, our Ummah, our Allah. Muslims need to do *something* because there's so much evil in the world. America, the Jews and the Hindus are bent upon destroying the Muslims. Our Muslim brothers are being massacred in Palestine, Bosnia and Kashmir. Muslims, who are the chosen people of Allah, have forgotten His message. Strict observance of a pure Islam is the only way out of these problems.'

He had the oratorical panache of an expert imam, although he had forgotten that the Bosnian War had ended years ago. I looked around to see his effect on his audience. It was difficult to say if they believed what he was saying or if any of them had any counterarguments. I looked at Ram. He was amused, as he always was when he encountered new ideas. I hoped he wouldn't raise his hand, as he did in the classroom, to announce he was a Hindu or to present his viewpoint. Hasan looked pensive.

'To return to Allah's message, we must create a milieu that's conducive to Islam,' Faisal continued. 'That's why our Jamaat, the Talaba, invites all students to the meetings of *Shab-e-Juma*, a religious congregation, on Thursday nights in various mosques or Islamic centres. Many Muslims don't know that in the Islamic calendar, the day starts with the sunset. That's why it's called Shab-e-Juma, meaning "Friday night". If you want to return to the right path, if you wish to correct yourself and this world, and if you want to fight the forces of evil, I urge you all to say yes to Shab-e-Juma. Please, brothers, say you want to go. Raise your hands if you want to go this coming Thursday.'

Only a few hands went up. Everyone looked at the others, looking unsure. 'I understand, brothers, that everyone has commitments and chores. But try to make up your mind and let me know when you're ready. Say *Insha Allah* and Allah will help you decide. Say it even if you don't want to, now.'

A few murmurs of *Insha Allah* were heard.

'Wait, wait, wait!' Someone spoke from the crowd. I couldn't see who the speaker was. Faisal paused, looking surprised. 'If I don't want to go, why should I say *Insha Allah?*'

Everyone turned around to look at the audacious speaker. I had seen him a few times. He was a squat, stocky boy with confidence oozing out of him. He continued, 'Look, *Insha Allah* means "If God is willing", right?'

'Yes. That's the whole point. You're acknowledging that Allah's will prevails over everything. You may not want to go, but you must remember that if Allah wills it, then nothing in the universe can stop it.'

The boy sat on his knees to raise himself. 'Well, that's another debate. But what's the point in saying *Insha Allah?* Will saying it change my mind?'

'Yes, of course. Allah's words are miraculous, brother.'

'That may be so, but I've a date with my girlfriend this Thursday. This one's new, so I can't say no.' A few people laughed while the others gaped at him.

Faisal looked embarrassed and in no mood to engage in a debate. 'If you don't want to go, it's your decision, brother.'

The boy, whose name I later found out was Yasir, was our classmate. Clean-shaven and with a sporty crew-cut, the boy was stylish and put on airs. He was one of the few in the college I saw with an iPhone; he also wore the most expensive looking clothes.

A few days after his first encounter with Faisal, Yasir confronted him again.

'The man in the middle is always bad, dangerous,' Faisal was speaking to a small gathering around the oak tree in front of the Admin block. Everyone called the tree *Dada Abbu* because it was old and its shadow was everywhere. 'Modern information technology has realized it only now. Islam knew it fourteen centuries ago.'

At that moment, I noticed Faisal eyeing someone and squirming in his place on the bench which encircled the huge tree trunk. I looked back to see who the newcomer was. It was Yasir, who had joined the group. Faisal resumed after a short pause. 'Have you heard of the term man-in-the-middle attack in computer networks? It's when some malicious person connects his device to a network you're connected to. It comes between you and the device you want to connect to. It can steal your data or even tamper with it. Right?' Some boys nodded. 'Islam has eliminated the man in the middle. No middleman is needed between man and Allah. Unlike in other religions, where you need priests or clergymen or sadhus, in Islam you have direct access to Allah. No VPN or router needed.' Faisal smiled, looking confident with his barrage of tech jargon.

'Excuse me, sir.' It was, as I had expected, Yasir. Before Faisal could speak, he continued, 'First, the analogy between religion and networks is pretty lousy. In networks, the man in the middle intervenes unwanted. No one asks him to step in. In the religions you mentioned, people willingly seek guidance from mystics and priests.' Yasir paused to catch his breath as all heads turned towards him and Faisal's face turned scarlet. 'Second, aren't you guys—people like you who proselytize—

middlemen too? Why don't you leave us alone and let us seek guidance from Allah directly?'

'No, Brother. We're here to guide people. Once people establish a direct link with Allah, we don't intervene. But you've made some good points. Thanks.' Faisal looked around. 'We will continue the discussion some other time.' He vanished quickly. He had probably learnt that it was best to avoid Yasir.

* * *

'There's a wave coming, a change. See the Arab uprising, which the West calls the Arab Spring.' The maulana who was speaking was soft-spoken but animated. He sat in the inner hall in front of which was a long veranda, and beyond that, the spacious playground where Hasan, Ram, I and many others sat on straw mats, listening to the sermon emanating from various loudspeakers. It was a small mosque with a large and dusty open space in front of it. Several cricket pitches suggested it might have been a cricket ground, now dotted with numerous sleeping bags and tents. These belonged to the Tablighis, who had come from afar to attend the Shab-e-Juma and proselytize in the mosque. Faisal had invited us to the event.

'But it's not a short battle,' the maulana's voice continued. 'It's not even a war. It's a jihad, one that will last for years to come. We might be weaker. We might be fewer in number. Remember, though, that there were only 313 Muslims against thousands of infidels in the Battle of Badr but it was Islam that claimed victory. Why? Because Allah was with them. And Allah will be with us again if we follow his prescribed path. Do not be afraid, for the victory will be ours, *Insha Allah*. Are you all brave enough to join this jihad?'

A roar of 'Yes!' resounded in the mosque.

'Do you have any doubt that the victory will be ours?'

'No!'

Shivers ran down my spine. I didn't know something like this was happening not far from my home. I looked around and felt alienated. Was I the only one who was not responding to the maulana? I looked at Hasan. He was quiet but looked interested. Ram was amused, as expected.

I didn't want to go to this congregation, but Hasan said we had to give it a try. He suggested we tell our parents that we were in each other's houses, sleeping over for night study. I had never lied to my parents, but Hasan said we were grown-ups and in the interest of trying out new things, we could lie to our parents. I agreed reluctantly. When I told Ammi about the plan for the evening, she was surprised we were studying late into the night when the academic year had just begun. I said we needed to submit an assignment. The weird part for me, though, was when Ram asked if he could come too, and Hasan agreed. He asked Faisal if Ram, a Hindu, could attend. Faisal pondered over the matter for a while and then said yes. Ram couldn't step inside the mosque, though, but would sit outside, where we were now.

After *Isha*, the night prayer, and the enthused lecture by Maulana Saleem Ur Rehman, we now sat on a large mat in the playground and listened to Faisal, who said, 'This world tends to take us farther away from the deen. It is full of temptations and attractions, which pull us away from the righteous life. The purpose of this Shab-e-Juma is for us to spend some time away from the attractions of the mundane world and come closer to the deen. It's like meditation. It's what our prophet used to do when he went to the mountains and sat in isolation.'

'Hindu gurus also prescribe meditation in isolation. Several things are common among religions.' All eyes turned to Ram, who had said this. Not everyone knew he was a Hindu. Ram grew self-conscious as he saw everyone staring at him. Droplets of sweat appeared on his forehead, and the back of his left hand went to his nose.

Faisal managed to diffuse the tension. 'Our friend Ram is a Hindu, but he's very much interested in Islam, so we invited him to this Shab-e-Juma.' Faisal exchanged glances with some other men, but no one said anything.

As we lay down to sleep, we found we weren't adequately prepared for October nights. It was that time of the year when the warm days lied about the chill of the nights. Hasan's phone had rung for the second time in the last half hour. He looked at me, and I motioned him to take the call. It was Jawad, his brother. After a brief conversation in which he uttered a mixture of lies and truths, Hasan ended the call and said we needed to go. He then got up and looked for Faisal among the people who slept on the playground. People were sprawled all over the place, and it took us some time to find him. Faisal said he would try to arrange transport for us, but after some time it became obvious he could not. Hasan called his brother again and asked him to pick us up.

'You should've answered the phone the first time,' I said to Hasan the next morning, after a night of reprimands from our parents. 'When you didn't return the call, your parents got worried. Then your brother called my father. Anyway, it was never a good idea to lie to our parents.' It was one of those rare occasions when Hasan tacitly admitted his mistake.

While the Shab-e-Juma issue was settled and soon forgotten, our encounter with the Talaba, the student wing of a religious political party, was not the last.

5

Waqas

Present day

My phone rang. It was Fareeha. 'Vickie, your girlfriend's on TV. She says your case is connected to the blasphemy case,' she said.

'What? Girlfriend? Who?' I stammered. Oh, she meant Amber. 'Wait, wait. Is she on TV? Which channel?'

Furqan and I had returned to the hotel as he told his story. I asked the man at the hotel to switch to another channel. The burly man took ages to exercise his limbs and press the remote-control button as he delivered instructions and curses to the hotel boys, just in time for me to see Amber disappearing from the screen and to wonder if she was wearing the same kurta I saw in the morning.

I said to Fareeha, 'Look, you shouldn't worry about what she said. My case has got nothing to do with blasphemy and lynching.' I looked at the boy as I said this on the phone, but his face was vacuous. I continued, 'You know how these media people like to create a sensation.'

'Where are you?'

'I'm meeting someone. It has nothing to do with this case. Don't worry. I'll be back home soon. Meanwhile, watch something on Hum TV. Which play do we have today? It's *Humsafar* tonight, right? We'll watch it together.'

I rose to my feet and said to Furqan, 'We need to stop now, young man. It's getting late for you too, I guess. Thanks for your time and cooperation. But I need more of them soon, maybe tomorrow. I'll let you know.' Furqan also got up, and we quickly said goodbye.

A bookshop attracted my attention as I drove off on my motorcycle. I hadn't read much poetry since I joined the police force. The Meeraji book had also been on my mind since the morning when I saw it in Maulana Saleem's madrasah. Although I had read little of Meeraji, I knew he had a reputation for obscenity. Why would Saleem have his book?

I parked my motorcycle in front of the shop—Danish Kada was its name. It was next to a chicken *karahi* house sprawled on a large expanse of the footpath and there was a parking lot in front of it. People sat around tables and ate under hanging tube lights, while cats and dogs scavenged from the leftovers thrown under the tables. The lights illuminated the thick layer of dust sitting just above people's heads. The dust pervaded the whole town but was not discernible. It obscured things and limited visibility. The light exposed the dust to anyone who cared to see it. But did everyone see it?

The young man behind the bookshop counter was busy with his mobile phone. I asked him if he had any books by Meeraji.

'You mean the actress Meera? Has she written a book or did someone write a book about her?'

That dashed my hopes of finding the book. But I persisted. 'I'm talking about the poet Meeraji. He lived in the early twentieth century.'

'Who reads poetry these days? Knowledge lies in the deen, and we have a large collection of religious books.' The young man who had a small beard eyed the shelves neatly stacked with stationery items mostly and some books.

'No, thank you.'

As I turned to leave, he said, 'In the street behind this one is a library inside a homoeopathy shop. You may find poetry there. It's a bit late, but you can try.'

'What's the name of the man who's running the shop?'

'Karamat, I guess. Not sure.'

Most shops were closing as I drove to the street the young man had told me about. The call to evening prayer emanated simultaneously from many loudspeakers. Most streetlights didn't work, and it was with difficulty that I spotted Karamat's homoeopathy shop. The man's back was towards me as he pulled down the shutter door with a clang.

'You're closing for the day?' I asked.

He turned around slowly, placing a bunch of jingling keys inside the pocket of his grey kurta. In the darkness around us, I could hardly see his face, but he appeared to be of average height and squat build. A small beard gave him a rugged look.

'What ails you?' he asked rolling his kurta sleeves up to his elbows.

'Nothing. I'm looking for a book on Meeraji.'

The man considered me for a while. In the dim light of a street lamp, his appearance reminded me neither of a doctor nor a librarian but of a tonga wallah.

'Which religious party are you from, Bhai?'

Saleem's dusty bookshelf flashed through my mind again. 'What makes you think I'm from a religious party?'

The call to prayer ended, causing a sudden quiet to descend on the place.

'Hmm . . . Never mind. I have a few books on him, but I won't sell or lend them to you. You can sit here and read, but not today. I must leave for dinner.'

'No problem. I'll come back another day, at a more reasonable time. Thanks.'

I walked away towards my motorcycle, thinking of Furqan's description of Karamat. While driving home, I phoned Ashraf and told him I needed the blasphemy case files on my table before I reported to the office the next morning. As my motorcycle passed under a banner saying, 'Down with the blasphemer!'—one of many amid eateries glittering with bulbs and tube lights—I was reminded of what happened in the town a few months ago.

* * *

'Vickie, how can you not fall asleep immediately after a tiring day?' Fareeha asked when she saw me staring at the ceiling as I lay on my bed after a shower and dinner.

'That's because I haven't held you in my arms yet.'

'If you wait for that, you might miss a few hours' sleep. Remember, the children's holidays have begun, and they won't sleep early. Expect them to barge in anytime.'

'A few hours? I can wait for a lifetime, sweetheart. But do come here this very minute.'

'Do they coach policemen in the art of seduction?' Fareeha asked, as she tidied up the bedroom. The smile on her lips and the dimples on her pink cheeks sweetened her face.

'By the way, how are the children doing? I felt they weren't happy with our move to the new place.'

'Rameez complained and argued; he's your carbon copy. Wasif and Roshni are more docile. Don't worry about them. Listen, I'm afraid you think too much about the blasphemy case, and that girlfriend of yours has put bad ideas in your mind. Throw them out, please.' She sat opposite me on the bed. Her smile had disappeared.

'You mean: get *her* out of my mind?'

Her way of ignoring my insinuations about other women and similar naughty things was adorable. Just when I started to kiss her, the kids stormed in. The boys circled the bed while Roshni bounced on it. Fareeha told them to go back to their beds. It took them some time to obey, after they had hugged Fareeha and me.

'Has she married?' Fareeha asked, adjusting the bed-sheet after the kids' stampede. She was a cleanliness freak, smoothening a wrinkle as soon as she spotted one.

'No. She's still waiting for me. That's one thing she likes about Islam. It allows men to have more than one wife.' I winked.

She ignored my joke and said, 'By the way, to me, you two—you and she—look poles apart. I never understood how you two could have been friends.'

I had often wondered why I had fallen for her. She wasn't pretty. Perhaps with her height, I-don't-give-a-fuck attitude and audacious dressing, she had redefined the standards of female attractiveness. And she made sure men found her repulsive. I once asked her if she was interested in women. Never one to worry about what other people thought about her, she said maybe she was.

I said, 'I used to read a lot of poetry. She was interested in that too, although her Urdu was horrible—the English-medium class, you know. She used to ask me to read Faiz's poems to her. In return, she read some English stuff to me. That's how . . .'

We sit side by side on our favorite bench in the university, with books in our hands. The winter sun feels like a plush, warm blanket. I read and she listens. When she reads, I watch her more than I listen.

'Her parents divorced when she was very young, isn't that so?' I nodded, and Fareeha continued while pulling out bed-sheets from a carton. 'Poor woman. Such a childhood affects you all your life.'

'Ammi was also wary of Amber, citing the same reason you mentioned. I don't think there's anything wrong with that. And she's sexy.' I winked at Fareeha, wondering if I was faking things or believed in what I said.

Fareeha changed the topic. 'You said the case—about the boy's death in Shanti Nagar—is closed. Amber sounded like it will start a new fiasco.'

'They always do that—these media people. Didn't I tell you, Fari?'

'But you also said Amber's different.'

I recalled the first time I introduced the two women. Amber said she wanted to meet Fareeha. Perhaps Amber wanted to show that our break-up had not jolted her. Fareeha broke into a cold sweat, when I told her a female friend of mine would come to see her. The very idea of my friendship with a woman was weird to her. The poor woman could hardly utter a word in response to Amber's frank sense of humor and repeated use of the word *yaar*.

'Well, she's different. You've seen her. But she must stick to her channel's policies.'

Fareeha was quiet for a long time—not the quietness that comes with thoughtfulness but one that's characteristic of her obedience. 'I know it's difficult for you to ignore the blasphemy case, but unless you try not to, you'll keep getting involved.'

'I know. I just want to dig into a few details before I close the case,' I said. I was sure she wasn't convinced. She would continue to worry about me. If I told her the details, though, she would ask me to do as Shakir wanted.

'Oh, I nearly forgot.' Fareeha had an animated way of dealing with memory lapses, getting excited over things she suddenly remembered and fretting over what she couldn't recall. 'Bhabhi called.'

'Oh, nice! After ages, it seems.'

'Yeah. Finally, she found time for me. That surprised me; you know it's considered my duty to call.'

'All good?' I ignored the rivalry of the sisters-in-law. 'How's Bhai Jaan?'

'Good. Bhabhi said he wanted to talk to you. So you had better call him.'

'I'll do that right away. I hope he's not asleep.'

He wasn't. After the preliminaries, he asked, 'Where have you gotten yourself posted?' There he was, sounding like Ammi again.

'I didn't get myself posted. The posting order came, and I moved. What else can I do?'

'Good officers can do a lot.'

'Well, if you consider me a good police officer, think again.'

'When will you learn to be an obedient policeman?'

'Probably never. I'll leave the police force soon.'

There was a long pause at the other end, during which I heard Bhabhi, his wife, admonishing her kids. 'Oh, God!

Waqas, when will you settle down? There's nothing wrong with this job!'

'I know where the wrong lies.'

'I don't know about the wrong, but the right lies in lying low and doing as the world does. It's simple, and you'll see it's the secret to success. Just speak when it's needed.'

'Yeah, the way I never spoke after Abba's death because no one needed it, right?'

Silence again at the other end.

I'm tidying up Abba's stuff—books, notebooks and pens. Nothing compares to being his assistant in the small office of his madrasah. He sits there at his table writing, working on his articles for the madrasah magazine. I saunter around, doing his chores. I hope he will dictate some stuff to me, and I'll write it. Won't that be great?

Some friends of Abba enter. Ibraheem is among them. I call him Chacha. They talk. Then the discussion turns ugly. Are they debating or quarrelling? They utter some words again and again: jihad, proxy wars, bloodshed.

Bhai Jaan's words pulled me back to the present, 'Are you listening, Waqas? It's useless talking to you.' He hung up. I was not sure when Fareeha came and sat on the bed near me, her hand on my knee.

'Why did you have to say that? You know it hurts him.' Fareeha spoke timidly.

'Why does he have to remind me that I'm no good? I know I'm not good. I couldn't get the jobs I want; gambling was the only way I could earn money, and my police career isn't great. But he doesn't have to throw that in my face every time we talk.'

'Okay, just forget it. Call him again tomorrow and make up with him, please,' she said as she rose to her feet. 'The goat legs are on the stove. Tomorrow's lunch. You know they take all night to cook. I'll be back in a minute, but please don't fret.'

While she rushed to the kitchen, my mind wandered off to Abba as I leaned against the bed's headboard and stared at the ceiling fan.

I sit on the front crossbar as Abba rides the bicycle. The November night air hits me on the face and feels cold, though, in the bazaar, it's warmer. The front wheel is steered by an unknown force; just as it appears to hit someone, making me gasp, it finds its way around people. Abba stops at Rasheed Sweets and buys barfi for me. He puts the paper bag in the right-hand side pocket of his coat, and as he rides again, now and then he puts a bite-sized piece of barfi into my mouth. With the barfi, Abba's green Rahber bicycle, and his rust-coloured tweed coat arms on both sides of me, life couldn't be better.

When Fareeha returned from her food rescue mission with whiffs of the goat curry and sat on the bed facing me, I said, 'Fari, you remember when we watched the movie *Lion King* with the boys? Roshni hadn't been born yet then, right? I could empathize with Simba in the scene where his father, while trying to save him, is stampeded by the wildebeest. My father, though, was stampeded by a herd of humans, who were supposed to know what they were doing. The wildebeest didn't even know they could kill someone.'

'There's something about a mob. It's probably no better than a herd of animals. And that's what people like Scar— wasn't that the name of the bad lion?—exploit. But Waqas, please forget all this. It's not going to do you any good. And that's what Bhai Jaan wants you to do . . .'

'No!'

My utterance was so emphatic, it jolted poor Fareeha. She took her hand away from where it had rested on mine. I sat up from a reclining position.

'No,' I continued, 'I don't want to forget it, Fari. Do you hear me? All my life I've wanted to talk about Abba. He deserved some words said about him. Bhai never had the courage to describe what Abba went through—he witnessed it—and we never had the courage to ask. We recited a lot of the Quran, day in and day out—it was just us and the extended family. The neighbours had tacitly boycotted us. Many of them didn't come to the funeral. But we did not speak about Abba. In his own language, Punjabi, or even in Urdu. As though he had sinned.'

Fareeha's face contorted. She looked tormented by my misery. But I continued to talk, not to her but to myself. 'Ammi said reciting the Quran would help. To be honest, it didn't. I wanted to know if Abba had done something wrong. He deserved to be remembered. We should have talked about his death and the circumstances surrounding it. It was suffocating for me. I was just eight years old then.'

'Religious issues are something we don't talk about. Blasphemy, in particular. You know that, Vickie.' Fareeha's voice rang with helplessness at not being able to convince me. All she could do was worry. She never shared my feelings. Amber was a discerning listener when I told her all this in our university days.

'True. There's a fear associated with them. But fear of what? I ask. Of accidentally insulting Allah or the Holy Prophet, they say. But how can you *accidentally* commit sacrilege against them? Why this fear? It's like a smog that settles down on us in the winters in Punjab. It's pervasive and intrusive. It's so ubiquitous we stop worrying about it.'

'I was very young when Ammi told me about what had happened to your Abba. But I didn't understand much. It would've been so difficult for you to live in that neighborhood. That's why you moved, right? You must've felt like an uprooted tree. Can it grow somewhere else?'

This time her words felt like poetry to my ears. I knew she had listened to all this before but for my sake she told me to go on.

'Yes, it was terrible living where we had lived for years.' I reclined on the pillow again. 'But fortunately, humans are not trees. They can start growing elsewhere. We moved to Lahore; Bhai requested his railways' bosses to post him out of our hometown. Maybe his bosses also didn't want him there. But this thing—I don't know what to call it—is so insidious. Why the hell doesn't it let me go?! Or maybe there's something in me that doesn't want to let go of it.'

I paused as I remembered something and continued, 'In my new school, my teacher, Miss Nida—I told you about her, didn't I?—asked me to introduce myself in my first class. The interview inevitably led to Abba. I said he was no more. She said she was sorry to hear that, and she asked how he died. I was speechless, utterly blank. What should I say? By then my mind had become attuned to not talking. The silence was unbearable. It lasted only a few moments, during which all eyes were on me. 'Make it up,' Ammi used to say to me when an occasion warranted fibs. But I couldn't. That would have been so unfair to Abba. Miss Nida realized my unease and moved on to another topic.'

'Tell me again about her.' She had heard of it before, but she knew I wanted to talk about Miss Nida.

'She's the most beautiful woman I have known in my life, more beautiful than you even.'

Fareeha smiled broadly, pleased not because of the praise but because my humour told her I was at ease. She played along, holding both of my hands in hers. 'More beautiful than Amber too?'

Nice joke. I laughed as a show of admiration and slid down on the bed. 'Amber's not pretty. No match to you, really. You have the most edible cheeks.'

'Never mind. Tell me about Miss Nida.' Fareeha made herself comfortable on the edge of the bed; her thigh against my shins could take away all the harshness of my life.

'She had a warmth about her, a glow in her eyes and a smile that spread like watercolour dropped in water. She made a huge difference to me. After that first class, she called me to her room and asked me again about Abba. She was the first person I talked to about Abba's tragedy. God! It was like releasing a pressure cooker—I was able to breathe after many years.' I paused as I tried to recall things. 'She used to read poetry to me. She was studying for a Master's in Urdu Literature. And she introduced me to the pleasures of stories on Radio Pakistan. She told me about a channel that aired weekly stories for children. I listened in a trance to a lady narrate a fairy tale every Thursday at six in the evening—never missed one. What a joy it was listening to her voice emanate from our radio set—you remember those large sets of the '80s with two knobs and a netted front? Her modulated voice was like Ammi's lullaby to me. But it came from another world. And her pauses took me to a fairyland.'

'Sweet! Did you meet Ms Nida after those school days?'

'No. I think of her whenever I go to Lahore. She's still teaching, and she's still the most beautiful woman I've ever seen. I saw her photo on Punjab University's website.'

'Why don't you meet her?'

I sighed. 'I messed it up. It was the poetry perhaps that prompted me to ask Ammi one day why we didn't tell people that Abba had done nothing wrong. Why did we not go to the police? Why did the police not do anything? She asked me who I was talking to. The goof that I was, I told her.'

Fareeha snuggled in the bed beside me and cradled my head with her arm. I kissed her hand and watched the ceiling on which the wilting whitewash made intriguing designs.

Ammi sits on the prayer mat. She turns her head right and then left . . . that means she has finished the prayer . . .

'Ammi, when Abba died, err . . . did we report it to the police?' She won't scold me while she is sitting on the prayer mat. Allah will not allow her.

Ammi looks at me. She recites something—Quranic verses— and blows at me, her way of warding off evil. 'The police would not have done anything.' At least she's talking about it.

'You mean the police couldn't catch the killers?'

She's thinking again. The white dupatta wrapped tightly around her face and covering her head gives her a pristine look. 'Are you talking to someone about it?'

'My teacher . . . Miss Nida. She said I shouldn't be afraid of talking.'

Bhai stands in the doorway. He usually doesn't want anything to worry him after a long day's work. He and Ammi look at me and then at each other. My feet and eyes are glued to the floor. Have I said something bad?

'Read Sura-e-Naas often,' Ammi says. 'It's one of my favourite recitations from the Quran—all are my favourites, but this one marginally more—and it rids you of bad thoughts.' I've read the Urdu translation of the Sura. It talks about how Allah's name gets rid of trepidation. But mine was no trepidation or bad thoughts.

Were thoughts about Abba bad? Why couldn't we talk about his death?

A few days later . . .

I sit outside her office on a bench. Through the open door, I can see her face as she patiently listens to Ammi. She looks at me suddenly. I hope she understands that I didn't complain to Ammi about her. She looks hurt. I can never forget the look on her face.'

Fareeha did not ask me to narrate the whole story, but I did. 'Miss Nida didn't call me to her office after that. I became even quieter about the matter, and since then, I've seldom talked to her—maybe a few times—despite my knowledge of her whereabouts. I can't face her.'

She smoothed back the hair from my forehead. 'It wasn't your fault, Vickie. You were a child. You shouldn't feel guilty.'

'Maybe you're right. Maybe.' I continued to look at the ceiling.

'But you can see her now, can't you? Why don't we go and meet her? Lahore isn't far.'

'Yes, we should. She'll be pleased to see you and the kids. I hope I can find time for that soon.'

'Let's plan it as soon as we can. Hope you don't regret it like Munir Niazi,' she said with a warm smile.

'I won't. But well said,' I responded with a smile and kissed her on her neck. She was alluding to Munir Niazi's poem:

Hamesha der kar deta huun main har kaam karne mein
zaruri baat kehni ho koi vaada nibhana ho

[I'm always late in doing things I have to do.
In saying something important to someone, in fulfilling a promise.]

'And remember, no one can tell you you're not good. For me, you're the best. Do you know that my sisters used to say I'm so lucky to be marrying you, that you look like Humayun Saeed? You have the same wide forehead, the same high cheekbones, the same smile . . .'

Even as I recalled that Furqan had said something similar, I laughed and said, 'And the same height.'

'Oh, come on, Vickie. Please don't be a cynic.'

'Okay. Thank you for the baby talk, but please . . . No more.'

She placed her head on my chest and was snoring gently within seconds. Cursing myself for pushing her away, I adjusted my head on the pillow, wrapped my arm around her, and tried to sleep.

Is that a dream, my fantasy or real memories invading me? Memories of Amber would invariably be there, visiting me in the shithole of a room that was my gambling den. Thank God none of my friends were there when she visited or it would've given them the wrong ideas. Wrong ideas, really? I'm embarrassed by its filth and mine . . . I must've smelled of cheap cigarettes—were they also drugged?—but she got into bed with me under the red and blue blanket—it must have smelled foul too—and we explored each other's bodies—the only time I touched her breasts under her grey top—why did she wear androgynous colours? Did she say I took up gambling to make her feel sorry? Did I tell her she had no right to pity me? Did she leave so fast? . . . I'm drowning in an ocean. I pedal my arms and legs frantically and every time my head bobs up above the surface, I see water everywhere . . . no one to rescue me.

6

Waqas

Present day

'Sir, I thought we've closed the case?' Ashraf asked as I walked into my office the next morning. Two ungainly piles of files sat on my table, with dog-eared enclosures peeping out of the covers and paperweights on top of them. The small cubicle office looked even smaller with the mountains of files that threatened to fall at any moment.

'I need to confirm a couple of things, Ashraf. You can help me with that. Find out if this boy Hasan was among those the police rounded up in the blasphemy case, after the riot.'

Ashraf was probably sullen, but he didn't say anything in protest. Sitting in a chair next to the table, he began to examine the files. His square face was calm. Only his thick moustache twitched.

'Please keep the files on my table so we can work together. I've found some evidence that he was among the rioters, but I need to confirm it.' I could take Ashraf into my confidence.

'Sir, may I ask you something? What if he was among those who did the lynching? I believe this case has nothing to do with that one.'

'Sorry, Ashraf. I think you're wrong there,' I said, as I pulled down a very old calendar from the wall, tore it to pieces and binned it. It was the best I could do to make my office tolerable.

I continued as I walked towards my chair, 'If we find out Hasan was involved in the riot, it is likely that incident engendered whatever happened yesterday—or maybe the previous night, whatever. If Hasan was involved in lynching the Hindu guy, wouldn't someone from the victim's family want to avenge his death?'

'Why Hasan alone? It was a mob that attacked the Hindu guy.'

'Maybe because he was at the forefront of the attack. Maybe he's the first in a series. The two knew each other. That makes Hasan an easily identifiable target for revenge.'

'How do you know that, sir?'

'Forget about me. Didn't you know that?'

'What?'

'That Hasan and the Hindu guy knew each other very well. What else?'

I looked up from a file to survey Ashraf's face. Why does everyone want to close this case? But then, didn't I also want the same till I met Amber and Furqan yesterday?

'No, sir. How could I have known? But I'm surprised you haven't closed the case yet. Did you find a witness?'

'Maybe. But let me confirm a few things first.'

'I'll dig into the files, sir.'

After a few minutes, during which I cleaned my table drawers off the junk the previous occupant of the office had stuffed into them—as well as a dead lizard that made me grimace—Ashraf placed a file in front of me. Under the high-speed ceiling fan, it was difficult to keep the file enclosures in place. 'Yes, sir. Hasan Zubair. That's his name on the list.'

'So he was apprehended,' I said, while surveying the report. 'Then all of them were released. Anything on that?'

'Nobody takes responsibility for that kind of thing. You know that, sir. I remember that SHO Sahib conveyed verbal orders when these men had been in prison for a few days. A couple of days only, I think.'

As I browsed the file, Ashraf continued, 'You know, sir, there was also a Hindu mob there, armed with sticks and stones. Somebody said there were guns too. The arrests were made mainly to prevent things from turning ugly. But then the police feared a greater backlash from the Deen and Millat parties who were furious because many of their party members were arrested, while only a few Hindus were rounded up. The orders must've come from the top.'

'There's one more thing,' I said, reclining against the back of the seat. 'Who let the Hindu guy out when everyone knew the Deen was baying for his blood? He was arrested without any charges, but that was for his own safety, right? But then, why was he released?'

'You mean, who released him from prison the day he was lynched? I think that, too, was on SHO Sahib's orders, sir. That was a mistake. Or perhaps it was an irresponsible act. Or perhaps he was just following orders. But then who bothers about that, sir? Who cares? If my boss tells me to do something that I know will have dire consequences, would I bother to argue with him? Isn't he supposed to know better than I do? Unless it's going to affect me, I won't think twice before following orders.'

I listened quietly to Ashraf's speech; he continued, 'Even now, if you ask me to reopen this case, I won't warn you that you'd be fiddling with beehives. It's not my responsibility to set things right when people have other ideas.'

'Other ideas? You mean I want to spoil things while you want to correct them?'

'Sir, don't you know what a blasphemy accusation means in this country? Even if the Hindu guy was innocent, it was better to leave him in prison for it meant that a town would remain at peace, right? So even if a few lives were lost, it's better not to seek justice for them at the cost of more lives. Sir, all I'm saying is that the best policy in this country is to let things run as they are.'

Ashraf's insolent harangue annoyed me, but I listened as he continued, 'Sir, I've studied some Physics. The other day, while I was helping my child with his homework, I came across Newton's Laws of Motion again. It's been a long time since I studied them in school. Our society is in inertia. It doesn't like change. And I don't have the force to disrupt the inertia.'

This time Ashraf's analogy amused me. 'You're right, but I'll do what I must, Ashraf. Something in me makes me oblivious to the laws of Physics. I may not reopen the case, but I need to ascertain some facts. Did you record the statements of the Zubair family, Ashraf?'

'No, sir. I thought we had closed the case.'

'I want you to do that. In fact, I'll go with you. While you're making your preparations, I'll see how to request the autopsy.'

'We decided yesterday to close the case. What has turned up since then?' Shakir, as expected, was annoyed to hear that I wanted an autopsy done on Hasan.

'Sir, I need to find out a few things. I'll most probably keep the case closed.'

'What? Do you get a kick out of autopsies? What's the point of having an autopsy done if you're not going to pursue the case? Waqas, talk some sense.' Shakir paraded around his office as if in search of something. That's how he tidied things up and presumably felt he had done something productive. A big tummy on a frail body looked ungainly on him.

Standing because Shakir was on his feet, I watched him helplessly. He had a point.

'Sir, let me go ahead with the autopsy. If we find concrete evidence that it wasn't suicide, then we can discuss a further course of action.'

'But we're not going for any further course of action, regardless of whether it was suicide or not. Even DSP Sahib has agreed to it. I don't want to have anything to do with those mullahs. Do you hear me?'

I reminded myself not to lose my temper. *I've decided what I want to do, and I'll do it no matter what Shakir says. I won't rest in peace until I've done it.*

I thanked Shakir and returned to my office, where I asked Ashraf and his team to accompany me to Hasan's house.

* * *

While my team was recording the family's statements, I unlocked and entered Hasan's room, which reeked of a suffocating odour. I felt as if I had stepped into an oven. I waited a few seconds for the ventilation to work before I stepped in and switched on the light. Dust, melancholy and—now that there was a blasphemy connection—fear sat on everything. Two things I

didn't pay much attention to the previous morning were a study
table and a cupboard. A few books lay on the table. One was
on Physics, another on Calculus—pre-Engineering textbooks
probably, things I hated in college. There were a few on Islamic
hadith and *fiqah*. A copy of Sahih Bukhari, a few volumes of
Maulana Maududi's Quranic *tafseer*. Dr Israr Ahmed's book
on the Islamic Renaissance. A thin layer of dust lay on all the
books as if it was a part of them. I ran a finger along the front of
the Renaissance book, opening a narrow window to the shinier
cover. What was Hasan reading in his last few days? What was
he thinking? What was his role in Mohan's death? Furqan told
me he and Hasan admired Mohan so much. How then could
Hasan have been behind Mohan's death?

I turned towards the cupboard fixed against the opposite
wall and opened it. It was untidy, with clothes almost thrown
around in various drawers. Socks, underwear, T-shirts and tying
cords for shalwars rolled into balls. I rummaged through all the
drawers but found nothing of interest. One drawer was locked.

I walked out of the room, where Jawad stood waiting
for instructions, if any. Today his hair was neatly combed,
revealing a broad forehead, which lent an air of handsomeness
to his face. As compared to yesterday, he also appeared to be at
ease talking to me. I told him to look for the key to the drawer.
While Jawad went downstairs, I resumed my exploration of
Hasan's belongings. One book was on Pakistan's madrasahs. I
leafed through it and read the back cover. The book was based
on research work on the Islamic educational system and the
madrasah's source of funds.

Funding was the reason for discord in Abba's madrasah, I
recalled. More than once, Ibraheem Chacha and a few others
argued with Abba. During those discussions, Abba would

tell me to leave the room. I overheard some things but could not make sense of them. Years later I understood that Abba's friends did not mind where the funds came from as long as they came; on the other hand, Abba's viewpoint was that such funding came from sources linked to jihad and that was why their madrasah should not accept it.

Jawad knocked on the door. He had not found the key to Hasan's drawer. He suggested sheepishly, 'It may be in the pocket of the clothes he was wearing. The body is not with us.'

'Was there a suicide note?'

'No. We didn't see any.'

I called Ashraf and asked him to have the lock broken. 'Have you had the fingerprints taken?' I asked him when he entered Hasan's room.

'Not yet, sir,' Ashraf said.

'Get that done before you break the lock. Call the forensics team here. I want the contents of the locked drawer in my office.'

After a few hours, Ashraf reached the police station with a bagful of Hasan's stuff and placed it on the table. I asked Ashraf to send the dead body for a post-mortem.

'Has Shakir Sahib endorsed it?' Ashraf looked surprised.

'You said this morning that when you receive orders, you don't bother about the who and how and why.'

'I'm sorry, sir. I won't ask any questions,' he said, with an apologetic smile and left. He had a way of getting sufficiently— but no more—chummy with his superiors.

The bag contained some cash, a diary, photos and newspaper cuttings. I leafed through the diary. It was a thick blue one, smaller than A4 size. There were several entries. Hasan wrote often, and sometimes in detail. The first entry was about three years old. Considering its age, the diary was in decent shape. I browsed through the journal entries and read their opening sentences. Many of them dealt with arts and Islam while some were on Islamic history. One was titled 'Why can't America leave us alone?' Another one started with 'Why are the modern arts un-Islamic?' I read a few lines and jumped to the more recent ones. The last one was dated two days before his death. It consisted of two pages and began with the title 'Notes from the AK article. Who's right about the Blasphemy Law?'

Who was AK?

7

Lubna

Nine months ago

'Our next assignment is titled *pir-e-tasma-pa*. What does that mean? Who can tell me? Who knows Urdu well enough to understand this?' The semester had just begun, and Mohan was bubbling with excitement.

Mohan, who had recently joined the Asian Institute of Fine Arts as a lecturer on his return from America, knew me as Hasan's sister. Our two families had met a few times, once in the boys' school and another time at an Eid mela. But did he recognize me? I was not sure.

'Is that a character in the Sinbad story, sir?' a boy asked from the back of the small auditorium. It was more a question than an answer.

'Excellent! Some people have read *Alif Laila* or *One Thousand and One Nights*, as it's called in English.'

'Sir, to be honest, I haven't read it. I saw it in my younger brother's textbook.' Everyone, including Mohan, laughed.

'Full marks for honesty. But what does it mean?' He looked around. No answer. Again, I was undecided as I knew part of the answer. Why do we girls become wary of men's eyes as we grow up?

Mohan continued, '*Pir* means 'old man'; *tasma* means 'shoelaces,' and *pa* means . . .'

'Feet.' A lot of voices rose. Some laughed. This was schoolkid stuff.

'Good! The old man with feet laced together.' He waited a while to let this sink in.

In class, Mohan was an actor on a stage. Or a great orator. Or perhaps a supremely confident lawyer advocating his case, not pleading it but making his audience understand.

'The story goes like this. Sinbad was stranded on an island where he met an emaciated old man who asked him to take him to another place on the island. Sinbad lifted the old man onto his shoulders, where he sat with his legs crossed across Sinbad's chest, like shoelaces. Hence, the name.'

Mohan paused, strolled around behind the lectern, and continued. 'Now it happened that the old man became a source of misery for poor Sinbad. He refused to get down from Sinbad's shoulders. For many days, Sinbad plodded around the island with the old man's legs locked around his neck.'

Mohan paused again and then resumed. 'Your assignment, ladies and gentlemen, is to draw or paint an image based on the phrase *pir-e-tasma-pa*. Think of it and read about it. Ponder over what this phrase conveys to you. What images, emotions, thoughts or reactions does it evoke in you? Then transform that emotion or idea into a painting.'

I felt tingling all over my body. It was palpable all over the auditorium, so real I would have been astonished if another student told me he or she couldn't feel it. Hasan had told me that Mohan was a walking encyclopaedia, that he knew something about nearly everything. But I never knew he could do this to people. He could do it to some people, I know, but of course some of them were interested only in passing the exam, those who merely wanted to get over the line, to get the passing mark. I called them Impressionists because they were creating a false impression of being artists.

'Sir, there's a similar story in Hindu mythology, that of Vikram and Baital,' a boy in the front row said. 'You must be aware of it.'

'Excellent!' Mohan was always encouraging and excitable. 'I didn't want to mention it yet as I wanted people to do their research. But now that this gentleman has mentioned it, let's talk about it. Baital was a mischievous spirit who demonized a certain country and terrorized its people. So the Raja of the country, Vikram, took it upon himself to capture Baital. He brought the spirit home, carrying him on his back and shoulders, somewhat like *pir-e-tasma-pa*, to be incarcerated. This is the prologue.'

Another pause. An excited clap of hands. A stroll in front of the class.

'The real story revolves around how, on the way back, the villainous Baital tells Vikram that he—Baital, I mean—would fly away the moment Vikram uttered a word. The only way to stop Baital from escaping was for Vikram to stay mum during the journey home. To make Vikram speak, the fiendish Baital tells him a story at the end of which there's an intriguing question that could test a man's wits. Now, Vikram, besides being brave, is a wise man; he loves solving riddles and puzzles. He can't restrain himself from speaking at the end of the story because he can decipher the puzzle. But as soon as he has given his answer, which is correct, Baital flies away, mocking Vikram for his wisdom and naivety at the same time.'

A pause.

'Like *Alif Laila*, this legend consists of a series of stories. In each chapter, Baital is captured, tells Vikram a story, and poses a bewildering question. In each chapter, Vikram can give the correct answer but falls into Baital's trap, enabling him to escape.

'Think about how the two stories are similar to each other and how they're different.' He resumed after a long pause. 'How are the two old men different? And how are they alike? But here's the caveat. Don't use a Google image or any other image-based hint because it would influence the image that's supposed to form in your head. Simply put, no cheating. Of course, I can't watch you while you're in your respective homes. But I trust you. Be honest. Read as much as you can, but don't search for images. Fair enough?'

'Yes, sir!' Fairly energetic voices arose.

'Good! We will have an initial exchange of ideas next week, on Wednesday. Is that okay? And two weeks after that, you submit your masterpieces. Enough time?'

The following Wednesday, Mohan asked us about the assignment, his eyes shining with excitement.

'Any thoughts? Any research?' He looked around but no one spoke, each one looking at the others.

Despite the initial excitement he had generated, Mohan could not motivate the students to do their homework. I had done some work, but I wasn't sure if it was good enough. Mohan looked disappointed, so I had to say something. I raised my hand.

'Yes, Ms Lubna.' He looked at me.

'Sir, could the old man symbolize religious fundamentalism, which impedes independent thinking? I chanced upon a poem by Kaifi Azmi with the same title . . .'

'Wonderful!' he cried, as if he had found what he was desperately looking for. 'Yes! Azmi sees religious bigotry as a yoke we've taken upon ourselves, like Sinbad's old man. Very good, Ms Lubna! Anything else?'

'Sir, in the same token,' I went on, 'could Baital be interpreted as a demon who punishes someone for speaking?'

'Why not? It could indeed be interpreted as such. There's no right or wrong here, Ms Lubna. If it resonates with hearts and minds, people will heed it. It certainly resonates with mine. I'm loving it! You have more?'

All eyes were on me. I couldn't speak for a while. Then I said, 'Sir, I was thinking of painting a female Sinbad—or a female Vikram. I mean to ask if *he* could be a *she*?'

'Superb! This is original, ladies and gentlemen.' He looked around at the class. Everyone was silent. 'We have a very innovative thinker among us. So, Ms Lubna, you want to portray womanhood fettered by the old man of tradition, bigotry and fundamentalism. I like it! I love it!'

Arifa, who always sat next to me, gave me a tacit thumbs up.

All through the day, as I walked back home, helped Ammi in the kitchen and sat down with the rest of my family for dinner, the thought of Mohan smiled on my lips, for anyone who cared to see.

Two weeks later, I submitted my painting, an oil work depicting the idea I had proposed in the class. Oh, God! I wanted it to be good. I spent so many hours trying to make it perfect. But I knew it wasn't.

Mohan said he loved it. 'You're good at portraits, and you can capture the mood, the feelings. Well done!'

I sat in his small office.

'I don't think it came off very well. But yes, I love doing portraits. My little sister and I play a lot of games themed around portraits—doodles, drawing from memory, drawing from description. Those kinds of things.'

'Then it runs in the family?' Mohan laughed. A restrained laughter. So avuncular, so wise beyond his age.

'Maybe. My sister is better than I am at doing portraits from memory.'

'By the way, are you a religious rebel?' he asked, tentatively.

'I am, I guess. I've mellowed with age, but yes, I am. I was freakish when I was younger.'

'Oh, really? What were you like then?'

'Once I cut the power connection to the loudspeakers of a nearby mosque. They were so loud I couldn't study for my exams.'

'And you disconnected the power cables?'

'Yes. With a pair of scissors.' He sat astounded as I giggled sheepishly. 'They were blurting out *na'at* hymns—I'm not sure you know what a *na'at* is; it's a poem in praise of our prophet— in tunes stolen from Bollywood songs. Can you imagine that? The very songs they deem infidel are inspirations for their hymns. Could anything be more hypocritical?'

Oh, poor man! He didn't know how to react to the anecdote. He surely found it funny and audacious. But a Hindu laughing over an Islamic thing? He knew the risks.

'Hasan said you loved Meeraji,' I said, eyeing his books in the tall, narrow bookshelf behind him. There was something special about his office. The way he had used the vertical space was smart, the piles of his artwork and the books placed on makeshift shelves nailed to the walls and going nearly to the ceiling. Hanging in a corner was his bag of dull brown leather. One side of it had the logo of a conference in Chicago. He must have attended it while he was in America. There was something about the way he slung it over his shoulder and across his chest. I knew he didn't show off. It just clicked. The best thing about the office, though, was its odour, the musty smell of the books and the aroma of the oil paints.

'Meeraji is one of my favorites. You know about him? He's not well known and is even less understood.'

'I've read a bit of him. Intriguingly difficult. You've never asked us to paint anything from his poetry. I thought you would.'

He smiled, his eyes wide with excitement. 'Several times I tried to pick a theme from his poetry, but I find him so abstract. I feel that any of his poetry depicted in painting will fall short of what he's conveying. One critic said he's like a railway station where myriad lines end and start from. He's full of possibilities. If you want to read about him, I can give you a book I have at home—a collection of essays on him.'

'I'd love to read more about him. Lovely simile, this railway station and Meeraji. Railway stations fascinate me—they evoke images of parting, meeting, yearning and nostalgia. There's a romance about them—like they belong to an earlier, more placid era.'

'Yes, true. I can bring you the Meeraji book. When's our next class? Hmm,' he said to himself, looking at the calendar on the wall. 'Right. Wednesday, you'll have it.'

Arifa told me people were talking about Mohan and me. She was a nerd—head covered with oiled hair wrapped in a dupatta—and was always worried about exams. I didn't pay much heed to what she said, but she repeated it. She said that the new bearded boy told a group of boys I had become a teacher's pet. What? What did he mean by that? And who was he to comment? But I stopped visiting Mohan's office and saw him only in the classroom. He glanced at me askance. Did he wonder why I hadn't collected the book he brought for me? Should I reach out to him and explain?

8

Furqan

Present day

'Who was the man you were talking to in the park, Furqan?'
As I entered my home, I heard Abba speaking from his room.

'Must be his friend. Was he, Furqan?' Ammi asked, perhaps
alarmed by Abba's tone, as I entered the room.

She was rummaging through the clothes stuffed inside
a narrow cupboard. It was a small room in which everything
competed for space, like an overcrowded bus. Two single
beds, separated by a hardly visible side table, were small by
themselves but too large for the room. In a corner behind the
beds stood the faded silver cupboard, from which the clothes
were always about to spill out. Everything was dropping out
from somewhere. You'd open a cupboard to fetch a notebook
and a few unwanted ones would plop out. While taking care of
them, you forgot what you came for.

'I guess he is a police officer, isn't he?' Abba asked. He was perusing some documents—office stuff—spread in front of him on the bed, his glasses pushed up to his forehead.

'Police officer?' Ammi asked. She paused her work and sat on the bed. She usually sat down when she was under stress.

'Does it have something to do with Hasan's death?' Abba asked, bringing the glasses back to his nose while staring at me.

'Yes.' I had to say something. How did Abba guess that? Inspector Waqas was not in the police's uniform. Perhaps his body language—he carried himself with great authority—his thickset physique, and authoritative demeanour betrayed him.

'But how did he find you? How did he know you were Hasan's friend?'

Ammi said, 'Hasan's family might've told the police.'

'Can you be quiet for a while?' Abba asked Ammi, visibly irritated. He looked at me again and asked, 'How did the police reach you so quickly? And why did he talk to you in the park?'

When I didn't reply, Abba continued, 'Did you approach him?' I nodded, leaning against the bed. Throwing a piece of paper furtively in the police jeep, which tested my heartbeat and nerves, now looked even more daring to me. The three of us were now speechless. Abba looked close to exasperation. He rarely lost his temper, but any father would get mad about this issue.

'Listen, son,' he finally said, surprisingly composed. 'The blasphemy issue is an extremely dangerous affair in this country. So many people have lost their lives because they were either accused of blasphemy or they just sympathized with the accused. We've lost two lives because of it—any idiot can guess Hasan was also its victim. And police business always means trouble.'

'I know, Abba.' I sat on the bed. 'Those two were my best friends. I want to help the police find the culprits. This police inspector is different. Looks like he wants to get to the truth. Let me help him, Abba.'

'You're so naïve, Furqan, and Mohan stuffed a good deal of idealism in you. But no, I can't allow you. Don't see the police officer unless you can't avoid him.' Then Abba went quiet with a sigh. He didn't like treating me this way.

Ammi walked towards me and said, 'Don't expose yourself. Be safe. Okay?' She ran her hand through my hair. I nodded. 'Let's eat. I've cooked bhindi.'

After a quiet dinner in the kitchen with Ammi—both of us sitting on step-stools in front of the stove so she could offer me freshly toasted rotis—I trudged to my room, which I shared with Bhai, who was asleep—he had a tough field job in the telephone company and went to bed early. Without switching on the light, I sat on my bed for a long time, staring into the darkness.

I took out my phone and flicked through the photo collection. I jumped to one of Mohan, Ram and Hasan. I had bought this Samsung phone a few days before the photo was taken. It was my first smartphone. Hasan had been insisting that I should have one, but I always said such a phone was a luxury. To be honest, I didn't have enough money to buy one and I didn't want to ask Abba or Bhai for it. If nothing else, it will help you take photos, Hasan had said. And there's a new app called WhatsApp that will allow you free calls and messages with anyone anywhere in the world. I had saved some of the money I earned through the evening tuition service I gave to the neighbouring kids. When I got the phone, we went to the irrigation canal for a dip. In the photo, all three

were without shirts, soaking and smiling. I adjusted the pillow
and rested my head on it as I looked at the picture on the
phone screen. I would touch the screen every few seconds so
the picture wouldn't disappear behind the screen saver. How
I wished friends could be secured against death this way, with
the touch of a finger!

* * *

'*Assalam-o-Alaikum*, Uncle. Thank you for your visit. It means so
much to us. Furqan has been like Hasan to us.' Hasan's brother,
Jawad, welcomed Abba and me. I let Abba offer words of
sympathy. I never knew what to say when offering condolences.
How did people manage big words on such occasions?

The drawing room was crowded and hot and smelled
of perspiration. Someone had pulled aside the curtains and
opened the windows to let some air in. It was past *Zuhr* prayer
time, and the sun encroached on the room. The people who
were there to offer their condolences sat in various corners of
the room. Maulana Saleem sat in the middle of the room on
the sofa, Saleem's hand on Hasan's father's shoulder. Zameer,
my college classmate, sat on the other side of Saleem. Ammi
had gone inside the house to talk to the women; a buzz of
conversation, punctuated with wails, could be heard from there.
Abba and I stood for a while surveying the room. Hasan's father
stood and ushered Abba towards the sofa beside them. Zameer
vacated a seat for Abba and joined me. We stood against the
wall and talked about Hasan.

'Thanks for being here,' Zameer said, leaning against the
wall. 'I feel more at ease with you around.' Zameer, who was a
serious and stiff-looking boy, never looked at ease.

'We—Abba, Ammi, and I—planned to visit anyway, and now was a good time. The police have been all around the place since yesterday morning.'

'I can't believe he took his own life.'

I decided it wasn't the best time to argue over that. My voice would have come out hoarse if I wanted to speak. I couldn't believe Hasan would never again walk in through the door. Was the dust on the light blue leather sofa the only thing that looked odd? My heart sank when I noticed Lubna's drawings on the walls were gone too. I looked around the room and found some photo frames placed upside down on the coffee table that had been pushed against the wall. Why were they placed like this? Perhaps Maulana Saleem told the family that the depiction of human faces had brought them Allah's wrath.

Zameer continued, 'You three had always helped me a lot. Hasan always took the lead. He approached me when I needed help with Maths, although it was Ram and you who explained the algorithms. But Hasan was the spokesman, wasn't he?'

I couldn't utter a word. I didn't even look at Zameer. When he first came to college, Zameer was like a child who had lost his way at a funfair. He told us that, having a rustic background, he was intimidated by the city and college life. His greatest phobia was the English language. Some classmates, including Yasir, would pull his leg. The three of us, led by Hasan, helped him a lot not only in his studies but also in terms of adjustment to college life.

Zameer probably noticed I was somewhere else. Did he see tears in my downcast eyes? Sounding awkward, he said, 'Without the three of you, I would've quit college. Sadly, Hasan's no more.'

I thought of Mohan. Who, other than his family and few friends, cried for him? I wished we could mention Mohan's death in the same breath.

Maulana Saleem began to recite a prayer in Arabic. His voice grew loud above the din of other conversations, until one voice held the house in its spell. Everyone became quiet and turned their chairs to face the centre of the room. They sat with their hands in front of them, in a gesture of praying. The house echoed with a chorus of 'Ameen' every time Saleem finished one piece of *dua*. He went on and on; I felt he would never stop. I recalled his lectures during Shab-e-Juma—the Thursday night when Hasan, Ram and I went to a mosque. Once he was the focus of attention, Saleem would not let go of it. His face was drenched in sweat, making his pinkish skin glow. Eyes closed and head bobbing back and forth gently, he seemed to be totally engrossed in his prayer.

Saleem appeared to have finished. I was relieved, but he started praying in Urdu, asking Allah to guide the young generation and to forgive Hasan's sin. He meant suicide, of course. I wondered how Hasan's father and brother, who sat next to him—their heads bowed, their hands covering their faces—felt. Did they wish they could have hidden the circumstances of Hasan's death? My mind wandered off towards Lubna. Did she hear Saleem? What was she going through?

After what seemed like ages, the *dua* ended. Everyone looked around quietly like they had lost any link with the past. Zameer suggested we bring water bottles for the visitors, as a help to the grieving family. That was considerate of him. Zameer and I zigzagged through a crowd of madrasah boys sitting on chairs and reading the Quran or just standing near the entrance. We walked towards a shop around the corner and brought a large carton of Nestlé water bottles—Zameer reminded the shopkeeper to give us the ones from the fridge. Jawad thanked us when we returned with the bottles, and the three of us distributed these.

As we walked back home, Ammi whispered to Abba, 'This girl Lubna, she's behind it all.' A few steps behind them, I had to strain my ears to listen.

'Behind what? The boy's death? I thought it's got something to do with Mohan's death,' Abba sounded astonished.

'Shh! Speak low. See those mullahs? They're all over the place.'

I looked around and wondered which ones Ammi was specifically referring to. Saleem had returned to his madrasah. So what were these boys doing here in the heat and dust?

'Both are connected, of course, but this girl is behind both deaths,' Ammi continued. 'Someone said something about how people needed to look after their daughters, not letting them walk free or the men will lose their lives. And you know what? The girl had the cheek to rebut. I'm not sure what she said, but she shouted and then ran to her room crying.'

'Only Allah knows the truth. Let's not judge anyone unwisely.'

When we reached home, I thought I should call Lubna. But would she be in the right state of mind to talk? I texted her, deleting and correcting my message many times. 'I'm sorry for Hasan's death. I know it's a difficult time for you, but you must be brave. It will pass. My prayers are with you and your family.'

That sounded so perfunctory. I waited for more than an hour, checking my phone and thinking about her a million times.

I recalled the first time I went to Hasan's house. It was raining buckets and he offered to drop me off on his bicycle. I agreed because I didn't have an umbrella or a raincoat. Hasan's raincoat was on our heads as he rode the bicycle, and I sat on the crossbar in front of it. I offered to take the driver's seat, repeating my offer amid the cacophony of raindrops on the coat. Shouting, Hassan asked if I would be able to pull his weight and mine. It was more an assertion than a question, so I kept quiet. Probably to make me feel useful, he told me to hold on to the raincoat, which kept slipping, and to be on the lookout for motorcyclists as he could hardly see ahead of him.

'There's a car coming,' I announced. He fitted his head under the raincoat just above my shoulder to monitor the oncoming car and navigated expertly through ankle-deep water. The rest of the journey was more placid, as the rain slowed to a drizzle. I leaned on the crossbar, watched the raindrops make circles in the water and heard the frogs croak.

'Well done! I couldn't have made it without you,' he said, when we safely reached his place, which was closer to the school.

He made me sit in his drawing room, which overawed me with its furniture and decoration. That's when Lubna walked in with two towels. We dried our heads with them while I was admiring the pencil sketches of Hasan's family members on the walls.

'I think you should have a cup of tea before you go,' Hasan said. 'By that time, the water will have receded. You live nearby, right? I can drop you off on my bicycle.'

'No, my place is only a few streets away. I'm good.'

The prospect of Hasan seeing my home with a torn curtain in front of the main door horrified me. When Lubna served me a cup of tea with a teabag floating inside it, I was clueless about how to drink it. Brewed tea was the only one I knew of. Not wanting to do anything that would betray my ignorance, I stared at the cup. She sensed my bewilderment. 'Keep the bag there. It will make a strong cup. One spoonful of sugar will do?'

'Thank you,' I said, thinking she was the sweetest girl I had ever met. When Hasan told me that the pencil sketches of his parents and grandparents on the walls of the drawing room walls were her work, I saw her as a virtuoso.

She rarely laughed, but when we played ludo during the summer holidays in Hasan's room, she laughed sometimes. Being self-important, Hasan usually chose little Sadia as his partner, while Lubna and I made up the other team. Victory had never tasted as sweet as when she high-fived me. Whenever she laughed, it was quick and would soon end, but for that instant, her expressionless face and eyes shone, radiating a light that lit everything. When she entered puberty, I would notice her growing bosom and posterior, and I would curse myself later for being a pervert. I hardly, if ever, noticed how small she was. She filled everything around me.

The phone buzzed. It was Lubna's text message. 'Thanks for the kind words.'

I hastened to reply so she would stay on the phone, 'I know it's an especially bad time for you. I'm also aware of how Hasan was acting up with Mohan and Ram. I could guess it had something to do with you.' I regretted the inadequacy of my message. I should've said more.

Her reply came a few minutes later. 'Why does everyone think I'm responsible for Hasan's death?'

'I didn't mean that. What I meant was that I know how bad the situation is for you, but I know Hasan's death wasn't your fault.'

My words were wanting in expression. When she didn't reply, I texted again, 'Did anyone blame you for it?'

I thought she might talk about today's incident that Ammi reported, but she didn't. Instead, she texted, 'Can we talk?'

I felt ecstatic for the first time since Hasan's death—since Mohan's death, in fact.

'Sure.'

I went to the rooftop, dragged a charpoy to a corner which was in shadow, sat down, and called her. 'Are you okay?'

She ignored my question. Did she think it was stupid? 'Your Ammi was here. Did she say something?'

Her voice sounded hoarse. I had always found her a brave girl. I couldn't imagine her crying. As she paused, I recalled how Hasan had taken her to play cricket years ago. We had fallen short of a player hours before the match. Never short of bright ideas, Hasan, the skipper, suggested the preposterous idea of Lubna filling in. Ram and I were speechless, and some of our players were sure the other team wouldn't accept a girl in the boys' team. Lubna had no problem with the idea when Hasan talked to her on the phone, although she had to make sure their parents didn't catch a whiff of it. When she reached the playground, the rival team didn't have any objection to Lubna playing. After all, what damage could a petite girl do to boys? However, when she smashed the ball to all parts of the ground, the members of the rival team quickly realized that she could do lots of damage to them. While most of the boys watched in amazement, a few of them raised a hue and cry, but they knew it was too late. The damage she did went far beyond the match. We heard that our rival team's strike bowler, whom Lubna had hit four fours in one over, had burnt his cricket kit and quit. In my eyes, Lubna was the epitome of economy in the construction of the human body. Despite her petite frame, she could achieve so much.

Returning from my reverie, I replied to Lubna, 'She said a woman had a sort of altercation with you. I can sense the focus could be on you.'

'Do you also think I'm responsible?'

Did that mean she expected better from me?

'No . . . No . . . Not at all. I want to assure you it's not your fault.'

I peeped into our courtyard below to make sure Ammi didn't overhear me. Why did she not like Lubna?

'But I *am* responsible! Mohan was lynched because of me! And Hasan killed himself because of Mohan's death! That means it was my fault again.'

'No . . . Listen . . . I'm pretty sure Hasan was killed. Don't . . .'

'How are you so sure about Hasan?'

'Because in his last few days, he sounded better. I think I was the one he talked to most in those days—not a great deal, but more than with others. I could tell he sounded better.'

'Oh, God! He did try to reach out to me, but I was mad at him. I didn't listen to him. I should have.'

'Okay, Lubna. Listen. Don't blame yourself for anything. The police officer in charge of the case appears to be a good man. He looks like he won't bow before mullah pressure. I suggest you cooperate with him. He can find out who's responsible for Mohan's and Hasan's deaths. Hopefully.'

'Okay.' Her reply was brief again. 'I've got to go.'

I desperately hoped I was right about what I had assured Lubna.

9

Waqas

Present day

Seated in my office, I tried to analyse the case. I was not much closer to cracking the case now than I was when I talked to Furqan last night. I shouldn't rule out a conflict within Hasan's family leading to his death. To understand Hasan's case, it was important to find out what led Hasan to be a part of Mohan's lynching. AK could be a clue.

'Was he upset a few days—maybe a few weeks—before his death?' I asked Jawad, who looked exasperated at my frequent visits to his home. A beard had sprouted up to pair with his unruly moustache. We sat in the drawing room on sofas facing each other.

He nodded, opened his mouth but shut it immediately.

'About what?' I continued, 'Was he upset because of the Hindu guy's death, the lynching?'

'Yes.' Finally, Jawad managed to say something. 'He showed signs of mood swings ever since that incident.'

'Was he involved in the lynching?'

'Maybe. I'm not sure. He wasn't like that. He fell into bad company.'

'Just answer my questions. Did you know he was getting involved before the incident?' I sat back on the sofa and placed my right leg over my left.

'No. We knew he met some deeply religious friends.' Jawad paused, wiped his brow, and continued, 'We talked about it in the family—Abba, Dadu and I. But we didn't think it was alarming. His friend Furqan—a good, sensible boy—told us Hasan might participate in the religious party's rally that would target Mohan. Abba questioned Hasan about it when he returned home that evening and advised him to talk to Mohan. I don't remember what Hasan said. Not much. He was never a good talker. Anyway, Abba decided to forget about it.'

Jawad sat back and continued, 'The day the lynching occurred, the news was all over town. I wanted to go out in the streets and find out for myself what it was about, but Abba, Ammi and Dadu—everyone—told me not to. You know how the lynching mobs are.'

Unfortunately, yes. Not many people know them as well as I do.

Jawad continued, '. . . We could hear slogans in the streets. It was horrifying to realize what was going to happen because we knew Mohan and his family were decent folk. We even shared gifts, like sending food to them on Eid; they returned delicacies on Diwali. The young ones went to each other's houses regularly. So we were worried. And then the realization that Hasan had not returned home terrified us. We told each other he must be with a friend, but the fear crept inside us that he was in the mob that wanted trouble. We didn't know how much he was involved in it. All we knew was that the police arrested him. That was trouble enough.'

'Did he talk to anyone about it when he returned from the police station?'

'We talked to him. We tried to get him to express himself. But he wanted to be left alone. Abba decided we should let him be. Gradually, he appeared to have become—kind of—more stable. Quieter but at peace with himself. At least, that's what we thought, until . . .'

'He must be attached to someone in the family, emotionally. Mother? Father?'

'Not really. Dadu and, to some extent, Lubna, our sister.'

I took some notes and said, 'I want to speak to both. If they want, I'll ask a lady police officer to be with us while I'm interviewing them. I hope that's not going to be a problem for your grandmother. I suppose she can walk. Please go and call them.'

Grandmother was the first. She entered, running the string of prayer beads through her wrinkled fingers. She said I didn't have to come to her room as she was strong enough to walk inside her home.

'He was a serious boy, not like other boys of his age. Responsible, a bit too worried about things—about poverty, about morals, about the country. We never needed to tell him to study. He never forgot what was expected of him.'

She paused, breathed heavily and coughed a few times. I wondered what she had wanted to say yesterday, but I did not ask her. 'I'm going to lie down, if the police officer won't mind.'

'I don't mind, Dadi. Can I make you comfortable?' I rose to my feet to help her.

'No, I can manage.' Her independence made her adorable. She placed a square, olive-green cushion where she could rest her head, and reclined on the sofa facing me, the beads dangling from her hand. A few adjustments to her position and clearing of her throat and she was ready to resume. 'Where was I? Ah, yes. Then he became too religious. Started arguing with his sisters, Lubna especially. He used to tell her that painting was un-Islamic. They had a few quarrels.'

Hasan's grandmother stopped for breath again, but apparently she relished this opportunity to talk, like most elders who were concerned that they were divorced from all important things. I admired how only a day after her beloved grandson's death, she appeared composed.

'But we were never worried about it till we heard that he was chanting slogans. Is Islam found on the streets and in slogans? Islam is in the heart. Islam fills you on the inside with a light. These kids have sat with me to pray during many a night, sometimes in Ramadan or on the twelfth of Rabi-ul-Awwal. How can one who has experienced the tranquillity, the beauty that *namaz* offers in the middle of the night, start to shout in the street, to force it upon others? I don't understand. I tried to talk to him. But there's only so much you can make a youngster understand.'

'Thanks, Dadi. Please tell me one more thing. Was there anything he spoke to you about in the last few days before his death? Anything about blasphemy and the punishment for it?'

'Yes. He asked me once or twice if blasphemy was pardonable. I said I didn't know the Islamic laws, but that Allah forgives everything other than *shirk*—worshipping someone other than Allah. Of course, no sin is bigger than *shirk*. I told him that misusing religion to hurt a human being was maybe a bigger sin than blasphemy. But he had a terrible time since Mohan died, so we didn't bring up the issue lest he be burdened by guilt.'

Lubna was next. She was short, so petite, that I wondered if they had misunderstood me and sent Hasan's younger sister. But she said she was the older sister, older than him by three-and-a-half years, she added. Despite her dishevelled dress—a light blue shalwar-kameez—she looked elegant. It was because of her face—the stern, confident look on it. She had her grandma's large eyes and broad forehead. Adjusting the dupatta on her head, she sat on the sofa. Perhaps the family had decided they didn't need the presence of a policewoman for this interview, or maybe they forgot to pursue the matter. With the drawing room door open, they were perhaps satisfied I could proceed alone.

'On what sort of terms were you with your brother, Hasan?'

Lubna's facial expressions indicated that she considered the question silly, the sort she expected from the police. Her body language said she wouldn't be impressed by anything. After a while, she said, 'Like all brothers and sisters, we were quite friendly.' In contrast with her height, her voice suggested maturity. If I had only heard her speak—a commanding, motherly voice—I'd have thought she was in her forties.

'Did you two ever have any quarrels about your taking up Fine Arts?'

She was surprised—perhaps wondering who had told me about that—and took some time to answer. 'Yes. He said it was un-Islamic and he didn't like it. But are you suspecting me of . . .?' There was noticeable aggression in her voice.

'Not at all. I believe Hasan's death—suicide or whatever—was related to some of the events that transpired in the last few months: Mohan's death, blasphemy charges, etc. So I want to decipher these events.'

Lubna continued to look surprised, this time probably at my friendly way of explaining myself. She still sat on the edge of the sofa, knees together and hands on her lap, but her perpetual attempts to adjust the dupatta on her head ceased.

'One more thing.' I leaned forward. 'Did the difference of opinion between you two on Fine Arts affect his relationship with Mohan? I understand Mohan was teaching you Fine Arts. Hasan might've believed Mohan was motivating you to pursue Fine Arts.'

'He mentioned it a couple of times. He said Mohan was an infidel and I shouldn't let him mislead me. I told him that Fine Arts were my passion, that Mohan was only coaching me and that he was not putting things in my head. As for whether his relationship with Mohan changed or not, I can't comment on it.'

'What made Hasan think the situation was dangerous?' I asked. In response to Lubna's quizzical looks, I took out Hasan's diary from my bag and added, 'He says it in here. Have you seen this?'

'That's Hasan's diary, I guess. What does it say?' Shadows of worry lingered on her face like cobwebs on a picture.

I opened the diary on the page I had read earlier and read aloud the few lines I wanted Lubna to hear: 'Islam prohibits any form of illustration of the human face or body. The study of human anatomy forms an integral part of the modern fine arts. Students draw nude human figures, including those of women. How can Islam allow that when it forbids pictures of faces? The only arts permissible in Islam are calligraphy and architecture. Why doesn't Lubna understand? Mohan is a

Hindu. There's no point convincing him. But Lubna . . . This
is getting dangerous . . .'

'Can I see?' she asked.

I rose and handed over the diary to her. She read the lines
and returned the diary to me, the cobwebs of doubts on her face
now denser. She did well to sound composed when she said,
'This was many months ago. I can't say what prompted him to
write this.'

'What's your opinion about Mohan?'

She coughed and cleared her throat. Then adjusting the
dupatta on her head, she said, 'What about him? He was a well
read man. He was my teacher. Our families knew each other.
That's about it. What does my opinion about Mohan have to
do with Hasan's death?'

'I asked because of Hasan's use of the word *dangerous*.'

Lubna's brief and calculated answers to my questions
suggested she was hiding something. I wanted to probe further
but did not want to sound offensive. Only Furqan could reveal
what she did not. I decided to end the interview. 'Anyway,
thanks for now. I might have to talk to you again soon.'

Returning to my office, I phoned Furqan. He said he would be
free soon. Having sent a driver to pick up Furqan, I had lunch.

When Furqan arrived, I asked him to resume his story.

10

Furqan

Nine months ago

The Talaba had a strong presence in the college. They demonstrated the awe they commanded through boycott rallies. During a lecture, we would hear the gradually rising slogans of 'Boycott! Boycott!' from a megaphone, and upon hearing them, the instructor would call off the class. No one dared to question their boycott. I remember that student rallyists once stepped inside the classroom to remind our instructor to discontinue the class. He didn't dare defy them; he took only a few minutes to pack up his things. Sitting at the back of the class, I could not believe how meekly the teachers obeyed the Talaba. No one else seemed to mind. No one, not even the teachers, could ask those boys why they hampered the classes. Interestingly, most of the students never bothered about what was being boycotted. What mattered to them was that there would be no more classes that day and they could go home or play cricket in the numerous playgrounds of the college.

Hasan and I once saw two Talaba boys cornering a boy behind a hostel building. We had lost our way around the hostel area and walked into this scene—one that looked like it was from a mafia movie. One of the Talaba boys had a hand on the wall next to the boy's face. When the Talaba boys saw us, the one doing the talking snapped his fingers and said, 'Take a walk, boys. This is none of your business.' Hasan and I walked away without a whimper, as if we had not seen anything.

We later learnt that this was not uncommon. Others had witnessed such scenes too. Rumour was that the boys being questioned were usually from the Red Brigade, a secular student party the Talaba hated.

Our next interaction with the Talaba was through our Maths teacher, Mr Abid. A small man dressed in plain shalwar-kameez, he looked quintessentially old school. He showed zero tolerance for the young generation's ways and expected pin-drop silence in the classroom. To penalize students for not meeting his expectations, he announced the names of the students during a roll call in a barely audible voice. Consequently, many students failed to hear their names called and were marked absent. If a student protested, Mr Abid calmly replied that it was the student's fault that he and his classmates hadn't observed silence in the classroom.

Yasir, the boy who often tried to get under Faisal's skin, postulated one day, 'You know, guys, through some abstruse algorithm, Mr Abid has computed the minimum audible level, accurate to fractions of decibels, and can prove his students scientifically and thus legally wrong if they try to formally challenge him.'

Mr Abid followed a similar policy of allowing minimum arguments from students during his lectures. He turned acerbic if students failed to grasp his lectures, for which he blamed their lack of understanding of the previous topics. We had recently learnt the concept of iota, which was the square root of negative one and the basic unit of complex numbers. So, one student coined *iota* as a new name for Mr Abid, a complex man.

We didn't mind Mr Abid's demeanour in the beginning. Many of us found him one of a kind and enjoyed his eccentricities. But two months after we joined his class, we took the first Maths test. The little fun Mr Abid's personality offered was over. We found out that most of us had flunked the test. For the first time in my life, I scored as low as thirty percent in Maths. Ram scored the highest, but even he wasn't proud of his score although everyone else looked at him in awe.

After we had poked fun at ourselves and others, we discussed what to do about it. Sitting in the front row, Zameer looked back and spoke for the first time, 'Maths is our main subject. We're all pre-Engineering students. Without Maths, there's no Engineering. Do you guys know what the lowest marks admitted to the University of Engineering and Technology, Lahore, this year were? Eighty-eight percent. Life is tough, friends. This college and its teachers are not going to help us.'

He looked genuinely worried, sitting in his chair, sometimes looking in front of him and sometimes over his shoulder. He was presumably the sort who assumed that sitting in the front rows of the classroom benefited their understanding.

'Engineering is not the only option,' another boy, Nasir, said. He was the busiest cricketer of the college. Whenever we went to the cricket ground or walked past it, we were sure to find him there. He said he would have opted for cricket studies, had any institute in Pakistan offered them. He took up Engineering when he realized that Mathematics and Physics were necessary to understand the intricacies of cricket: the art of reverse swing, the ball-tracking mechanism and, not to forget, the controversial Duckworth and Lewis method, which he planned to challenge. He hoped that by the time he graduated, some institute somewhere in the world would offer a PhD in cricket.

'Yes, cricket is certainly an option. Who needs engineering when cricketers earn better than engineers do?' someone quipped. Everyone laughed. Students were moving around the class, packing their bags to leave.

Zameer looked sombre. He tilted himself in the chair slightly and cross-questioned the cricket lover who sat behind him, 'I'm sure you don't mean cricket. But then what option did you mean?'

Nasir grinned and said, 'For me, cricket is not only an option but the first choice, but because we're talking about ordinary mortals, how about a Bachelor's in Physics, followed by a Master's degree?'

'And what job would you get? A teacher's? What will you earn? Peanuts.'

'You imply that the engineers in this country are earning millions, Mickle.' Yasir said to Zameer from the back of the classroom, talking while texting on his phone. Zameer usually wore shoes which had the popstar Michael Jackson's name inscribed on them, but with *Michael* misspelled as *Mickle*. Zameer had told us the shoes belonged to his father, who bought them in the eighties when the singer was a rage. No matter how much people like Yasir made fun of him, Zameer said he would continue to wear them because they were his father's.

Yasir continued, 'My friend, there are no jobs for engineers. Teaching may be a better option. You're more likely to get a teaching job. This country's funny. Nobody knows how many engineers it needs but engineering universities are springing up like mushrooms.'

At Yasir's supportive argument, Nasir celebrated by pumping his elbows backward, like a bowler who had dismissed a batsman. I laughed at his gesture and looked around. It seemed no one else found it funny.

Yasir added, 'Guys, do yourselves a favour. Stop coming to this bloody college. Join some academy and you'll get a better education. Perhaps when they see empty classrooms, the authorities will worry and do something to improve the education they're offering.'

'Why should I pay an academy's fee when I'm already paying this college?' Zameer was adamant. 'And everyone knows that the same teachers who don't teach properly in the colleges help academy students score record marks. I won't let this education system fleece me.'

'Suit yourself. Enjoy the wonderful feeling of having outwitted the education system, and let your career be ruined.' Yasir scoffed and plugged back his earphones, returning to whatever he was doing on his mobile phone. Hasan, Ram, I and many other boys looked around, wondering who was right.

Hasan cleared his throat and said, 'As Ram has scored the highest marks, I invite him to come to the front and offer us some advice.' Everyone clapped.

'Advice? On what?' Ram had a sheepish, ear-to-ear grin on his face. He was busy with his favourite pastime: solving a crossword.

'Say anything, yaar. Come on, come on.' Hasan patted him on the back.

Ram walked towards the whiteboard and faced the class, self-conscious but enjoying the moment. 'I guess most people cannot grasp the complex-number concept. I can try to explain it.' He picked up a marker and approached the whiteboard.

'Oh no! Please, no!' someone in the front row said. 'I can't stand this iota. Spare me the complex numbers!'

'What do we do then?' Ram looked confused, but the endearing smile never left his face.

'Tell us about jobs. This engineering versus teaching debate. Which field will fetch me a job?' the boy asked.

'This is an interesting problem. The answer is not binary, though. It's ideally suited to fuzzification. You see, we can understand . . .'

Hasan and I looked at each other and smiled. Ram was an adorable geek.

The boy had no patience. 'Oye yaar, we can't understand college Maths and you're teaching us fuzzy logic!'

'Okay, I'll try to make it simpler. But you must be a little patient, okay? Look,' he went to the board and started to sketch a graph. He blew his nose repeatedly with a tissue paper that he put inside his trouser pocket as he spoke and wrote on the board. His parachute-like T-shirt and trousers made him look comical. 'See, if we try to plot the number of jobs in various fields year-wise, we can predict the trend in the coming years provided we have data from the previous few years, decades maybe, which we don't have . . .'

'You mean you can't predict?'

'Ah, yes,' he said, and everyone laughed. 'But I believe artificial intelligence and machine learning are going to be super-attractive fields of study, and they're so mouth-watering.'

'Sir, the class time is over. Please leave,' another boy joined in the fun. 'But sir, have you considered applying your fuzzification technique to curing your perennial flu?' Everyone burst into laughter at this.

'Fascinating!' Ram mimicked Mr Spock of *Star Trek* fame. He was always up for some fun, even at his own expense. 'That's another interesting application. I had never thought of it.'

'I say,' Yasir spoke in his characteristically loud manner. 'You'll be a popular teacher. You know why? Because half of the time in the lecture, you'll blow your nose.' Ram sniffed once more, and everyone laughed again.

But Zameer was his usual worried self, his longish face looking even more elongated. 'Gentlemen, if we don't act, we can't blame anyone for not correcting the system. We have to do something, else the system will continue to rot.' He regarded the classroom. Ram returned to his chair.

'Do *something*? What does it mean?' another boy asked the question I also wanted the answer to.

Zameer said, 'Talk to the Talaba's *nazim*, the head of the student body.' Everyone went quiet. Zameer continued, 'Believe me, they have a solution to everything. They're not just a student body. They'll help you with everything, from admin issues to academic ones. Everyone goes to them, and they're always willing to help.'

Yasir said, 'What are we going to ask them to do? *Oh please, nazim bhai, would you correct the education system for us, and this country too?* Sure enough, he would recite a few verses, and whoosh—the college and this country would become paragons of prosperity, like Hazrat Umer's caliphate.'

Yasir was now in his element, as he was when he questioned Faisal. The boy next to him elbowed him with a 'Shh!' No one talked like that about the Talaba, as they had the support of the Deen-e-Kamil. Some faculty members also backed them. Not even the college authorities challenged them. Zameer didn't reply. I looked around to find some boys exchanging furtive glances. I was worried for Yasir.

'Let's forget all this and play cricket.' Nasir had had enough of this discussion. A few people laughed as he left.

'Who wants to go to the Talaba's nazim for help?' Zameer suddenly asked while looking around the room. 'There are better teachers in this college than Abid Sahib. The nazim can ask the authorities to assign another instructor. Trust me.'

I didn't know student bodies could meddle in faculty affairs. Did the backing of a religious party make the Talaba so powerful? I, too, looked in front and then at the back rows. A few hands went up slowly. Hasan raised his hand and looked at me with furrows appearing on his brow, coaxing me to do the same.

'Remember, Faisal helped us with the forms. He's a member of the Talaba,' he whispered to me.

I raised my hand too. We didn't expect Ram to raise his hand, but he did.

Several students in our class, including the three of us, went in a procession towards the nazim's office in one of the newer buildings. Zameer and a few boys went into his office, a small room, while the rest waited outside. A few minutes later, the nazim came out to listen to us. With a stout build, a stately beard and an expensive looking waistcoat on top of a neatly pressed shalwar-kameez, he looked more like a teacher than a student. I'd have addressed him as 'Uncle' if we had met elsewhere. He listened patiently to our complaints about Mr Abid and said he would talk to the teacher right away. A few students passing by had become curious and joined the procession, which, led by the nazim, marched towards Mr Abid's office. While we waited outside, feeling like a scientific breakthrough was nigh, the nazim went in and returned in a little while accompanied by Mr Abid, whom he dwarfed. We weren't sure what exactly they said, but it amounted to the nazim assuring us that Mr Abid would help the students as much as possible and that the students should also behave well and cooperate with the teacher. Feeling triumphant at having done *something*, we returned to our homes.

However, we got nothing out of the *something* that Zameer wanted to do. Mr Abid was more accommodating for a few lectures following that episode, but he soon returned to his former ways. The students no longer cared much. Many of them joined evening prep academies if they hadn't already. Only a few boys besides the three of us sat in the Maths class, which was sparse like a small crowd watching a boring cricket match. Zameer became a fan of Ram, who was often surrounded by Maths-phobic students—there were quite a few of them who declared calculus problems venomous because the integral symbol resembled a snake.

The incident involving Mr Abid, however, was instrumental in an unexpected way. It was a precursor to a series of events that centred on Mohan.

* * *

'You guys complained about a teacher to a student?' Mohan asked us when we told him about our story.

We gaped at each other, befuddled. Mohan had recently secured a job in our college, alongside his evening classes in the

Asian Institute of Fine Arts where Lubna was studying. We sat in a conference room, one corner of which was his makeshift office.

After a while, Hasan said, 'Mr Abid leaves us no option. We want to learn, and we want good grades. Did we come to college to hear his sarcastic one-liners? How else can we correct the system?'

Mohan looked amused. He pondered and said, 'Look. Part of the problem is that student bodies—they're backed by political parties, you guys know that—have become too strong. They're literally bullies. See, Mr Abid may be an unforgiving man, but he's your teacher and he's old enough to be our father. And he's good at his profession. You must be patient with him. Make him believe you guys need his help. I wonder what will come out of what your nazim sahib did. Do you think that will change Mr Abid?'

We looked at each other again. I asked, 'So there's no way a student can complain about a teacher? There must be some checks and balances.'

'Good point. There are several options. You can talk to the head of the department or the principal. You can write to them. But the first step you should've taken was to talk to the teacher himself. Many issues can be resolved by talking to the person who's ostensibly the source of your problem. That would've made him feel good. He probably needs some respect and attention. That's all. But you've done the opposite. Put yourself in his shoes. Imagine a student leader coming to tell you you're not teaching well. How would you feel? I won't be surprised if he gets vindictive. Do you know he has had another brush with the Talaba guys?'

'What happened?' Ram asked.

'You've seen the Talaba guys boycott classes, how they go to each classroom to make sure the lecture doesn't proceed?' We nodded. He continued, 'I've heard they once went to Mr Abid's class. He continued to lecture as two Talaba boys entered and asked him to stop. He gave them a piece of his mind, which led to an altercation. Thankfully, it was resolved, but the Talaba don't like him.' Mohan looked at the three of us and resumed, 'I guess your nazim took this current episode as an opportunity to embarrass Mr Abid one more time. That would've hurt, right? Anyone else—someone saner—would've advised you guys on how to tackle this problem properly. This guy, the nazim, took you along to tell a seasoned teacher that he wasn't doing his job well.'

I recalled how prompt the nazim's action was. And we thought he was so helpful. Oh, we should've known better! I glanced at Hasan and Ram. They also looked remorseful.

'Should we apologize to him?' Hasan asked.

'Considering how hurt he must be, he'd probably think you're there to make fun of him. He's a cynic, I know. There's not much you can do now except learning your lesson.'

While we were pondering about what we had done and what we could do now, a girl peeked in through the door and said something to Mohan mostly in rapid-fire English and in an upper-class accent we couldn't understand much. She left as quickly as she came, leaving Hasan and me with our mouths agape. Ram smiled and told us she was Madiha, Mohan's assistant. Mohan was helping the college build a Fine Arts department; Madiha had recently completed her A-level and the college had hired her as an intern for this project. He said she was passionate about Fine Arts and that she wanted to pursue a career like Mohan, whom she idolized. For Hasan and me, Mohan became a celebrity. Ram also impressed Madiha because he told her about Hindu mythology, the origin of zero, the Fibonacci series and other mysteries of Mathematics.

* * *

A few weeks later, the Talaba boys held another boycott session. Placards in their hands, they stood in front of the Admin block. When they started to march from the red-brick library building towards the academic blocks, I noticed that the placards said something like not accepting a Fine Arts department in the college.

'I hope that has nothing to do with Mohan,' I said. When Hasan looked at me, I pointed towards the procession.

Hasan thought about it and said, 'If it's Fine Arts, it has everything to do with Mohan.'

'I guess the Talaba don't like Mohan,' Ram added in a barely audible voice. The Talaba boys were now shouting slogans.

'Why do you say that?' Hasan asked.

'Remember the incident with Mr Abid?'

'Yes, but what does that have to do with Mohan and the Talaba?'

'Somehow the Talaba found out that Mohan criticized students for taking up the matter to the Talaba.'

'What?'

The procession, led by a boy with a megaphone, passed in front of us. He periodically shouted what sounded like rejection of a Fine Arts department. In response, his followers shouted: '*Namanzoor! Namanzoor!*'

The shouts were deafening, and for a while, all we could do was to wait for the procession to pass. It was scary to talk about the Talaba when they were within touching distance.

'What did you say? How did the Talaba find out? What did they do?' Hasan asked as the noise ebbed, leaning his ear towards Ram. I also tried to snuggle closer as I pressed Hasan's hand to remind him that the people we were talking about were within earshot.

'I've no idea how they found out,' Ram said, one hand pressed to his right ear. 'I might've mentioned it to Zameer. That Mohan had this and that opinion about the episode. It sounded trivial then. I never thought it would reach them. Mohan told me the Talaba came to his office and told him to keep his ideas to himself and not to corrupt young minds.'

'Oh, no!' Hasan said.

The procession had crawled to the front of the green-coloured Humanities building—each department had a different colour. The target was ostensibly Mohan, whose office was in the same building. A stout man climbed up the flight of stairs leading to the department entrance while the rest of the procession quickly coalesced itself—like a living organism—in a semicircle in front of the department building. The nazim stood quietly behind the stout man, observing everything, appearing to be in control.

'Let's go there!' Hasan said and rushed towards the Humanities department, with Ram and I at his heels.

'. . . While we're not against modern technological education, we categorically condemn the satanic fields of studies the Western world is thrusting upon us,' the stout man said. 'Fine Arts is a hotbed of nudity and obscenity. We won't allow a department of this filth in this college. This country and everything in it are founded in the name of Islam. We can't permit anything that Islam doesn't allow!'

The young man had great oratorical skills. He was big and loud—he didn't need the megaphone. 'We don't want pictures of naked girls!'

'Oh, yes, we do,' someone whispered behind me.

I looked back and saw Yasir winking at me, amid a sea of furious faces. What a crazy guy! He didn't even know which side I belonged to. Perhaps because I was friends with Ram, whom he was fond of, he thought it was safe for him to share his feelings with me. Or he probably didn't care.

The Talaba leader said, 'It's absolutely against Islam, and we can't allow anything un-Islamic!'

He paused, then continued, 'But we're giving our enemies a chance. We don't want any trouble. Even Muhammad—may peace be upon him—always sent emissaries with a message of peace before any jihad. We will talk to him first. Don't worry, brothers. The Talaba will not allow the evil designs of Zionist lackeys to succeed!'

He paused and looked at the nazim and his companions, most of them bearded and white-capped, standing solemnly a few steps behind him. They whispered some things among themselves.

'They're going to talk to Mohan,' Hasan said, turning around to look at me and Ram. 'Is he in his office today?'

'Yes,' Ram replied.

'Let's go!' Hasan rushed towards Mohan's office.

11

Lubna

Six months ago

I owed Mohan an explanation. I planned to visit him at his home. Oh, God! To this day I'm amazed at how I mustered the courage to do it. But I had to. I told Ammi I wanted to discuss some course content with him and that I'd go with Hasan. Ammi thought a lot before she agreed. So did Hasan.

'Should we take the car?' Hasan asked. 'Boys ogle at girls in that locality.'

Why did he try to suggest *that* locality was different from ours? As if we lived worlds apart. There was a time when I didn't care two hoots about oglers. Now I tried not to cross paths with them.

Hasan added, 'But don't you think taking the car would be inappropriate considering the small street they live in?'

'Yes, I see what you mean. And it would probably draw more attention. Let's just walk.'

Mohan looked surprised, although I texted him before I left home. His parents and brother acted like I was a VIP, making sure I was comfortable on the sofa, which they wiped clean with a cloth before I sat on it. The sofa was perhaps very old, and it sank when I sat on it. I sat erect and tense so it wouldn't show. What would they say after I had left? Would Mohan and I stir gossip everywhere we were together?

While his father disappeared inside the house after the greetings, his mother, a diminutive woman dressed in colours that, like her, seemed to shy away from the limelight, sat with me for a while and asked about how my family was doing. She looked genuinely happy to see me but why was there hesitation in her demeanour, the contaminant of her happiness? Maybe the alienation was bred by the difference of faiths. She left after serving tea and mithai. Hasan had gone upstairs with Ram.

I adjusted my dupatta on my head and my shirt around my knees as I sat on the edge of the sofa, sipping tea. 'Sir, I came to tell you why I no longer visit your office,' I said to Mohan.

'Alright. What is it?' Mohan asked.

'People were talking about how I visit your office too often.'

'I think you did well by stopping the visits. We shouldn't give people a reason to talk.'

'The tea is very good', was all I could think of saying after the initial conversation.

'Thank you. Ma's mithai is also tasty. Try it.'

The presentation of the mithai was not great—the small stainless steel saucer that held it was clean but lustreless—but the aroma of the mithai was irresistible. I had heard some good words from Hasan about it. I pecked a bit of the creamy white barfi and put it in my mouth. It was delicious. I'd rather not touch the dark gulab jamun or I wouldn't stop. I couldn't make myself too chummy on my first visit. Would it not look unseemly?

Before today, I had seen Mohan only in shirt and trousers, which he wore to school. Sometimes he also wore a maroon coat, which was slightly big for him. He must have gotten it from a thrift shop. Not that it lessened the esteem I had for him. Dressed now in casual clothes—a white pyjama and kurta—he looked informal but still distant. I noticed his appearance for the first time. He was frail and had a disproportionately big, bulging forehead. But something about him was attractive. What was it? Perhaps it wasn't in his face or his body.

After an awkward silence, I asked, 'Can I see your room?'

He appeared amused at my request.

I continued, 'I want to see your books and get the one you wanted to give me.'

'Okay. Come along.'

As we left the sitting room and entered the inner house, I noticed a decoration on the floor in front of a small door.

'How beautiful! This is for Diwali, right?' I asked Mohan, my unease disappearing.

The design was a lamp done in bright orange and yellow rangoli colors, nearly a foot long in each dimension.

'Yes, this is our *pooja* (worship)-cum-storeroom. We made the design in October, I guess, and it has remained since.'

I peeked inside the room. In a corner, there was an idol placed on a wooden platform. Some boxes sat in another corner, nicely arranged but out of place.

He said, 'It's Lord Ganesh. Ideally, it must be in the northern part of the house and facing the south. And if you peek inside, there's also a Lakshmi in the right corner. The two of them are paired at Diwali.'

I peeped inside at the other idol and said, 'Interesting. There's something about colours. They stay while lighting and fireworks don't. I'm sure you designed this.'

I squatted and examined the design of the lamp on the floor, touching the powder with my fingertips, taking away some of the colours on my finger.

'Ma and I.'

He smiled the way one smiles on seeing a child, his eyes telling me he loved my interest in his house.

I stood up again. 'I used to love firecrackers, when I was a kid. I read somewhere that Moghul kings introduced fireworks in Diwali celebrations. Emperor Akbar was the one who took them to a great level, and Shah Jahan introduced the Akash Diya tradition, the sky lamp. Funny how we Muslims believe that the Hindus corrupted our traditions.'

Mohan looked behind me, unease evident in his gaze. I turned around to face Hasan, who had probably heard my last sentence.

Mohan said, 'Well, I think it's just two cultures inspiring each other.' Was he trying to propitiate Hasan? Hasan went back to talk to Ram. Why the hell did he come down for a moment and then return upstairs? Was he spying on me?

Mohan led me through a small veranda up a narrow staircase—everything in the house was dark, small, narrow, or all of these.

'Watch your feet; the cement at the edge of some of the stairs has worn off.' A quick movement of his hand suggested he considered holding it out for me but decided against it. Was it because his parents stood at the bottom of the stairs, looking concerned for my safety?

Hasan and Ram were on the rooftop, leaning against the bulwark, talking. Both stared at me, surprised.

'Another one joining our club?' Ram asked.

I laughed. 'I wish I could.'

Ram was even slenderer than Mohan and had the same comforting smile.

'You can benefit from his company while you're at school, Lubna,' Hasan said.

I nodded. What if he knew Mohan and I were already the talk of the school? It would be a catastrophe.

Mohan led me to his room, which Hasan had told me about—about how it appeared to be an unfinished building's grey structure but how it was their abode for stories, discussions and homework. What I had in mind was a room built with books—books everywhere instead of bricks, in the walls, floor and ceiling—which, though old and worn out, were sturdy, hardcover tomes with the tenacity of bricks. The reality didn't seem too far from the image. I scrutinized the books one by one, caressing one, leafing through another, bending to survey the spine of one, blowing the dust off another. I could see from the corner of my eye that Mohan was standing in the doorway, arms crossed on his chest, a blissful smile on his face.

'What are those paintings?' I asked, pointing to several frames placed on a shelf facing the wall. 'Can I see them?'

'I don't think so.' He paused and added, 'They're nudes.'

'They're works of art, right? You're an artist . . .'

'Not really. I admit they're erotica. You won't find much art in them.'

'But what's the inspiration? Your imagination?'

'Primarily. I try to copy ancient Indian erotic art and reproduce sculptures on paper, mainly from Khajuraho temples.'

'It's called grisaille, an art form, right?'

Mohan's eyes lit up perhaps at the possibility of a discussion on art. But he asked, 'Can we drop this discussion?'

As I returned the frame, Hasan walked in saying, 'Lubna, shall we go home now?'

Was there anxiety on Mohan's face? Had Hasan seen those paintings? Did Mohan not want Hasan to think I had seen them too? Did Hasan note the anxiety too? He appeared to have stopped short of saying something.

Fidgeting with my dupatta, I said, 'Yes, let's get going.'

12

Furqan

Eight months ago

'They're coming to talk to you,' Hasan said, breathing heavily as we rushed in.

Mohan was in his office and ostensibly aware of what was happening outside the building. He sat back in his chair, doing nothing. The office—recently allotted to him—was small, just a cubicle inside a large conference room. There was barely room for a small table, a few chairs and a bookshelf. Mohan's books and art pads occupied the shelves.

'Good of them!' Mohan smiled. 'Why are you guys in a hurry?'

He pretended to sound unperturbed, but he wasn't. I felt sorry for him as the repeated finger-combing of his hair betrayed his feelings. A little while later, we heard footsteps in the corridor. The Talaba guys were here. The door opened with a creak and in marched the nazim with Akbar, the fiery and stout speaker, at his heels.

'May I come in?' asked the nazim, while standing in the doorway.

'Yes, please.'

The three of us went to a corner of the room, feeling like prisoners in a cell. As the nazim entered, followed by Akbar, Mohan asked, 'So you opt to forgo the word *sir*?'

The nazim looked taken aback, but he replied calmly, 'I asked for permission to enter. Is that not enough of a show of respect to a rookie teacher who's probably younger than I am?'

'It's up to you. Asking for permission to enter someone's home or office is an essential and minimum courtesy one can show. Age has nothing to do with respect or wisdom. A teacher is a teacher, no matter how young. But have a seat and tell me what I can do for you.'

The nazim's pursed lips indicated he was nonplussed, but he sat down. Akbar, whose hands on his hips suggested even greater perturbation, took the other chair. He filled it and most of the small room. One of them or both had just had a dip in a pool of perfume, which pervaded the small room.

The nazim began in his slow and measured manner. 'Sir, I'm sure you know what this is all about. I understand you're not a Muslim, and I respect your religion. But this country is nothing without Islam. We can't allow a Fine Arts department here when the country needs Islam and Islamic studies. We request you to withdraw the case for your department.'

'How can I do that? The college employed me for this department. It's the college's plan, not mine. As soon as I joined the college as a faculty member, the dean assigned me the responsibility of its planning.' Mohan sat back, seemingly relieved that the conversation was over.

'If we can convince the college authorities, you won't have any problem?'

'I didn't say that. Of course, I want this department to be set up, and the college has already invested in the project. The building is almost complete. They have obtained funding from the government to send two faculty members to the US for Master's studies. A few more faculty members are being inducted, not to mention some other staff.'

Hasan and I looked at each other. Was he also thinking of Madiha?

'We can take care of everything. The building will be used for the Islamic studies department, and the college will be asked to stop the induction of the two new faculty members. Whenever they return—I have doubts, though, that they will— they will be asked to seek a job elsewhere, not in this college.'

Mohan's brow was furrowed. 'This means it's alright if they teach Fine Arts elsewhere? Strange!'

The nazim and Akbar had no answer to that.

Mohan continued, 'And so many colleges in Pakistan are teaching Fine Arts. What about them? By the way, what's un-Islamic about it?'

'An image, particularly of a human, is forbidden in Islam. Other than calligraphy, all other arts are un-Islamic. As for other institutes, we can't do anything about them now. If Allah wills it, though, we will take care of them in the future. Right now, however, this college is our responsibility,' the nazim said, as if he had announced a verdict.

Mohan paused, then said, 'Look. This college isn't your responsibility. There are people who know how to run this college. Let them decide which department they want to establish.'

'You listen to me, Mr Mohan.' This time, Akbar dragged himself forward in his chair. My heart missed a beat as I thought he was going to punch Mohan across the table. 'If the American poodles who held the reins of this country's education system did their job, our education today wouldn't be in a shambles. If the disgustingly corrupt leaders of this country knew their job, it wouldn't be stinking as it is now. This country has survived only because Allah has been taking care of it. But Allah won't allow this complacency for long. We have to do something.'

The nazim put a restraining hand on his colleague's arm. He then said to Mohan, 'Leave that to us. We will convince the college bosses.'

'That's also what I want. Let's present our respective cases to the college authorities, and whoever has a more solid case will win. I know it's a flawed system, but let's play our respective roles the best way we can and hope the system delivers.'

'This Westernized system will never deliver.' Akbar took over again.

'Then what will? How will you correct it?'

Akbar paused for a while to collect his thoughts and said, 'Islam has a solution to everything, to every problem.'

'Okay. May I know what Islam says about correcting a college or an educational system?'

'Do you think Islam does not offer a solution?'

'I didn't say that. All I want to know is what road map Islam prescribes. I don't know it, and I want to learn from you. What will you do to correct things? After all, I'm a faculty member here. I have the right to know what you plan to do about it. By the way, what qualifications or credentials do you have to claim to correct it?'

Akbar again mumbled something. The nazim spoke instead, 'We have a think tank that has road maps for everything.'

'Oh, nice. Who are they, and can I hear their plans?'

'Don't worry about that. The best option for this country is to trust us and Islam.'

'As far as I know, Islam didn't prescribe a political system. So how can we entrust the entire country to you?'

'Of course, Islam has a political system,' Akbar said again. 'What makes you think it doesn't? It's *khilafat*, of course. Non-Muslims are on a mission to malign Islam. I'm not sure about your intentions either.'

Suddenly, Hasan rebutted, pointing his finger at Akbar, 'How can you talk to him like this? Don't you dare! For your information, he's more Muslim than many so-called Muslims!'

Akbar looked over his shoulder, aghast. Mohan, Akbar and the nazim dragged their chairs and rose to their feet.

'Who's this behan chod?' Akbar fumed.

I put an arm around Hasan's shoulders and pulled him back. A commotion ensued, as Mohan and the nazim tried to calm things down.

'Hasan, please chill. You might like to step out and take a deep breath. Ram, Furqan. Please accompany him.' Mohan was surprisingly composed.

'No, I want to be right here!' I had never seen Hasan so livid.

'Sir, please tell the kids to leave,' the nazim said.

'No. They'll stay here. Please mind your language, gentlemen.' Mohan looked around with authority. I loved him for his aplomb, despite how frail he looked.

'And rest assured, gentlemen, I have no intention of maligning your religion. I only want to understand. What are the key things in this *khilafat*? How's it different from, say, democracy?'

Mohan looked at Akbar, as if nothing had happened and they had just been interrupted during an intellectual discussion.

'In *khilafat*, there are no elections, unlike in a democracy, in which every person, whether he's a criminal, uneducated or whatever, has a single vote. Islam doesn't prescribe this system. Its ultimate yardstick is piety.' Akbar was still fuming so the nazim replied instead.

'And how do you measure this piety? How do we know this one is more pious than the other one?'

Akbar tried to interfere, but the nazim was sharp enough to see that the arguments would not go in their favour and that Akbar could make things worse. He said in a tone of finality, 'You don't have to worry about any of these things. We have think tanks working out solutions to all problems. Of course, our knowledge is limited. But if you're interested, we can help you meet some learned scholars who will answer all your questions. You want to present your case to the college? Sure, go ahead. We thought we could put an end to the matter through a discussion, but you obviously don't want it. Thank you for your time.'

After the Talaba guys left, Mohan told us to sit down and said, 'Gentlemen, what you've just witnessed here is a form of well-disguised bullying.' He tried to appear calm, but he wasn't. 'And the worst part of it is they don't even know it. They don't understand that all the people in this world have the right to dream and to strive to realize their dreams. They believe that everyone who differs from them is wrong. Why not talk and listen to each other? No, that's not their way. Hasan, I can't thank you enough for what you did, but you need to be careful. Akbar won't forget this insult.'

I also expected a backlash from Akbar or his friends. On a few occasions, when we came across him, I was sure he would come at Hasan. Surprisingly, he didn't. The next few weeks went alright, but we didn't know Akbar and company had other ideas.

13

Lubna

Six months ago

I began to read the Meeraji book as soon as I reached home. The front cover had a monochrome drawing of the poet, eyes looking pensive and long hair neatly combed back, perfect for portraiture. I had read somewhere that he was a far less neat person. The first poem I came across was *Silsila-e-roz-o-shab*, meaning 'Succession of days and nights'.

Khuda ne alao jalaya hua hai
usse kuch dikhai nahi de raha hai
hur ik simt uss ke khala hi khala hai
simatte huay wo sochta hai
Taajub ke nur-e-azal mit chuka hai

[God has lit a flame
He cannot see anything
All around Him is a void

He shrinks into Himself and thinks
He's surprised that eternity has faded into darkness]

'Does Meeraji allude to Prometheus in his poem *Silsila-e-roz-o-shab?*' I texted Mohan on WhatsApp the following day. I waited for his reply which came much later in the evening.

'I'm impressed.'

'By what?'

'By your knowledge—that you know about Prometheus.'

'Thanks. The answer, please.'

'That's a possible explanation. Or he talks about man burning his own flame, independent of God's—thinking for himself and doing away with dogmas. A religious rebel, like you.'

'Why is he afraid of ecstasy?' I referred to Meeraji's poem *Mein darta hoon musarrat se.*

'Not sure. But here lies the beauty of poetry—Meeraji's, especially. If you've read the next few lines of the poem, you would've noticed he says he doesn't want to be like a god and doesn't want to forget the bitterness of life. Maybe he's shunning the life that seeks refuge in the lap of dogmas and determinism. From the complacency that religion lulls man into.'

'Nice. That makes sense. But what prompted Meeraji to write this? Was he at odds with the mullahs?'

'Not really. I've read him, but I couldn't understand him without the guidance of learned people. Most critics think his poetry revolves around the colonial experience, and more so around the Muslims' response to colonialism. This response consisted of seeking refuge in their glorious past.'

'I want to paint Meeraji's poetry. Please help me.'

'As I've said, I couldn't think of any way of putting his abstract ideas on canvas. You're full of ideas. Maybe you can think of something. Also consider Noon Meem Rashid's poetry. He's full of imagery.'

Starting that day, I found I could open that book and enter a world—like Alice's wonderland—where I would meet Mohan. Not only that book. There were other books and the notes he had written on the sidelines, which talked to me . . . a handwritten phrase in neat green here, a highlight in green there, lots of negative spaces thrown over the pages . . . my photographic memory stored the pages more as pictures and shapes—of a meandering stream or an hourglass or a silhouette of a tree— than as text. So what if we couldn't meet? We found emails, WhatsApp texting and sometimes phone calls unhindered means of communication.

Once, I texted him, 'About your nudes . . .'

'What of them?' he replied briefly. Was he mad at me?

'Eroticism is part of the Hindu religion. Some say it's a path to divine love. You don't have to hide your work.'

'Why do you insist? Are you curious?'

'No. I want you to not hide them.'

'I must. Most people won't approve of them.'

'Meeraji approved of eroticism. He found earthly humanity in it.'

A long pause before his reply. 'M is typing . . .' kept me on edge. 'People don't approve of Meeraji either.'

Did he seek his Indian roots—like Meeraji perhaps, whose poetry was replete with Hindu mythology? Did he shroud his yearning in a country that had turned its face towards the Arab world in the last few decades, away from its Indian origins? And

when Mohan admired Meeraji's multiplicity of meanings—
like abstract art on a wide canvas that has no single correct
interpretation—was he, like me, preferring it over the rigidity
of religion? He never said it because he was afraid of offending
a Muslim. I wished he would confide in me!

* * *

'Do you know that the depiction of the human face is forbidden
in Islam?' Hasan asked one day when he saw me working on a
portrait. He stood outside my door, which was open.

I could see it coming. First, the *namaz*—he wouldn't miss
any of the five prayers of the day. Sadia and I teased him for
acting so saintly, but he didn't seem to like the joke. We stopped.
He started to tell me and Sadia to cover our heads when we
stepped outside our home. How could he do that? That put me
off. But even then, I didn't retaliate. Now, the time for niceties
was over. I put aside my pencil and said, 'Hasan, I don't think
you need to tell me what Islam is.'

'I thought being your brother, I have some rights over you.'

His face was grave. How long his beard had grown! Why
hadn't I noticed it before? He had grown up to be a stranger.
Where was the Hasan I played cricket and flew kites with on
our rooftop? He didn't mind when boys stared at me from the
neighbouring rooftops. I had to tell him I shouldn't invite the
attention of boys. And he was so caring, almost condescending
towards me—I didn't mind it because I knew it was his way of
showing brotherly love. When he learnt to drive Jawad Bhai's
motorcycle, he picked me up and dropped me at my school
whenever he could, so I did not have to walk or resort to public
transport.

'Look here, Hasan. I've been going to school for more than four years and no one—Abbu, Ammi, Dadu or Jawad Bhai—has forced me to cover my head. No one except you and, if you remember, we had a few scuffles over it. Now, don't play brother–sister after having brought things to this.'

He changed the topic. Yeah, this one was not working for him. 'What did Mohan show you last month when we visited their place? The paintings you hid from me when I entered his room?'

I couldn't believe my ears. 'I didn't hide anything from you.'

'Those are indecent paintings. I know about them.'

I dragged my chair and turned it so I could face him. He still stood in the doorway. I hoped Sadia did not overhear this exchange of pleasantries between her elder siblings.

'Why do you think you can see them, and I can't?'

He averted his gaze and pretended he was surveying the room. 'I didn't see them, but I could guess from the way Mohan has been hiding them.'

'Well, don't jump to conclusions until you've seen them.'

'Did you see them?'

'I don't have to reply to it.'

'Okay. Don't. I can only advise you.' He turned away.

'What's wrong with you, Hasan? What do you have against Fine Arts?'

He paused and replied before walking away. 'It's forbidden in Islam for a reason, which you don't understand now. You will, but it might be too late.'

A few weeks later, Hasan saw Meeraji's book on my table. 'This is Mohan's, right?'

I sat on my bed, reading a textbook. Which book did he mean? Oh, that one. I said, 'Yes.'

'Do you know Meeraji is an obscene poet?'

Hasan stood near the doorway, next to the table. I didn't invite him in. When was the last time he walked into my room? 'What?'

'Yes. I can't talk to you about the things he writes. They're filth.'

'Well, I didn't know it.'

'Then why did Mohan give you this book?'

What could I say in reply? 'What nonsense are you uttering, Hasan? And who gave you the right to ask me all these questions?'

'Look, Lubna. You must stay away from Mohan and such books if he gives them to you.'

Slamming my book shut and throwing it on the bed where it bounced, I blurted out, 'By the way, how do you know Meeraji writes the things you said? Did you read them?'

'Yes. A friend pointed out the obscene stuff to me. I read them myself.'

'And who was that friend? One of those mullahs you've been hanging around with?'

'You shouldn't talk about my friends this way.'

'Well, if you can allege baseless things against my friend, I can do the same with your friends.'

'A Hindu can't be your friend.'

'Oh God, Hasan! You're beyond comprehension! Please leave my room and don't talk to me again!'

* * *

'By the way, you rearranged my books—probably subconsciously—when you visited my place.' Mohan called me on the phone one day, a reason for me to rejoice. 'I could see you were kind of sleepwalking into it. Do you know?'

'I do, sir.'

'Oh, then it was deliberate.'

'No. What I mean is that when I do it, it's almost instinctive—subconsciously, as you said.' I had this habit of reordering things—books, stationery, writing stuff mostly—without realizing what I was doing. 'But yes, I was aware I had done it to your books. Did you dislike my new order?'

'Not at all. You did a fantastic job, really. You put the Urdu books together, poetry and prose in separate piles. And you did the same thing with the Fine Arts books. It's a pity you didn't have time for the rest. You have an elderly *rooh* in you—Ma uses this term to mean someone who acts older than her age.'

I adjusted myself on my bed and placed a pillow behind my back. 'I have, indeed. You know what? I've never met my Dada—grandpa. He died before I was born. But I've heard a great deal about him from Dadu—what he read, what he wrote in his diaries. Dadu says I'm like him.'

'Interesting. Was he artistic?'

'Yes. She says he was very artistic. He used to do wood etching, and he was so good that the Mayo School of Industrial Arts in Lahore—it's called National College of Arts now, I'm sure you know—hired him as a part-time instructor. Dadu says no one among their children was artistic and Dada was disappointed. But she told him they could wait till the next generation. She was delighted to see me delving into the arts. But too bad Dada died before I was born. I didn't see him except in photographs, but I still dream of him.'

'Fascinating because I had a similar relationship with my Dadi. She was great at pottery.'

'Sweet!'

What was it about Mohan that made me talk so much? Anyone who knew me would ask, if they heard me now, where was the girl who spoke so few words.

I continued, 'She still has all his diaries, and we read them together often. Her eyesight is not good now, and I read to her. She tells me those stories about the train journeys at the time of the partition—when Pakistan and India won independence. That's what has made me so connected to the past—to old-fashioned things, to cute-looking notebooks rather than to computer word processing. Connected to sketchbooks, to the sound of pencil on paper . . .'

'Beautiful! How Ghalibian! *Sareer-e-Khaama nawa-e-sarosh hai.*'

'It's Persian, right? What does it mean?'

'It's a line from Ghalib's ghazal. The scratching of a pen on paper is an angel's sound. Ghalib says the sound brings fresh ideas to his mind.'

I visualized a winged angel whispering in my ear. Such was the magic of Mohan's words. I often smelt oil paint as he talked to me.

'Oh, so profound! I used to think your knowledge was mostly about Indian history. How wrong I was! Is there anything you don't know?'

'Lots. And I'm glad there is lots yet to know if death permits. By the way, the book I gave you, it's from a library. I need to return it. That's why I called. I've already exceeded my time. The guy doesn't mind, but I don't like to exceed my time.'

'Guy? Who?'

'There's this man named Karamat Ali. He has a collection of the most precious books. It's his personal library that he has opened to the public.'

'Oh, yeah. Hasan told me about him. Interesting man, isn't he?'

'He is. You can go in there, sit and read in his clinic-cum-library. You may pay if you want to, but you can't take the books away. That's something he has allowed me and some of my friends—Hasan and others, I mean. We can borrow books, but we must return them in time and pay him.'

'Who reads Meeraji these days? I'm sure Mr Karamat Ali won't mind.'

'Well, if I keep his books to myself, it's certain no one else will read them.'

'Alright, I'll bring the book to school.'

* * *

At the dinner table a month later, Hasan brought up the Fine Arts topic again.

'I believe Lubna should not study Fine Arts. It is forbidden in Islam,' he said, lifting his eyes briefly from his plate.

What? I was speechless because I had never argued with my parents. Ammi and Jawad squirmed in their chairs. Sitting opposite me, Hasan did not look at me for even a second. As if my opinion did not matter.

'Can't you study something else?' Abbu asked, looking diagonally across the dining table at me.

Luckily, Dadu, sitting at the head of the table, intervened. Between morsels and coughs, she asked, 'Why should *she* quit a profession? Aren't thousands of Muslims all over the world taking it up?'

'At least, it will restore some peace to our household, Amma,' Abbu said, as much to Hasan and me as to Dadu.

'Not her fault,' Dadu said, waving her left hand towards me.

'Fine Arts is just a fad, Amma. Eventually, she will marry and go to her in-laws.'

'Art is no fad. For your father, it was a profession, even more than that. He was devoted to his work. At least someone in the family follows in his footsteps.'

Dadu told Hasan that he could only counsel me, that he couldn't force anyone into anything, and that if I refused to listen, it would be my loss. Hasan looked like a grumpy child.

Little did I know what things would come to. If I did, I might have done something about them. But what could I have done?

14

Furqan

Five months ago

Hasan had begun to change . . .

One day, Ram asked for advice on what he should wear on his date with Madiha. She had asked him to take her to a Sankranti celebration. Beaming from ear to ear, Ram insisted that the outing was a date. The bad part was he didn't have anything good to wear.

'You can borrow a sweater from Hasan. He's got a few in his wardrobe.'

Ram hadn't borrowed clothes from Hasan, but he readily agreed.

We met Hasan in the library, where Ram put forward his request.

'Where are you going?' Hasan whispered, in compliance with the library rules. We took our seats around the table where he sat, and Ram told him about his date. Suddenly—to me, it was conspicuous—Hasan's countenance changed. Did he like Madiha? I wasn't sure. What he said to Ram was rude: 'If you want to look like a scarecrow on your so-called date, you're welcome to borrow my sweater.'

Ram was his typical humble self. 'But it would still be better than looking like a scarecrow in one of my sweaters.'

'Alright, suit yourself. Come and get it from my home.'

There was no attempt to sound courteous. Ram noticed the cold shoulder. He walked away, leaving me with a brooding Hasan.

'Why are you misbehaving with Ram? What's gotten into you?'

'What's gotten into me? Nothing.' We were whispering because we were still in the library. But Hasan's anger, though subdued, was noticeable.

'That was no way to treat a friend.'

'Really? And that's no way to woo a Muslim girl. Can't you see what he's up to?'

'Are you insane, Hasan? They're just friends. And why do you think Madiha's your responsibility?'

'Enough. We're disturbing the people here. The librarian's staring at us. I must study. Please go.'

* * *

'Akbar wants to talk to you.'

A boy approached Ram one day while he and I were walking past the large oak tree. The boy walked away, and we looked around to find Akbar sitting under the oak tree with another boy, ostensibly a Talaba member. It sounded rude, Akbar treating Ram like a child. We looked at each other and then at Akbar, who beckoned Ram with a finger. I gestured to Ram that we should listen to him. Akbar was not a guy you would mess with unnecessarily. We inched towards him. He sat cross-legged yoga style but looked like he was going to interview a candidate.

'I didn't call you,' he said to me. Muscular and stout, he was more a wrestler than a student.

'I'm his friend.' I fidgeted with the hem of my shirt.

He weighed my answer for a while and turned towards Ram, saying, 'What are you up to with that girl Madiha? What's going on between you two?'

Ram looked at me as if seeking assistance with a tough Maths question. I was as clueless as he was. Akbar perhaps took that as a sign of guilt. 'Why are you flirting with her?'

'Flirting?' Ram finally spoke. 'I'm not flirting with her. She's interested in Sankranti, so I took her to a celebration. She asked me to.'

'Why is she interested?'

We had no answer to this question. Ram and I looked at each other again. And again, Akbar might have interpreted our silence as a sign of guilt.

He said, 'I heard you were dating her.'

Akbar was constantly twisting the ends of his moustache, which reminded me of the steering handle of a Harley–Davidson.

'Look. There's a difference between going on a date— which I did—and dating a girl—which I didn't,' Ram spoke the way he did to his Maths tutees. I thought he acted bravely when he said this.

'Don't teach me what dating is. I know all about it.' Akbar floundered, probably thinking that his statement might be deemed an admission of womanizing. He was so quick at judging and misjudging. 'I mean I know what you're up to.'

Ram was up to nothing, though he was excited about his date with a girl. Who wouldn't be? But we had no answer to most of Akbar's questions. Akbar adjusted his enormous off-white *khaddar* kurta, folded his right leg with the knee next to his face, and twisted both ends of his moustache again. Ram and I shifted from one leg to the other. I didn't know how many people were watching us, but if anyone was, they would've deduced that this was a bullying session, something the Talaba had claimed to put an end to.

Akbar said, 'You stay away from her, alright? Now, go.'

Ram perhaps considered arguing and mumbled something before Akbar reminded him with a wave of his hand that the meeting was over.

We decided to tell Mohan about it and went to him after our next class.

'You should report the matter to the head of the department,' I said to Mohan, frustrated at not having given Akbar a piece of my mind.

'No. That would blow things up. I can explain things to Akbar and his friends, and hopefully, they'll understand,' Mohan replied. The brothers preferred courtesy to fairness in religious matters.

'You're wrong there, Mohan Bhai. They won't back down.'

'Hasan is friends with some of these guys. Maybe he can convince them.'

Ram and I exchanged looks, but we didn't mention that Hasan had changed for the worse. I brought up another excuse. 'They won't listen to him either.'

Finally, Mohan requested Madiha to end her internship prematurely and leave the college, which she did.

* * *

Oh, why didn't I see it coming? I could have stopped it, maybe. The Talaba deeply influenced Hasan. He saw Faisal more often. Hasan still met me, but he avoided Ram. He had the courtesy to be polite with Ram, but courtesy was the only thing that remained between them. The books he was reading changed. Islamic history and *fiqah* replaced English and Urdu Literature. He had also begun growing a beard a month ago. I had noticed the change, but I didn't say anything.

But that day, I had to say something.

'Where are they going?' I asked Hasan, as he rose to his feet after a group session in a meeting room with Faisal and another Talaba boy. The group dispersed, and Hasan stopped to answer me.

'Afghanistan and Iraq,' he replied, as if the two countries were places near Rawalpindi.

'What for?'

'Why, of course, to help our injured and homeless Muslim brethren, and maybe to fight alongside the Mujahideen.'

We walked out of the room and into a corridor. I thought for a while before I said, 'And the boys have volunteered?'

'Yes, of course.' He looked askance at me, as surprised at my questions as I was at the idea of going to Afghanistan and Iraq.

'Who takes care of the visa? Will they follow a legal passage?'

'The Deen takes care of everything.'

'Oh, really? Have the boys' parents allowed them to go?'

'Oh, Furqan! Come off it! You don't ask parents for everything you want to do, especially when it's that important.'

'Many of these boys, including us, aren't even adults yet. I hope you're not going.'

'I sure am.'

'Are you out of your mind, Hasan?' We walked past the oak tree, where several boys stood in groups. For a while, that was the only thing I could utter in a faint voice. 'You do know what they'll put you up to in the guise of aid work, right?'

'What will they put me up to? And how do you know?' Hasan continued to walk. Our discussion didn't seem to matter to him.

'Everyone knows. Those militants are recruiting young men like you and me. Do you want to become a terrorist?' I looked around to make sure no one was within earshot. Ram joined us and walked alongside us. I was between the other two.

'Terrorist? Who's a terrorist? For America, any Muslim freedom fighter is a terrorist. If that's the one you're talking about, I'll happily be a terrorist.'

'Hasan, you've no idea who's fighting whom over there! No one understands it. Would it not be sensible to pick your side wisely before you join the fight?'

'So we sit smugly in our bedrooms and drawing rooms and figure out who's fighting whom, and meanwhile, hundreds and thousands of our Muslim brethren die? Is that what you're suggesting?'

'It's still better than falling into the hands of militants. Let's see what Ram has to say about this.' I tried to diffuse the tension and looked at Ram, who had been following the debate quietly.

Before Ram could speak, Hasan asked, 'You expect a Hindu to empathize with Muslims?'

'Hasan, what has gotten into you? Let this be a scholarly discussion and let him join. We've never discriminated against him.'

'This isn't a scholarly discussion. I'm done with scholarly discussions. It's time to do something for your Ummah. Do you want to join or not?' He stressed every word as he stopped in front of the library.

I took a deep breath to calm myself down and said, 'At least, talk to your parents. Have you done that?'

'That's my business.'

I tried another way. 'Hasan, do you know what these Talaba guys are up to? They recently picked up Yasir. You know that guy, right? He's Ram's friend—sort of.'

Yasir disappeared one day and returned after many days, visibly shaken. Although he never said a word, there were whispers that the Talaba suspected him of being a member of the Red Brigade.

'Who says he was picked up? And who can prove the Talaba did it? Don't believe in rumours, Furqan.'

The discussion was going nowhere. I said goodbye to Hasan and left with Ram.

Fortunately, Hasan's intended adventures never materialized for reasons best known to the Deen guys, who were supposed to sponsor the trip. But the schism between Hasan and the two of us had widened. I tried to talk to him about the change in his behaviour, but all we could do was exchange harsh words, so I decided not to bring up the topic again.

And then came the incident which proved to be the tipping point. It drove a wedge between Hasan and Ram, who, I discovered, held grudges though he did not show them until the day when he brought Mohan's art pad to the college. He said he had to deliver it to Mohan in his office. We sat in an auditorium, waiting for a lecture to begin. Very few students were around. Hasan sat on my left while Ram sat on my right.

Hasan pretended to ignore Ram and focused on his book while Ram leafed through the art pad and skimmed through the drawings Mohan had made.

'See, this one resembles Lubna, doesn't it?' Ram asked.

It was unmistakably Lubna's face, but what was significant about the painting was it was seductive, besides being artistic. Lubna, or the woman in the painting, wore a diaphanous, light-yellow shirt—a kind of kurta—whose few upper buttons were undone so that some part of her breasts showed. It was a beautiful pose—the head tilted forward, a hint of a smile playing on her lips, dreaminess lurking in her eyes, and a backlight on her hair—I wondered how artists could create such an effect. It was a stunningly beautiful work done probably in acrylic paint.

When Ram mentioned Lubna's name, it was loud— undoubtedly deliberate. Did he want Hasan to hear and see? Hasan looked in our direction and saw the painting despite my attempt to quickly flip over the page. Hasan pretended he hadn't noticed anything, but I saw him blush. The worst part was that Faisal had just joined us and sat in the row immediately behind us. Had he seen anything? I wasn't sure. Hasan left the room, followed by Faisal who whispered something in his ear.

* * *

The maelstrom that swept everything away began with the news that Mohan had said something offensive about Islam. I felt like my breath had been constricted when one morning, I saw banners placed at various locations in our college—on walls, noticeboards, everywhere. They condemned the blasphemous utterances of a certain Hindu teacher.

It can't be Mohan. That was my first thought. A bit like someone who was not willing to accept or believe they had been diagnosed with cancer. But everywhere I went in college, those banners stared back at me. Some of them called Muslims to unite against Hindu designs. *Ya Allah! Let this be someone else. Not Mohan, not him . . . please . . . please.* My heart prayed quietly, until I saw one banner that read: Arrest Mohan Lal! It said in blood-red, hastily written Urdu words on a white poster.

It was unmistakable now. Like the final diagnostic test that confirmed the patient was going to die. I watched the death report for I didn't know how long. I suddenly realized I might be watched. I looked around to see if someone noticed me standing alone in front of the banner. *Would my face not tell them how I felt about it?*

I never found out what exactly Mohan said, but the rumours went around that he had uttered something blasphemous during his lecture at the Asian Institute of Fine Arts, where he taught in the evenings.

None of my friends were in college. I went home and called Mohan, Ram and then Hasan. None of them replied. I called Yasir, who told me he had just returned from the college where he witnessed the Talaba organizing a rally which Hasan had also joined. *What was Hasan doing in a rally targeting Mohan?*

That afternoon, Ram rang to tell me the police had arrested Mohan. My heart sinking, I called Hasan again. Still no answer. I imagined the worst things that could happen to Mohan. My face would've betrayed my feelings. Ammi and Abba asked me what was going on. They must have also seen some banners around town. I told Abba about it, and it started a commotion in our house.

'Stay out of it, Furqan. Don't go to college tomorrow. Just stay home.' He stressed with a wag of his finger.

'Abba, nobody knows what Mohan had said. I'm sure it's a misunderstanding. I need to visit them, to see how his parents are doing. They must be worried sick. Abba, please let me go.'

Ammi and Abba argued for a while before he said he would go along with me; he probably discerned it when I wanted something badly. Mohan's parents looked like convicts about to be hanged. His father swore that Mohan had not said anything bad about Islam. How could he have?

'Don't you know him?' he asked, as his eyes darted towards me. His short and frail body looked even more miserable. Ram's mother stood behind her husband, sobbing. Ram's father held my hands in his and asked, 'Furqan *beta*, can you talk to someone in the Deen party? Ram told me Hasan had some friends there. Please! Can you do something?'

His desperate pleas were heartbreaking. The realization that I was being asked to save a human life, the life of a great friend, shook me. Never in my life had I felt so helpless; never in my life had I cursed myself so much for my ineptitude. I looked at Abba who said everything would be fine. Did he sound hollow only to me?

'Is anyone allowed to meet him in the *thana*?' Abba asked Ram's father.

'No, not even his parents can meet him.'

We had no way of listening to Mohan's version of the events. But did it matter?

Ram had been standing a few steps away as the rest of us stood in their small drawing room and talked. His eyes were downcast, but I could tell there was accusation in them.

Whenever I looked at him, I felt even more disgusted with myself than before. Before we departed, I walked over to him and embraced him, but he resisted my attempt to hug him and his frail body felt limp in my arms. Abba patted Ram's father's clenched fists and shoulder, but I could see he was in a hurry to get away from their house.

'You don't understand what kind of people these Deen men are. They won't even spare the sympathizers of Mohan's family,' Abba said, as we hurried back home. I had never seen him walk so fast, his eyes looking restless and wary.

I looked around to find out what had scared him. I felt as if we were in a zombie land—similar to those I had seen in Hollywood movies, in which humans turned into zombies one by one and you couldn't be sure whether another person was a normal human being or a zombie. All eyes seemed to be piercing through Abba and me, trying to determine if we were like them or not. I dared not look back but felt their eyes were fixed on my back.

Things simmered in our college the next morning. Rumours and whispers flew around. Someone said Mohan had insulted our Prophet Muhammad. Why would he? I thought. There were more banners on display, condemning insults to Islam. Both Ram and Hasan were absent from college. I preferred not to talk to anyone. I felt as if I was amid wolves.

Then I heard slogans and chants, which sounded ominous like distant drums of war. Everyone crawled towards the sprawling old oak tree—once my favourite place in college, an oasis of peace, calm and cool shadow. In front of the Admin block, a large crowd was building up, their faces seething with rage. Many of them held placards and banners. They were shouting slogans against those who had insulted Islam. They looked like stage actors in a melodrama.

'Fine Arts are Satanic arts!' read one placard. I saw Akbar emerge from the crowd. He stood on the concrete bench built around the oak. Soon, the nazim joined him. Both eyed the sea of followers that was building up fast; both looked arrogant like political demagogues.

'Mohan has been released from jail,' someone in the crowd in front of me whispered. *That's why the Talaba are protesting.*

'Did you go to Mohan's yesterday?' A voice whispered in my ear, as I stood a few yards away from the protesting crowd. I looked over my shoulder and saw Faisal's face, his eyes looking—as always—like they were kohled.

He said, 'As your sincere friend, I warn you not to go there again. Go home and stay put.'

There was concern in his dark eyes and sweet voice. I wanted to ask him what would happen to Mohan, but my voice was nowhere to be found, neither in my throat nor in my gut.

My home was not far from the college. Most of the time, Hasan, Ram and I walked to and from the college. But that day, I wanted to disappear, to be invisible. I took a bus and hid myself in the crowd. It was always safer to go with the crowd. Some eyes in the bus seemed to pierce through me, though. I averted my gaze but saw faces everywhere, inches away, each one staring in the distance.

Disembarking from the bus, I thought of turning towards Mohan's house to tell him they were coming for him. But Faisal's kohled eyes blocked my way. I went home. Ammi said something, I'm not sure what. I went to my room and buried myself in a quilt. The spring was warm, but I was desperate for a cover. In the darkness of the room, I tried to lose myself in the flowery patterns on the red quilt. For a while, I succeeded in insulating myself from the reality that was chasing me. But then I heard slogans that slowly grew louder. They were marching towards Mohan's house. As the chants grew louder, I buried myself in thicker layers of the quilt.

15

Waqas

Present day

'What happened after the lynching?' I asked.

Furqan looked shaken. He reached out and took a few sips of water from the glass on the table. He said, 'Some Hindus protested. They tried to hold rallies. I'm not sure. We heard rumours all the time. Abba had told me to stay out of it. Strictly. The police apprehended some men from the Deen party. Hasan was one of them. But in a day or two, I think, they were released.'

I recalled having read newspaper stories about the town simmering in those days. The Deen-e-Kamil wouldn't allow any Hindus to protest. A bloody clash between the two groups was around the corner. Finally, a Hindu provincial minister stepped in and placated his community with promises of justice for Mohan, promises that were never meant to be fulfilled.

I asked, 'Tell me about Hasan—when he returned.'

'Hasan went into a shell after his return from jail.' Furqan sat back sometimes and then leaned forward as he talked, looking restless. 'I was worried about him. I tried to talk to him, to tell him that Mohan had deserved to be heard before he was declared guilty by the Deen. But he avoided any discussion on it. Then very slowly, he picked himself up. One day, he said to me in college that he had read something about the Blasphemy Law. It wasn't like he wanted a conversation, though. He wanted to tell me that he had opened a window, that some communication was possible. But unfortunately, I had to go to Karachi to help my brother, who was there for work and had an accident. We didn't talk much after that.'

'Why do you think Hasan was influenced by the Talaba? I mean, you weren't.'

'I remember pondering over it when Hasan had begun to change. I think Hasan didn't have a strong bond with his family. An extrovert outside, he was an introvert at home. He didn't share much with his family, except perhaps with his Dadu and Lubna. I remember discussing with my father whether I should go with the Talaba to their weekly proselytizing trips. Abba began by chiding me. Then he knew he needed to explain to me why I shouldn't. As I was a fragile boy, he was doubly worried about exposing me to strangers.' Furqan laughed, blushed and continued. 'Hasan had no one to discuss things with, except his Dadu.'

I took some notes. The day was ending. I rose from my chair and switched on the lights. As most of the day staff had packed up, the humdrum and noise of the police station had ebbed. The ceiling fan creaked, as if complaining about having to run at full speed all day. I ordered the canteen guy—a lean man I admired for his cleanliness—to bring two lemonades as the electric power had shut down.

'I didn't know there's electricity load shedding for the police too.' Furqan smiled.

'There is. Usually for fewer hours than the public has to put up with.'

We sipped the lemonades. I watched the ice cubes floating in the cold tumbler and wrapped my hands around the tumbler and caressed it against my cheek and forehead. In this heat, one needed every nugget of cold one could grab.

I said, 'Tell me about that guy, Karamat.'

'I could never figure him out. He was kind of mysterious but full of knowledge. What Mohan was to us, he was to Mohan. We helped him move in and arranged his books and discussed them with him, as we did with Mohan. It was lots of fun. He's also a homoeopath, and Mohan consulted him often about his parents' health, about the efficacy of nux vomica, bryonia and carbo veg for his father's stomach and other such ailments.'

I laughed. 'You've learnt a few names. He moved from Islampura to Shanti Nagar, right? Didn't you guys find it strange? Two people or families doing it within months?'

'We did. I remember, Hasan asked why everyone from Islampura migrated to Shanti Nagar. He had this flippant manner as if he were mocking others. "Not everyone, only those who didn't fit in well over there," Karamat replied—words to that effect. Don't know what he meant. He often muttered things—to no one in particular. Maybe to himself. Once, he said something like: minorities in our country are so estranged, I wonder why they are not afflicted with more allergies.'

'Tell me more about him and Mohan.'

'Karamat was not a talker. I think it was months after we met him that we mustered the courage to ask him how he

got the limp. Mohan was in America in those days. So we
talked with Karamat more often. Hasan asked him about the
limp; he usually took the initiative. Karamat replied with his
characteristic aloofness; the police's baton charge on him and a
few other journalists went a bit too far during a protest against
General Musharraf's government.

'His world revolved around books and writing. He would
pick up a book from his shelf, dust it with a pat of his hand
if it was a hardcover or with a puff of air from his mouth if it
was not, and he would recommend it to Mohan with hardly a
word from his lips. I was amused to realize how, amid tongas
and rickshaws and the humdrum of mundane commercial life,
we talked about stories; Mahabharata, Panchatantra, Jataka
and all that. But not only stories of Hindu origin. Mohan and
Karamat had also read stories of Arab and Western origin,
about the Arabian nights, Amir Hamza, *Tilism-e-Hoshurba*,
Urdu masters, Greek mythology, Hercules, Ulysses, Cyclops
and whatnot.'

The boy was a good storyteller. I asked him to go on about
Mohan.

'All of us had some favourites. Mine were stories; Hasan
wanted ideas, -isms and verdicts regarding which system was
right and which was wrong; and Ram loved clever things, such
as information about Science and Maths. Mohan was more
into poetry. He loved Meeraji. He recited this poem often. I
liked it, so I remember.

Mein darta hoon musarrat se
Kahin ye meri hasti ko
Bhula kar talkhiyan saari
Bana de dewataon saa.

ff

[I'm scared of ecstasy
Lest it should make me forget all bitterness
And transform my existence
Into something like gods'].'

Recalling the Meeraji book on Saleem's shelf, I asked Furqan to continue.

'Poetry and Fine Arts, those were Mohan's favorites. I saw these lines written on a painting in Mohan's room one day:

Ye tamannaon ka bepayan alao gar na ho
Iss laq-o-daq mein nikal aayen kahin bhairiye
Iss alao ko sada roshan rakho.

[If this unending fire of desires vanishes,
Wolves will appear in this wilderness.
Always keep this fire burning.]'

'It's Noon Meem Rashid's poetry,' I said. My mind travelled back to when Miss Nida read poetry to me. She used to read it to me and smile, not expecting me to understand it but to be inspired by it, as I was to this day.

'I didn't know that. The painting was interesting. I saw it during the time when Hasan had been estranged from me so I went to Mohan's alone. It was a large oil painting and was kind of scary. It painted the scene depicted in these lines: two people sitting around a fire—one a man and the other a woman—in a jungle perhaps, and wolves at some distance from the fire, waiting for their chance to pounce. The contrast between the fire's light and the surrounding darkness was superb. There was no way you couldn't notice the painting. The strange thing about it was that the wolves had beards. I asked Mohan what the painting and the poetry meant. He didn't say much, probably because he was busy. The painting was initialed 'LZ,' which obviously meant Lubna Zubair.' The boy blushed as he said this. Was it at the mention of the girl's name? There was a long pause, after which I asked, 'Hasan's diary mentions an article by AK. Does this name ring a bell?'

'AK? I don't think so. But we can find out easily if it's an article on the Internet. Let me check on my mobile phone.'

He worked on his phone for a while, complaining about how slow the Internet connection was. 'There,' he finally said after some searching and browsing. 'There are some articles related to blasphemy by a certain Mr Arshad Karim. I guess AK stands for Arshad Karim. It will take some time to read them, but I guess Hasan was doing that too.'

'What does the gentleman say?' I asked, pulling up a chair alongside Furqan's, and staring at his phone screen. 'I hate reading from the phone.'

He pushed up his glasses, wiped his nose bridge, and let the glasses fall back. 'From what I can read, he has discussed the origin of the Blasphemy Law in Pakistan. Do you want me to print them? You have a printer, don't you? And a computer with an Internet connection?'

'Yes, but I'm not sure if they're good enough. We police wallahs are not tech-savvy. I know we have a broadband subscription, but I'm not sure if it's working. There's one guy here who's good at it and who takes care of the computer stuff. If we're lucky, he might be on duty.' I called a peon and asked about Ashraf who, it turned out, was away.

'Never mind,' said Furqan. 'Show me the computer and I'll try to kick-start it.'

Accompanied by Furqan and a constable, I went to another room where a primitive-looking desktop computer stood on a table. After a few minutes of playing with the cables, settings and passwords, Furqan managed to switch it on and connected it to the Internet and the printer, although Furqan's face said it was taking ages. Finally, he managed to print some stuff, which he handed over to me.

'Thank you, young man. There are some lines across the printouts, but I guess it's the printer's fault. I can read them all right.'

'About Hasan distancing himself from Ram and Mohan,' I asked, 'do you think it has something to do with Lubna taking up Fine Arts and Mohan putting things in her head?'

Furqan thought a long time before he answered. 'Yes. That's just my guess, though, sir, so please take it as it is. This lemonade is great. Thank you.'

'Feels like it's from paradise, right?'

'Hasan had one reason—maybe two—for developing a dislike for Mohan. First, he deemed that drawing and painting are frowned upon by Islam, so he didn't like Lubna taking lessons from Mohan. Second, I think he was worried that the two—Lubna and Mohan—liked each other.'

'What makes you think so?' My cell phone rang. It was Fareeha. She wanted to know why I hadn't returned home. I told her I would be home shortly. I then said to Furqan, 'So Hasan had strong reasons for disliking Mohan, maybe even hating him. He could've been at the forefront of the lynching mob. Leader of the gang, maybe.'

'As I've said, I wasn't there to witness the lynching, sir, so I can't say. But I'm not so sure my friend could take a life. You see, a mob is like a sea; it carries the individual with itself.'

'True.' His use of the word *mob* took me three decades back. But I returned quickly and cleared my throat. 'Knowing whether Hasan was leading the pack can give us an idea about his state of mind. Who can tell us about it? Do you think Ram might be able to?'

'Yes, provided he was home when the lynching occurred, which is highly likely. You want to talk to him?'

'Yes. It's already on my to-do list. We can drive to the hotel where you and I sat. Can you call him and ask him to come there?'

After about an hour, during which I went home, repeated my it's-about-another-matter mantra to Fareeha, and changed into civvies, Ram, Furqan and I sat in the hotel. With most customers having left after dinner and the TV's volume turned low—an inconsequential T20 match between two county sides of England was playing—the place was quiet and had a welcoming coolness.

Ram had a dusky complexion and was so thin a waft of wind could blow him away. His most noticeable feature was his eyes; when he looked at me for a split second, I saw infinite sentiments in them—rage, resentment, despondency. Furqan had told me Ram had intelligent eyes; the intelligence was now buried somewhere beneath those myriad sentiments. I had asked Furqan to join the meeting so that Ram would feel more relaxed in his friend's presence. But Ram had a belligerent expression on his face; he looked neither at me nor at Furqan but at a wall, as if telling us he would rather be elsewhere, his way of shutting out the world. I wondered if the belligerence had always been there or appeared only during the last few months, after his family had gone through this ordeal.

'Hello, Ram.' I cleared my throat. 'Thanks for coming here. I need to ask you a few questions.'

'Am I a suspect in Hasan's death?' He spoke in a deep voice. He and Furqan sat side by side while I sat opposite them.

'You could be, but I don't interview murder suspects in hotels.' To show that this was far from an interrogation, I hailed a waiter and asked him to bring us three Coca Colas.

'My turn, Waqas Bhai,' Furqan interrupted. 'Allow me to pay for the drinks this time.'

Furqan's offer made the meeting convivial, so I nodded.

'Then what do you want from me?' Ram asked.

'I need some information.' I paused, then added, 'Let's start with the lynching or the events leading to it, shall we? When and how did the relationship between you and Hasan turn sour?'

Ram's account of how Hasan began to distance himself from him tallied with Furqan's.

'Didn't you try to talk to him about it? To ask him what had gone wrong with your friendship?'

'Why should I have? I knew exactly what bothered him. It's because I'm a Hindu and that's something that dawned on him after years of friendship. Suddenly, I was an infidel, unclean and a threat to his faith. That's why. I knew it. So why would I have asked him?'

'Did you and Furqan ever talk about it?' I looked at the boys one after the other.

Ram replied, 'No. We mentioned Hasan's weird behavior once or twice. Furqan did.' He looked at Furqan, who nodded. Then he continued, 'I wasn't bothered by it.'

'You made some new friends, didn't you?' In response to Ram's quizzical look, I continued, 'The Red Brigade, I mean.'

Ram picked up the Coke bottle and sipped on the straw. 'You can't call them friends. They were out to boost their following. They targeted the pseudo-liberals and the non-Muslims and tried to win them over. They aimed to counter the influence of the Talaba and the Deen.'

'They asked you to join them. Did you?'

'No.'

'Wasn't it a good chance to get even with Hasan? Joining the rival party?'

'As I've said, Hasan's estrangement did not bother me. Also, Mohan told me to stay away from student politics. Eventually, the Red Brigade was one reason that the Talaba and the Deen guys targeted Mohan.'

'In what way?'

'Hasan said to me one day in college that joining the Red Brigade would put me in trouble. I asked, "Really? What kind of trouble? You guys will punish me for that, won't you? What do you think you guys can do?" He said he was not threatening me and that it was just a warning. I told him to stop worrying about me. I believe that the Red Brigade was another reason why the Deen guys didn't like Mohan. They thought I was linked to the Reds and so was Mohan.'

'What else could've gotten Mohan in trouble? Did he love Lubna? If he did or if Hasan thought he did, that could've worked against him.' Someone in the hotel ordered kebabs. Before I heard the sizzle, the alluring aroma invaded my nostrils, and I remembered it was way past dinner time. Ram seemed to be thinking or maybe he did not want to talk about the things I mentioned. I averted my gaze to outside the hotel, where families and groups of children poured into the park, as the heat had lost some intensity while inside the hotel it was still humid.

'Lubna was one reason, I'm sure,' Ram said, after a long pause. I recalled the painting of the Lubna lookalike but didn't comment. 'Mohan mentioned Lubna so often in the house that Papa and Ma knew he liked her. Papa cautioned him, but I think it wasn't needed. Mohan said he wasn't even sure of Lubna's feelings.'

'So he didn't propose to her?'

'No. I asked him and he laughed. But poor Mohan! He was crucified for an undeclared love. Hasan knew about it and hated him for it, I'm sure. Even Papa suspected that Mohan had proposed to Lubna and that he was lynched because of it. To this day, Papa grumbles about it.'

'Tell me about the lynching.'

Ram regarded me for a long time. Then he said, 'Why do you want to know about it now when it hardly matters? Where were the police when it happened? Why was no one punished? No one was punished, right? It looks like a Muslim's blood is more precious than a Hindu's, that's why the police are so keen to investigate Hasan's death even though it was plainly a suicide.'

I didn't lose my composure. Nor did I try to explain much. 'I understand those are painful memories, and I won't defend the police for what they did or didn't do. Maybe you remember a few faces. Maybe we can book them.'

'Faces? You want to know if I remember any faces? They all looked alike. All I remember are faces mad with rage. Eyes throwing balls of fire . . . mouths spitting venom and shouting, the sinews on their throats stretched tautly . . . arms swinging wildly, looking for something they could tear apart. They were all alike.'

Ram looked around the table as if he was recalling a nightmare, as he spoke in slow, dogged words. I swallowed to push back my tears. Furqan looked as though he couldn't bear the words. He did a brave thing by putting an arm around Ram. 'Didn't you guys lock yourself in?' I finally managed to ask. 'We had. But Mohan insisted he would face them. Papa and Ma begged him not to. Ma threw herself on the floor and wrapped her arms around his legs. Mohan knew that if he didn't open the door, they would break it and might hurt Papa and Ma. I feared that the deafening shouts and slogans would break open the door. Mohan kept saying there was nothing to worry about. And he opened the door and stepped out. Within milliseconds, he disappeared. It felt like a giant reptile had lashed its tongue out and sucked him in.'

Memories of things seen decades ago and of some that I didn't even see came flooding into my mind. The only reason I managed to sit there was that I saw the boy was in greater agony than I was. As they often did, Faiz's words succoured me.

Bara hai dard ka rishta, yeh dil ghareeb sahi

[Though this heart is fragile, the bond of pain is so strong.]

I wished the words could heal Ram too, but I couldn't utter them. His head was bowed and his eyes were focused on something on the table, perhaps the Coke bottle. Only his voice told me he was sobbing. Furqan continued to rub his back. I tried to avert my gaze. A merry group of boys passed by, cricket bats and wooden stumps in their hands. One of them was repeatedly throwing a white-taped ball up in the air and catching it as the others chattered loudly.

I looked at Ram again. He lifted his eyes, which betrayed shame at having cried in front of me. The bond of pain didn't solace him. I asked, 'Can you tell me what was Hasan's role in the lynching?'

Ram took a deep breath and said, 'I'm sure he instigated it. He told Mohan's principal that Mohan tried to seduce his sister. What a lie!'

'I'm talking about the actual lynching; when the mob attacked Mohan. Where was Hasan then?'

'I didn't see him among the mob, but do you think I could recognize faces in those mad, frenzied moments? He was later picked up by the police, wasn't he? So he must've been there, somewhere in the mob.'

'But of course, he wasn't at the front of the mob. Else, you would've seen him . . .'

'Does that matter? Are you defending him? Do you mean to tell me he wasn't responsible? I'm telling you he was. He was responsible for the lynching. He was responsible for my brother's death. He was responsible for the terror with which we're living right now.'

The boy appeared irritated with himself for soliciting sympathy. He stood up, his hands on the table, his eyes fixed on me, and continued, 'He took the life of a friend, of an intelligent, talented and loving man. But that's not the end of our misery. My father doesn't sleep for many nights at a stretch. My Ma doesn't let me go out because she's scared that, being short-tempered, I might run into trouble with the Muslims. We talk about moving to another city, but we can't because we don't have enough money. We're a scared family, sir. We're terror-stricken. That's what Hasan's responsible for.' He paused and, with the back of his wrist, wiped his nose.

'You *jamadar bhangi*! You're not allowed to shout at places like this. Remember what happened to your brother, and don't invite something like that for yourself!' The fat man on the counter yelled.

Before I could turn around to shut him up, something flew across my face and narrowly missed the man, who ducked and disappeared behind the counter. It was a Coke bottle that crashed against the wall with an explosion, spreading thousands of shards all over the floor. The few customers present inside the hotel jumped up in alarm, stunned.

'Behan chod!' Ram ran around the table and rushed to the counter, but he had to pass in front of me, and I grabbed him.

'Hold him!' I shouted at Furqan to get hold of Ram, whose frail structure had suddenly amassed tremendous energy. Furqan wrapped his arms around Ram and managed to contain him.

'Let . . . me . . . go, Furqan!' Ram shouted, as Furqan whispered something in his ear to placate him.

I rushed to the counter and pulled the fat man from behind it, holding him by his vest strap, which came apart. The vest now fell limp from his left shoulder. The man's eyes were about to pop out. 'Don't you dare threaten him or I'll break your jaw!' I locked my hand around his face and squeezed it so hard the man winced, his face white. I could have been the angel of death for him. 'And don't forget, this is no hollow threat! I'm a policeman!'

16

Waqas

Present day

Abba and I are working in the same room. He's writing. I'm reading the Quran. The electricity goes out. I get up to open the windows and to get a candle for Abba. I can stop reading, but his work must continue. Ammi has told me so often to be careful with fire. I wish I had listened to her. I trip as I walk. The candle falls from my hand and lands, still burning, on the Quran. The Quran catches fire. I panic. I throw some water from a tumbler on the burning pages. Nothing works, and I scream at Abba, whose back is towards me. He turns around and picks up a rag to smother the flames. He's composed. Ibraheem marches in. He starts shouting, 'What has he done? He has defiled the Quran! Oh, what will you bring upon us?'

The fire has been put off, but a few pages are ashen and soaked. Ibraheem picks up the burnt pieces of paper and kisses them.

'What has he done? Did he do it?' he asks Abba, but eyes me.

'No, no. He didn't do anything. It was my fault. I lit a candle and it fell.'

'Qari Sahib, you should've known better. We care for the Holy Quran more than we care for our lives, and you were so utterly casual. This is disrespectful.'

Abba stands speechless for a while. Ibraheem leaves the room, shouting and beckoning people to come and see what has happened. I can't understand what he's up to. Yes, the Quran is sacred, but what if one accidentally drops it? Abba told me one day that in situations like this, 'just kiss the Quran and hold it near your heart. Allah forgives for He knows whether you just erred or did it deliberately.' Why then is Ibraheem Chacha creating a fuss over this? And why did Abba lie and say that he, not I, was at fault? Abba follows Ibraheem out into the veranda. Other people and students of the madrasah are rushing in. Abba tells me to go home. Some trouble is afoot. I want to stay, but he pushes me away with a stare, which is so out of place alongside his stately beard and kind face, like a smudge on a painting. 'Go! Just go!'

I run and run, stopping every now and then to look back. In the veranda, there's a storm—not a mob—gathering. As I run further and further away, I can see Abba's figure, clad in a white shalwar-kameez, being sucked in by the storm. But he's not fighting for his life, as one would when drowning in a sea. He stands there, firm, erect and dignified, then just disappears.

My heart feeling like it's going to implode, I rush inside my home. I want to shout to Ammi and Bhai, but something like a maelstrom has built up inside me. It's pulling everything into itself, and not even a whimper can escape it. All I can do is fall into Ammi's lap, sobbing. Bhai rushes towards the madrasah. Ammi's face is ashen, but she's quiet . . .

I didn't see it happen, just heard it from someone. Who told me about it? Not Bhai Jaan. No, he was tongue-tied. Some neighbors were whispering about it. An infuriated mob tied Abba to a motorcycle and dragged him till he died. How come I see it as if I were there? It runs like a film before my eyes. When Bhai reaches, probably a few seconds too late, the street where the madrasah is located, the motorcycle has already set off—a red and black Yamaha 100 croaking like a giant frog, more like a rickshaw engine. Three men are holding Bhai firmly while he cries and protests. A mob is just standing and watching.

When I woke up from the reverie, I was not sure how long I had been sitting on my motorcycle which stood in front of my home, the headlight making a circle of light on the door. I was not even sure how I had managed to drive through the evening traffic, my eyes not seeing what was in front of me but the events of three decades ago. Slowly, I switched off the engine and sleepwalked the motorcycle through the front door.

Fareeha fanned the sleeping children with a straw hand fan as the electricity was off. She didn't utter her customary welcome words. Sulking, surely. The flickering shadows cast by the candlelight made the home gloomier.

'I got delayed because of some errands. I thought I might finish them today,' I said, my voice unconvincing.

When she remained seated beside the sleeping children, I walked into the kitchen and looked around in the candlelight Fareeha had lit. A dinner tray sat next to it on the shelf. I brought it to the bedroom. The potato curry was cold but the rotis wrapped in a kitchen cloth were warm. I sat on the bed with the tray in my lap and finished my meal, thinking about the irony in how Ram's story felt like an antiseptic to my childhood memories.

I sat on the bed when Fareeha walked in and said, 'You're a bad liar, Vickie.'

She picked up a few papers from the bedside and waved them at me. They were the printouts Furqan had given me.

I sighed. 'Fari, I want to investigate this case. I want to know what happened.'

'Despite the danger to you or your family?'

I paused as I leaned against a pillow and picked my teeth with a toothpick, wondering how to explain. Ram's words echoed in my head and childhood memories kept dragging me down. I wanted to lighten things up or Fareeha would be worried.

I said, 'Come and sit here.' She trudged slowly and sat down opposite me on the bed. 'Have you seen how people drive in our country, Fari? You don't drive, but you must've noticed. Suppose you're driving down a main road and it's your right of way. Another vehicle appears from a side road or somewhere. Now, that guy would never stop at a safe distance to let you pass. He would keep coming until, intimidated by his vehicle, you stop. Or he finds out you haven't stopped so he knows it's no longer safe for him to continue; so he stops. I'm going to do the same in this case.'

Fareeha gawked at me. I couldn't help laughing and added, 'I'll go all the way till I find it's no longer safe to proceed further. At that point, I'll stop. As of now, however, there's nothing to be afraid of.'

Before I had finished, I saw tears in Fareeha's eyes. She said, 'You never take me seriously. I'm worried to death and all you can think of are your stupid philosophies.'

'First of all, my dear Begum, mine is no philosophy. It's an analogy which I thought might explain to you my approach . . .'

By now Fareeha was weeping. I said, 'Okay, okay. You know I can't think of endangering your life and the children's lives.' I shuffled closer and pulled her sobbing frame towards me. 'Now stop crying. When I come home, I want to see a smiling Begum.'

Poor Fareeha was still snivelling. My phone rang. It was Amber calling. After putting it off for a while, I took the call— she must have something related to the case. She spoke in her annoyingly slow manner, as if the listener had no other business but to listen to her. 'I went to see the principal of Islamia College, where this boy studied.'

'What happened?' I lowered my voice, though I knew Fareeha would guess what we were discussing.

'I talked to him about the blasphemy lynching. He was reluctant at first, seemingly surprised to hear about the case again. These bastards are so jubilant to see the issue fizzle out.' Amber was probably eating something, which made her pauses longer and more annoying.

'I told him that this boy had links with the Talaba, who were the bullies in his college, and to the party responsible for the lynching. The principal was hesitant at first but then began to talk. Here's what I found out. The Talaba wanted to build an Islamiyat department, but the principal had no sanction for it. The college received a grant for a Fine Arts department, with a focus on digital design and visual arts. You know, it's an *in* thing. The principal told those maulvis, "Nothing doing." I'm sure the Talaba removed Mohan because he was in their way. "Now that he's no more, what will happen?" I asked the principal. He was clueless. The department issue is in limbo.'

'I could guess that. Anything about Hasan's death?'

'You're not interested in Mohan's death? A Muslim's life is worth more than a Hindu's?' This was no moral lesson, merely her way of scoring a point.

Fareeha watched me with an expressionless face and waited
for me to finish the call, but when I didn't, she placed her head
on my lap and closed her eyes. An easy sleeper, she fell asleep
the moment she closed her eyes.

'Don't be silly. The police have already closed that case.
I read the file. They attributed the lynching to mob action,
stating that no individuals could be held responsible. I can focus
only on the case I've been assigned.'

Fareeha's back was all sweaty, and her kurta clung to her
back. I recalled how she had been wishing for the last few
summers that we had an air conditioner, which I couldn't buy.
But my angelic wife never complained. I peeled the kurta away
from her skin, wiped away the perspiration from her back with
her dupatta, and then fanned her with it.

'How egregious! The police can sweep a man's murder
under their files!'

'Oh! As if little Amber didn't know already. And what's the
media been doing about it? You guys have forgotten the issue
and are looking for more sensational stuff.'

'I'm not getting into this debate with you. Tell me how
Fareeha is doing. I might drop in to say hello sometime.'

'She's good.' Somehow, my physical proximity to Fareeha
while I talked to Amber excited me. 'Still trying to come to
terms with the audacious roaches, sneaky rats, burnt sockets
and clogged pipes in our new home. Once it's in better shape,
we'll invite you to dinner.'

I suddenly recalled our first kiss. Amber had initiated it in
the library, between two cupboards of Islamic philosophy books.
The quick pressing of her lips to mine left me dumbfounded for
some time but also assured me, when I thought about it a few
days later, that like me, she was a novice at kissing. It was like

an instructional kiss that said: *I have gone this far, hoping you can take it from here.* She also seemed to mock me for procrastinating for so many days. Her muffled giggle seemed to say, 'My poor gutless friend!'

'Nice try, sir. It won't work, though. I'll drop in anytime.'

'Be my guest.' I quickly returned from my reverie. 'Okay, listen. You know this guy Arshad Karim? He writes for English papers.'

'Arshad Karim? Ah, yes. He's a freelancer. Very interesting man. Hermit-like ways. He owns a bookshop and writes for various magazines and papers, mostly about religion. Why do you ask? Journalism still haunts you?'

'No. It's about this case. This boy Hasan mentions him in his diary. AK, with the words "blasphemy articles". AK must be the same guy.' Fareeha stirred, and I felt my left thigh pasted with perspiration where her head rested.

'Ah, yes, that reminds me. I saw him at the boy's house. Yesterday.'

'At Hasan's?'

'Yes. He was there to offer condolences. He must be a family friend.'

'Yes, it's likely. Can you meet him? You see, I don't want to alarm him. Perhaps you can drop in on him and find out what he says about Hasan.'

'Now you're asking me to do police work. Let me see. Got to go now.' A quick goodbye, so typical of her.

After many nights, the dream recurred . . .

I'm running in the Lion King wilderness, looking for Abba. Hands on my knees, I stop and pant. He's nowhere. A dust cloud is settling down where the herd of cattle disappeared. What are these things sailing in the air? They're paintings on pieces of paper flying away tantalizingly, dodging my attempts to grab them . . . seductive, elusive manoeuvres in the air. Is that Fareeha's softness pressed against my ribs? We're sweating, glued together by the perspiration. How uplifting the touch of her bosom is! Amber's small breasts felt so good too. Why did I tell her she came to take pity on me? Why did I drive her away? Why do I drive people away? Why did I quibble with Ammi before she died? . . . And then I'm drowning in the ocean.

17

Waqas

Present day

'Did you like Mohan?' I asked Lubna, who sat on her drawing room sofa opposite me.

The first thing I did after the mundane early morning tasks in the office was to go to Hasan's house. The family had just risen, and Jawad had a *not-again* look on his face when I knocked on their door. He brought me a glass of lemonade and expressed his apology that Lubna might need a few minutes to join me.

I had wanted to ask *Did you love Mohan?* but I decided to use *like*. Sleepy-eyed Lubna's face reflected the anger that rose inside her even before she spoke.

'What does that have to do with Hasan's death?' She had quickly splashed water on her face but couldn't dry it completely, leaving droplets on her chiselled nose, forehead and hair.

'If needed, I will explain it to you later. Right now, I don't think it's important for you to know. But please remember that

I can hold this interview in a police station, which I'm sure you and your family won't like. It will be better for you to correctly answer my questions now. Also, keep in mind that I have other sources who can confirm or refute what you'll say.'

A little boy clothed only in shorts came and stood by the door of the drawing room, leaning against the wall, one foot over the other. 'Who's he?' I asked. Lubna turned her head towards the door, smiled at the boy, and told me he was Jawad's son. Did he want something from Lubna? He was probably wondering about what had been going on in their house and who the stranger in khaki and black was.

Lubna waved the boy away, and he trudged off. She adjusted the dupatta on her head, wiped the perspiration and water from her forehead with its hem, and said, 'Yes.'

'Yes, what?'

'I liked him.' Lubna's reply was brief.

I controlled my temper. 'I want you to tell me everything in detail. Start from the first time you came to know him. Got it? But first, do you think Hasan was one of those who wanted to punish Mohan?' Lubna took a long time to ponder the question. I scanned her face for indications of whether she had earlier considered what I suggested, but I couldn't see any. I decided to elaborate: 'He had reasons to hate Mohan. Hasan was going down the road to bigotry. Mohan was leading his sister astray, even perhaps courting her. He was the exact antithesis of what Hasan saw in religion. He had perhaps enough reasons to kill Mohan, or enough to exploit the opportunity that the blasphemy lynching offered.'

'I can't comment.'

I could see she was hurt. I realized she could've been holding herself responsible for Mohan's death—and if so, for Hasan's too. If Hasan had reasons to kill Mohan, wouldn't that weigh like a mountain on her conscience? I asked, 'So you agree there's a possibility that Hasan manipulated the blasphemy events to get even with Mohan?'

'I said I can't say.'

'Alright. What happened after the painting episode?'

'What painting?' Lubna's reddening face told me she knew which painting I meant but she pretended otherwise.

'Your portrait that Mohan did. You know which one I mean.'

Lubna was close to tears.

'Who's telling you all this? About the portrait, I mean. Ram? Furqan? Who?'

'I told you I have Hasan's diary.' I lied.

'He wrote all this in his diary?'

'Never mind. Tell me, did he confront you over it? What did he say about the painting incident?'

'He returned from college one day and rushed into my room. He was furious and dropped this bombshell. He wanted to know if I posed for Mohan. I too lost my temper when I understood what he was saying. How could he even imagine it? But we didn't listen to each other. We clarified nothing and assumed a great deal. I rue that he died with those assumptions.' She paused and then asked, 'What does the diary say?'

I felt sorry for Lubna. I could understand the quandary she was in. It was obvious the painting was Mohan's imagination. Lubna never posed for him, at least not the way the painting depicted her. Lubna had probably not even seen the painting. She had no means of finding out what was in it that angered Hasan. If Hasan mentioned *nude* or similar words, Lubna might have been wondering how much of her body appeared naked in the painting. She couldn't ask Hasan, she probably never asked Mohan, and now she couldn't bring herself to ask the same thing of a stranger. Perhaps even Hasan knew the painting was a result of Mohan's imagination, but it was reason enough for him to be furious.

'And the painting on Rashid's poetry? Was it an assignment too?'

Lubna looked astonished. 'How do you know about it? Who's telling you all these things? This couldn't have been in Hasan's diary.'

'His friend Furqan told me about it and the previous painting too. Was it an assignment or a gift for him?'

She said it was an assignment.

My phone rang. It was Furqan. 'Waqas Bhai. I'm sorry to disturb you. But Ram is missing. His father called me and said Ram had not returned home since last night.'

'Didn't he sleep in his home last night?'

'His father says he sometimes leaves home and returns in the morning. He's been like this ever since Mohan died. But today, he hasn't returned.'

'It's still fairly early,' I said even as I recalled Ram could have been upset after last night's episode. 'But I'll see what I can do.'

'Is it about Ram?' Lubna asked, anxiously. 'I forgot to tell you he came to our place late last night—stood outside our door—and vented his anger.'

'What did he say?' I asked, standing up and putting my phone in my trouser pocket.

'He said justice had been done and that we had got what we deserved—words like those. He was shouting so I couldn't understand much. Abba went to the door. He didn't reply but closed the door.'

She paused and added, 'There were a few Deen-e-Kamil men near our door. They're at our door most of the time. They must've seen his outburst.'

'I've got to handle this first, but I'll be back.'

* * *

I knocked on the door of Saleem's madrasah. When he opened it, I asked, 'Is that boy Ram with you?' No time for formalities with this man.

'The Hindu boy?' He looked taken aback at my aggression.

'Yes.'

'Please come in. Well, he was unnecessarily worked up. We brought him here for some words of advice.' Saleem, who I noticed for the first time had a stout build, was his usual composed self. 'Would you like tea or a cold drink, Inspector Sahib? It's really hot, isn't it?' He removed the white turban from his head and wiped perspiration from his brow and hair.

I ignored the offer. 'You know you can't keep people in custody like this.'

'Custody? Not at all. He's like our guest.'

'Nice. Did you offer him tea or a beverage? And what did he do to deserve your hospitality?'

'He pestered a family that's already grieving a death. Won't you sit down?'

I ignored his sentence again. 'Who pesters whom is none of your business. Let the police handle it.'

'We thought the police might get unnecessarily nasty while we can make him understand like brothers. Anyway, I'll bring him to you.'

Saleem returned in a while with Ram, whose eyes carried even more emotions than they had the previous night.

'Are you alright?' I asked Ram.

'Will you arrest me?' His appearance did not suggest they had manhandled him, but the pressure cooker of anger steamed in his eyes.

Saleem's face bore a perennial smile as though we were a family gathering. I wished I could wipe that smile—smirk, in fact—or expose the daggers it cloaked. I was sure he had threatened Ram, for which I could charge Saleem. But it would have been futile because Ram, who had become hostile to everyone including me, would not cooperate. I decided to let it go and said to him, 'Go home.'

I was itching to hear the rest of Lubna's story. When I returned to her house, I asked her to tell me everything in detail.

18

Lubna

Three months ago

A student sitting in the front row raised his hand and said to Mohan one day, 'Sir, you said a few weeks ago that there's no right and wrong. But religion teaches us to differentiate between right and wrong. So how can we reconcile the two views?'

Arifa, who sat next to me, whispered in my ear. 'He's the one who has been talking about Mohan and you.'

'You are new to the class, aren't you?' Mohan asked.

'Yes, sir. I've recently joined the class.'

With a big beard, the guy had mullah stamped all over him. What was he doing in a Fine Arts class?

'Welcome to the class. I hope you'll find it enjoyable and useful. Would you like to introduce yourself to the class?'

'Sir, please answer my question first.'

The statement sounded impudent, but Mohan did not show he was offended.

'Sure. What was your question? Yes, right. Well, that's a long debate, my friend, and I want to shorten it to this: the two may not reconcile as art presents a point of view of life different from religion's.'

'Sir, does it mean art takes man away from religion?'

'Perhaps it does. But so does technology, many would say. Should we then abandon technology and go back to caves? Of course, we can't.'

Some students laughed.

'Then, sir, what should we do about our moral bankruptcy? We can't ignore the fact that the world is becoming a sinful place. The lack of religiosity, the rise of materialism, the exploitation of the third world by capitalists, etc. What I mean, sir, is that if the arts and, as you say, science, are taking us away from religion, we should perhaps consider that this drifting away may be the cause of our problems.'

'My friend, I think you're getting too worried about certain things. Your worldview is subjective. Others may not agree with it. For example, how can you say we're morally poor for having drifted away from religion? Yes, man is less religious now than he was, say, a century or two ago, but is he intellectually, socially or morally poorer? It's debatable. Hasn't mankind reduced disease and poverty considerably?'

'But the Fine Arts are promoting vulgarity. It's for everyone to see.'

'Then, my friend, you're sitting in the wrong place. No one has forced you to take Fine Arts.' As he said this, Mohan looked perturbed, as perhaps many of the students were.

The boy jumped to his feet. 'I haven't joined this class. I just came to see what filth you're spreading here. We must do something to stop it.' With this, he paraded out of the classroom, leaving everyone stunned.

What the hell was that? We? Who were we? Arifa and I looked at each other, foreheads creased.

* * *

A few days later, when I went to school, there were anxious faces all around. Arifa took me to a corner.

'The principal wants to see you,' she said.

She had a penchant for melodrama—an assignment was a catastrophe, an examination the day of judgment—so my initial guess was that she was needlessly worried. I only paid attention when she said someone had complained to the principal about Mohan.

'Who told you?'

'The principal Sahib's PA came to find out if you were in school. He requested us to inform you as soon as you come in.'

'But who told you about Mohan—and the complaint?'

'The boys were talking about it. Please don't waste time and see the PA now.'

'Chill, Arifa. What's the hurry? I'll see what it's about, but I'll go and see Mohan first.'

'He's not in his office. He's been with the principal since this morning.'

This was worrying. I went to the PA who sat next to the principal's office in a vestibule behind a small table with a computer and several phones placed on it. He talked to the principal on one of them and told me to wait in the school. The principal would convene a meeting soon, he said.

Nearly an hour went by as I wandered around the school corridors. Boys stood around in small groups, whispering. Were they stealing glances at me? *Negative spaces*, a term I liked in Fine Arts. Those people reminded me of it. Why were those boys, who were less interested in arts than in a scandal, in this department? Adjusting the dupatta on her head repeatedly, Arifa looked more worried than usual, not for me but for the world in general. Or probably for herself because she and I were usually together. Why was she in Fine Arts?

Finally, a peon came to usher me into the PA's room. It was crowded with bearded boys. All glared at me with fire in their eyes as I waited for them to make way for me. When I walked into the principal's office—a large almost square room with a shining tiled floor and a huge table against one wall—I spotted Mohan sitting in a chair in a row of many, looking lonely, and the principal sitting behind the large table. 'Come in, Ms Lubna.'

I thought he would ask me to sit, but he didn't, so I stood with my hands on the back of a chair. There was someone at the door behind me, to whom the principal motioned. In a while someone entered . . . Many pairs of feet dragged themselves on the floor. A chill ran down my spine. The principal motioned them to fit themselves in the spaces between the table, chairs and sofas. He continued, 'Ms Lubna, do you visit Mr Mohan's office often?'

What a silly thing to ask! I had not seen the principal often. The man was well dressed and looked educated, but his question was inane. 'Yes, sir. Is it not allowed? I thought students should discuss things with their instructors after class.'

'Yes. But there have been complaints that you spend too much time in his office.'

'Complaints, sir? Who complained? Did Mr Mohan complain? Did I take too much of his time?' I glanced towards Mohan. Was there a hint of a smile on his face, a tired smile that patted me on my back for my courage? 'Who else can complain?'

'Ms Lubna, there's no need for you to be sarcastic. You know the norms of this society. You must adhere to them.' The principal glared at me, his thick lips pressed together.

Something inside me was ready to explode, but I told myself to understand how people perceived my visits to Mohan's office. For Mohan's sake, I had to keep the storm inside me under a lid. I said, 'Sir, I'm aware of this society's norms and I don't think I've crossed the line. But I'll be more mindful of it.'

The principal probably deemed my statement as his victory. He sat back, motioned me to sit, and considered the people behind me, his eyes saying: *Isn't her explanation satisfactory?*

'Sir, ask her why she visited his home,' someone behind me said.

This blew the lid off. 'It's no one's business!' I glanced over my shoulder at the boys. I was in two minds about what to say to the principal. If I defended myself, I might appear guilty, but if I sounded bellicose, the issue might escalate. Again, Mohan's concern came to the fore. I said, 'Sir, my brother is Mohan's friend. My family has ties with his.' I paused, wondering if the two families would vouch for it. I tried to control my quivering voice as I added, 'Sir, it's unfair to drag my personal life here.'

The principal stared at the person who had spoken. 'I won't let her personal life be brought into disrepute.'

'Sir, Islam says Muslims cannot be friends with non-Muslims . . .'

'Excuse me, mister. You don't have to worry about her practice of Islam.'

'But sir, even the information she gave is incorrect. We've talked to her brother. His narrative differs from hers. Sir, this man—a Hindu—wants to trap a Muslim girl. We won't let this happen. So it's not just her personal life we're talking about. Our women are our honour. Muhammad bin Qasim came to India to rescue Muslim women . . .'

Luckily, the boy's history ran out. The principal's large face said I was not the only one exasperated. He removed his glasses and cleaned them with a silky napkin. Perhaps encouraged by the principal's gentle demeanour, other voices arose, leading to pandemonium.

'Quiet, everyone!' The principal had to intervene. His voice quivered, as mine did.

'Sir, if you'll allow us?' This was the same boy who initiated the arguments. He probably realized he would lose his opportunity to speak if the principal called the meeting off. 'Sir, this is an important issue. It's not my opinion alone. The whole school is worried. It's a matter of concern for the whole society. We won't let anyone defile Islam. We will protest if the school authorities don't do anything. And as I told you earlier, this is not the only issue. This man is also guilty of blaspheming Islam . . .'

'We'll talk about this later. As far as Ms Lubna's conduct is concerned, I don't see any problem. And she's one of our brightest students. Ms Lubna, you may go.'

But what was the other issue? I wanted to stay . . . for the other issue. But how could I? The principal's narrowed eyes seemed to ask why I was still there; am I not happy to be out of this? I finally spoke as I was about to leave, 'Sir, what about the other issue? What's wrong? I don't think Mr Mohan has said anything objectionable. If these people don't like what he teaches, why do they attend his class?' I was half sitting. Oh, God! What could I do? The more concern I showed for Mohan, the more difficult I made things for him.

'Sir, this is none of her business.' It was probably the same boy who had spoken earlier.

'You should leave,' the principal said to me, his stare showing he was desperate for me to be out of the way—with womenfolk involved, the issues get doubly thorny. I glanced at Mohan again who sat expressionless and, trying hard not to cry, I left the room. Did I hear the clank of daggers being unsheathed behind me?

* * *

'Why don't you look at me when I talk to you?' I followed Hasan as he left my room and entered his. 'What happened in my school? Did you go there today? What did you tell those bloody mullahs? Sons of bitches, that's what they are!'

'Stop degrading them! And mind your language! I can't believe my sister is talking this way.' He turned around and wagged a finger at me.

'And what are you and your respectable mullahs up to? Why are you after Mohan?'

'Stop shouting! You want to announce that to the whole neighbourhood?'

I realized he had a point. 'Hasan, please tell me what's going on. Please don't do anything to Mohan. He has done nothing wrong.'

But he slammed the door in my face. All evening, I paced up and down my room, much to Sadia's annoyance. She asked me what was wrong. How could I tell her that something evil was about to happen to an innocent man? I messaged Mohan that I wanted to see him.

'There's nothing to worry about,' he texted.

'Please. I want to see you. I'll come to your home at around midnight.'

His reply came after ages. 'No. I'll come to you. The empty plot behind your home.'

Those few hours before midnight were the longest in my life. No, nothing would happen to Mohan. Everything would turn out alright. The world was not devoid of reason, fairness, justice. And after all, there was Allah, making sure no harm would come to an innocent man. But . . .

Mohan arrived before me and texted. Thankfully, Sadia had gone to sleep. In the next room, Hasan was quiet. Was he asleep? I gently unlatched the door and slipped out. Down the stairs, out the back door, soundlessly, I hoped. The meeting place was stinking. It always stank. The chirping of the crickets sounded unusually loud.

'Thanks for being here,' I whispered as I approached his frail silhouette. I later realized that the *sir* had disappeared from my speech. 'What's going on in the school?'

'Nothing at all. Some misunderstanding.'

'It's not true.' I inched closer to him, whispering because we were not far from Hasan's room. 'What happened after I left? What did the principal tell those mullahs?'

He hesitated, started to say something, then stopped.

'Long story. In short, they think I've insulted Islam. I said if I have, I will apologize.'

'What?' I could hardly suppress my anger. 'Why do you have to apologize? I have heard all your lectures. You didn't say anything bad.'

'Lubna, try to understand.'

'Okay. Were they satisfied?'

'Hopefully.'

'All good, then?'

'Kind of.' He paused as I glanced towards my balcony in the darkness. Was someone standing there? I held Mohan's hand and hastened to a place where broken furniture was dumped. We might be camouflaged there. 'The principal has suspended me . . .'

'What! Why? What's going on?'

'Listen. He said it's for my own safety. To pacify them. Everything will be okay soon.'

To hear each other's whispers, we had huddled together, our arms almost touching, his breath warm on my forehead. 'I want to kill those mullahs! They're so unfair to you! Was Hasan there? Did he say something against you?'

'He was there, but he didn't say anything bad.'

'Why was he there then? Tell me the truth. He must've spoken ill about you. He's turned so mean.'

'No need to be so mad, silly girl.' He cupped my face in his hands. They were sweaty—it was way past midnight but still very humid. Or were those my tears? 'Everything will be alright.' We stared at each other, though in the darkness we saw little.

'You have a runny nose?' I asked. He was snuffling repeatedly. 'You always have.' I couldn't help giggling.

He muffled his laughter too. 'I forgot to bring my hanky. I usually keep one in my pocket as I never know when my nose will start running—even in the summer. Karamat says anti-allergies are not good for long-term use.' He lifted his left forearm to rub it across his nose. I grabbed his wrist and stopped him.

'Please don't. This is an artist's hand.' I cleaned his nose with my dupatta.

'Ma used to do it for me when I was a kid. No one has done it since then.' His muffled voice sounded happy.

For some moments, we stood motionless. Then he kissed me, an awkward kiss, with his lips searching for something on my face, cheeks, forehead, eyes. 'Everything will be alright,' he said as I kissed him back, standing on tiptoe, my heartbeat so loud I thought someone might hear it—Hasan could, for his room was nearby. Perhaps he did.

This was the last time I saw Mohan. I didn't wash that dupatta, leaving it in a corner of my cupboard.

When I sneaked back into the house and tiptoed up the stairs, Hasan's door opened and there he stood in front of his room, arms crossed on his chest. I jumped with fright and my feet froze. The light was low, but I could see the accusing look on his face.

'You've proven me right. I told your principal that Mohan had intentions about you and that he must be stopped.' He returned to his room and shut the door.

19

Waqas

Present day

My phone rang. It was Ashraf.

'Sir, Shakir Sahib wants to see you immediately.'

'What about? What's so urgent?'

'Sir, about the autopsy report you requested.'

'What about it? Has it arrived?'

'Yes, sir. But I haven't seen it. It's with Shakir Sahib. He wants to know who requested it. I told him you did. He asked me to call you.' Ashraf's voice maintained its usual languorous ease, as if everything in the world was boring.

'I'm in the middle of an interrogation. Tell him I'll see him when I'm done.'

'Where are you, sir? What should I tell him?'

'I told you I'm investigating Hasan's death.' As I ended the call, the little boy returned to where he stood a while ago. I asked Lubna, 'Does he want something from you?'

'Yes. He usually eats his breakfast with me. Sometimes, when he throws a tantrum, he listens only to me.'

I smiled. 'Alright, I won't keep the little one from his breakfast long. Just a few more questions.' I asked a few questions about Hasan's demeanour after the lynching. Lubna's account tallied with the ones I had heard before. 'Can you recognize the people who visited Hasan in his last few days?' As Lubna pondered over it, I continued, 'I've learnt that some friends visited him.'

'Yes. They did. What about them?'

'Can you help me identify them? What did they look like? You're an artist. Maybe you can draw their faces.'

'I didn't see them up close.' She was visibly disappointed with herself. 'But wait! Sadia, my sister, did. She said some of Hasan's friends visited her school too, for a religious sermon, I think. And she's also a good artist, probably better than I am when it comes to portraits.'

'Great! Can you call her? Let's ask her.'

Lubna went into the house and returned with a girl in her early teens. She wore white churidar pants, a lemon-yellow kurta, and a tie-and-die dupatta thrown across her shoulder. Her eyes and forehead were similar to Lubna's, but the lips were thinner and the face was pimpled. The expression on her face reminded me that seeing a police officer for the first time could be a horrifying experience.

I said, 'Please sit and relax, Sadia.'

Sadia wiped her face with her snake-like dupatta and sat down. Lubna, who sat next to her on the sofa, looked sideways at her and said, 'Sadia, the police inspector wants you to draw the faces of the men who came to see Hasan in his last few days.'

'I think I saw three of them,' Sadia said in a shrill voice. Her chin was tilted downward so that her restive eyes looked downcast. 'On separate occasions.'

I asked, 'You can tell one from the other, can you? You remember their faces?'

'Yes, I guess.'

'Good. And can you make sketches of their faces? I'm actually interested in the men who visited him days before . . . Hasan died. It'll be a great help, Sadia, if you can do this. This is the sort of work only experts can do.' I wanted to add that her sketches would help us catch her brother's killers, but I stopped short of making any promises.

I'm not sure if Sadia's confidence was boosted as much as I hoped, but she said meekly, 'I'll try.'

'She means she'll manage something for you,' Lubna said, with the first hint of a smile I saw on her face.

'Good!' I got up. 'Can I collect them this afternoon?' The girls nodded.

* * *

'Waqas, didn't I tell you we don't want an autopsy?' Shakir's face was crimson with rage; his nearly bald head glistened with sweat.

'Sir, first let me see the autopsy report. I told you if it hints at a murder, we'll continue the investigation; else, we'll abort it. What does the report say?'

'Never mind the autopsy report. Do you have any regard for what I said? I said we won't pursue this case. I told you categorically not to request an autopsy, did I not?' He wiped back the thin hair on his head with his right hand, almost as a gesture of helplessness. Then suddenly, he banged his right fist on his table; it thundered in response.

I could no longer ignore Shakir's ire. I sat down and said, 'Sir, the most important thing is the autopsy result. Let's see what it says.'

'Waqas, don't test my temper. Alright, if you're worried about the result, here it is. The report shows no abnormality before the death. Now you answer my question and explain why I shouldn't charge you with disobedience.'

I was so astounded I forgot Shakir was touching the limit of his patience. 'But sir, how is it possible? I'm sure he was murdered.'

Shakir exploded. 'Waqas, I want to know why you disobeyed my order. And why . . . I . . . should . . . not . . . charge . . . you . . . with . . . disobedience!' Every word of the last sentence was uttered with a bark which must have reached the bazaar behind the police station.

Furious about the unexpected result of the report, I responded in the same tone. 'Sir, how can you ignore a person's death? How can you sweep it under the rug? Are we so afraid of the mullahs that we would be willing to trample upon justice?'

Speechless, Shakir scratched his balding scalp. A barren skull had led to a barren exterior. He counter-attacked in his characteristic irrational manner, 'And what have you, the champion of justice, achieved in the last two days, besides letting Hindus run amok?'

So the news had reached him. I decided to ignore the last part. 'After your stiff resistance, you ask me what I've achieved? I hope you remember, sir, that I requested the autopsy report only yesterday. And sir, do you know that the media people are breathing down our necks? If we sweep this case under the rug, they will pull the same rug from under our feet. Are you ready to face the media, sir?'

Shakir chickened out. 'What are they saying? Whom did you meet?'

I leaned forward in my chair, sitting on the edge. 'Sir, they know this case has links to the blasphemy case. That Hasan—the boy whose body was found—was connected to the Deen is no secret. One doesn't have to be a Sherlock Holmes to connect the dots.'

I had probably overdone it. Shakir exploited my argument. 'All the more reason why we must bury this case. The autopsy report is enough to silence anyone fond of digging deeper.'

'Can I see it, sir?' I wished Shakir was lying.

'You don't believe me? Am I lying? Let me discuss it with DSP Sahib. Then I'll file it. You can see it later.'

Having averted a possible disciplinary action from Shakir, I was nonetheless worried. A negative autopsy report would confirm it was a suicide. But I wanted to see the report myself, which was not possible till later in the afternoon. But Shakir had no reason to lie about it. Or perhaps he had: to show me I was wrong.

'Sir, I hope the danger is averted.' Ashraf rose to his feet as I left Shakir's office and marched towards mine. Ashraf followed me.

'I can't say. I'm more worried about the autopsy report,' I said, dropping into my chair.

'What does it say?'

'I haven't seen it, but Shakir says it's perfectly normal.'

'Then Shakir Sahib will surely cool down. He'll be glad to win a victory over you. And I believe you're also going to cool down, sir, now that we know it's a suicide,' Ashraf said, while running his hands over his thick nylon belt.

'Yes, maybe.'

* * *

As Hasan's house was nearby, I decided to check if Sadia and Lubna had completed their sketches. They had, and the results were professional.

'Very good job! But the police usually prefer a more neutral mood,' I said to the girls sitting on the drawing room sofa, as I surveyed the two sketches. The sketches had a dark feel about them, probably reflecting the artist's mood.

Sadia's face showed that she couldn't understand my point. Lubna asked, 'You want us to do it all over again?'

'No, no. They're great. But you got my point, didn't you?' Lubna nodded.

I scrutinized the faces in the sketches. Both men were anywhere in their twenties and bearded. One of them looked familiar, but I couldn't recall where I had seen him. I thanked the girls, and as I rose to go, Hasan's father, Zubair, entered the room, dressed in a dhoti and a kurta.

'Son, I want to make a request,' he said, as he inched forward.

I stopped near the drawing room door.

'We don't want an investigation of this case. Please close it already. We don't want any post-mortem. Please, we've already lost a son.' The man appeared to be carrying a mountain on his shoulders, looking much older than he had the last time I saw him.

'Has someone threatened you?'

The old man's unshaven face was creased with helplessness. 'No. It's not that. We don't feel there's any use taking this matter further. What's bygone is bygone. Nothing can change it.'

Though I felt sorry for the man, I did not want any obstacle in the interrogation. 'Zubair Sahib, let the police do what it must. Technically speaking, everyone in your family is a suspect. Motive? The police can very well invent one. So please don't interfere. In fact, now that you've mentioned it, I'll send a few policemen. Please provide them with all the call records of your family in the last few days. Don't delete anything, I warn you, else the police can round up your whole family.'

I paused and looked at the two girls behind the old man. I added to Lubna, 'Please tell your father to cooperate. I want to trace the murderers.'

Leaving Hasan's house, I phoned Furqan and told him, 'I'll send you snapshots of sketches of two men's faces.'

'Okay.'

'See if you can recognize them. Hasan's sisters sketched them. They say these men visited Hasan in his last few days. Whoever's involved in Hasan's murder must've come to survey his room.'

'Makes sense. It's difficult to burgle a room one hasn't seen earlier.'

'Smart boy. So help me with these. They'll be on your phone in a minute if the signal isn't too bad.'

What next? I hadn't read the Arshad Karim articles yet. And I also wanted to see the autopsy report to confirm what Shakir said. Luckily, I found the file on my office table with the autopsy report inserted in it. To my dismay, the report didn't mention anything abnormal about Hasan's body before his death. Perhaps it was time I put my gut feeling to rest. *But how was it possible?* I put the file aside and went home.

'The case is over, I guess.' Fareeha was quick to sense my disappointment.

'Yes, it is.' I sighed. 'What's for dinner?'

'*Pakora* curry. But you're early, so you might have to wait a while. Are you hungry already?' Fareeha's voice rang with placid joy, obviously relieved to know the case was closed.

'I am, a bit, but I'll wait.' I walked into the kitchen and put my arms around her from behind as she ladled the cooking pot.

'I'm sweaty and smelly. This kitchen burns like hell!'

'But I don't mind it because hell holds the most beautiful houri. And I'm sweaty and smelly too. The poet says pleasure is doubled when wine mixes with wine.'

'*Uff!* I love this one. Fraz's, right? Read it to me after dinner.'

'Oh, my wife is in a poetic mood, which means in the mood for love!' I pressed myself against her from behind.

'Watch out! The kids might be around.'

'No, they're outside, in the street. I saw them. Even Roshni is making new friends. Perfect timing while I make love to my wife. Your body feels so good in my arms!'

'Not really. I'm afraid I'm putting on inches. Don't you feel the tire around my middle?' She laughed self-consciously.

'I adore those curves, my houri.' I kissed her nape.

'Okay, have a shower. When I finish my cooking, I'll shower too. Then we can have a lovely dinner. What do you say?'

'And what's for dessert? The sweetest and the most beautiful houri, I hope.'

I decided I might use this time to call the landlord and complain to him about the things on Fareeha's list, which was quite orderly and written in a neat handwriting. I'd often told Fareeha she would make an excellent staff member in my office as she did a much better job than some of the police clerks, who were miserable at making briefs, precis or reports. 'Why don't you train them?' she had asked. If I tried to, I told her, they wouldn't have time to do the chores of their—and my—superior officers; that would disrupt not only their careers but mine as well.

Bhai Jaan called while I was seated in the open veranda. He came straight to the point. 'You're worrying yourself about a blasphemy-related case?'

'Salam Bhai. How are you?'

'I'm good. You're dodging my question.' His deep voice sounded like a schoolmaster's.

'There's nothing to hide. Yes, I'm investigating a case.' I saw Fareeha peek through the kitchen door and disappear into the kitchen.

'You never learn. That's where our last conversation ended, and that's what I'm forced to repeat now.'

'Thanks for constantly reminding me I'm a bad officer.' I didn't like where this conversation was headed.

'Have you ever considered the possibility that I'm concerned about your safety?'

'*Safety first* is not a path that Abba chose. He offended people because he chose to pursue what he believed in.'

'I know, and you don't have to remind me. But remember, he paid the price.'

His words were punctuated with coughing which checked my rebuttal—his lungs were not great. I decided to ignore his second sentence. 'We keep reminding each other but never listen to each other. How are Bhabhi and the kids? As soon as

I've settled down here, we'll come over for a weekend. It's long overdue.'

'Yes, please do.'

'And if it makes you feel better, please know that the case is closed.'

I dropped the call and strode into the kitchen. 'Why don't you tell the entire world—if there's anyone left—that this behan chod Waqas doesn't listen to you?'

She turned around, tongs in one hand, a kitchen towel in the other, and tears in her eyes. 'Why are you shouting expletives?' She sniffled. 'And tell me how else I can ensure your safety?'

'I'm not a child! I can take care of myself.' My voice was so loud that Roshni, who had just skittered in, froze at the door, her perfect round eyes widening. The boys decided it was safer to turn about. *Waqas, rein yourself in.* 'Now that the case is over, stop telling the world about it.'

I thought I could play with the kids for a while and pretended I was in control of my temper, but they stayed away from me. Roshni stole glances at me to find out if she could trust me—she knew her Abbu well—and then went to her room for a shower. Fareeha was definitely sulking. She wasn't thinking of apologizing, I was sure. My anger unabated, I decided to be alone. The police station would be a quieter place. I left home on my motorcycle, enjoying the knowledge that I had punished Fareeha by blowing away her plans for a romantic dinner.

The duty constables sat on charpoys laid out in the courtyard. Both rose to their feet unwillingly.

'Your phone should be right next to you. What if someone calls for help?' I scolded them for not being alert enough while on duty, even as I realized where my anger stemmed from.

'Sir, we will run inside and take the call. Don't worry.' The senior man, a thickset fellow with an even thicker moustache, said.

'Shut up! I can see how fast you can run. Lazybones! Get the phone here or sit near it in the office. Hurry up!'

I went to my small cubicle office. Fareeha called a few times, but I didn't answer the phone. I wanted to smash it against the wall, as it rang incessantly.

Life felt infinitely dull. I picked up the articles on blasphemy from the table, hoping they might be interesting. One of the two said there were things about the Blasphemy Law that had been kept hidden from the public. Having gone through a few paragraphs, I stopped at a horizontal black line on the paper. A malfunction in the printer caused it, I recalled, when Furqan printed them. There were two of them in fact, and one of those lines masked a complete sentence. I picked up the other computer prints and found the lines exactly at the same places on all the papers. I slammed them back on the table. Nothing was working.

Wait a minute. Where else have I seen these lines? I jumped out of my chair. Of course! I had seen them only hours ago, on the autopsy report.

20

Waqas

Present day

I rushed to where the two constables sat in front of a noisy pedestal fan. They cowered in anticipation of another scolding and then stood up. 'Where are the keys to the filing cabinet?'

'What's up, sir?' the senior man asked. The other one watched.

'The keys, the keys. Where are they?'

The bulkier man was nimbler. He rushed in to get the key. 'There you are.'

I ran back, opened the filing cabinet, and rummaged through a few files but couldn't find the autopsy report.

'Who would know which file holds today's report?' I shouted at the two constables, who stepped back, alarmed. File work was not their domain. I wondered if they were any good at their own jobs. I found out I didn't have the phone number of the clerk taking care of the files. How silly of me! The time wasted looking for a contact could be crucial in police work. Fareeha was better than me at keeping a record of phone numbers. She said the manual phone directory was the best, and she always bought beautiful ones. I texted, then phoned Ashraf. He didn't know which clerk I was talking about.

Damn! I didn't know the names of all the staff even after five days at the new place! *Waqas, you are a useless policeman!*

'No worries,' Ashraf said. 'The weekly duty roster is on the noticeboard but I have a copy. I'll get back to you in a jiffy, sir.'

The guy was good, a rare breed in the police force. Before I rushed to the noticeboard, he had texted me the name and number of the clerk and saved me the trouble of browsing the roster. I called the clerk, and thankfully, he attended my call. I was sure he didn't have my number, but it turned out he did. He sounded startled, but he remembered and told me where he had filed the report.

It took me a few minutes to find the file. My breath bated, I looked at the autopsy report lying on the table. Indeed, there were lines on its three pages at the same place as the printouts Furqan took for me. The autopsy report was obviously printed on our station's printer.

'Did the autopsy report come by email?' I called the clerk again. I couldn't imagine he had ever heard of the word email, but he had. This was a day of epiphanies about the police staff.

'No, sir. They always send a hard copy. It's computer-generated so it won't need a signature. But they never email the original. We can request a copy by email, but it's always followed by the original. They send it through snail mail. But why do you ask, sir?'

'Who brought it?'

'Autopsy reports generally arrive through courier service. Sometimes the lab people send a peon, or if we're in a hurry, we send our man. Is something wrong, sir?'

Oh, God! What was going on in this police station! I sleepwalked to my office and sank into my chair. Someone printed the report here and made it look like it came by the usual mail. Who? I had an idea. *That son of a bitch!* But I shouldn't let anyone know I had detected the anomaly. *Get hold of the actual report first.*

I called the pathologist who worked in the lab that performed the autopsy. The phone numbers were at the bottom of the report. I tried a few of them in vain, my frustration rising—a feeling of being so close and yet so far—before I reached him. Rushing through the preliminaries, I found out who I was talking to and got to the point. 'Hafeez Sahib, do you remember an autopsy your lab did yesterday or probably today? A young boy, in his late teens.'

'I do. I did it myself. What about it?' The nasal voice was sing-song.

'May I know what the findings were?' A pause as my breathing ceased again.

'Ah, let me think. Yes, I guess the body was drugged before the man died. There were scratches on his throat. Nothing else, I believe.'

'Drugged?'

'Yes. He took propofol, or somebody administered it to him. The contents were still in his blood. The quantity was large, so it's obvious someone—whoever fed the sedative—was in a hurry. The death occurred due to asphyxiation, but the man was unconscious well before the death. You haven't gotten the report yet?'

I knew it! I knew the report I saw was wrong.

'We have, but it says there was nothing wrong with the body before the hanging.'

'It's not possible. I remember it quite well. One doesn't get to perform many autopsies, so I couldn't have made a mistake.'

'Hmm. Hafeez Sahib, I have an inkling that someone has tampered with the report to make the boy's death look like a suicide. The actual report hasn't reached us.'

'Who could've done it?' Hafeez's voice sounded like he had become defensive, anticipating that his lab would have to shoulder the blame for doctoring the report.

It was important not to lose the man's support, if I were to get hold of the correct report.

I said, 'I think it's someone from my police station. But my hunch is that someone from your department is an accomplice—a clerk or maybe a peon. It would've been difficult without the help of someone from there.'

'Oh.' The nasal voice trailed off.

'Please tell me one thing, Hafeez Sahib. Shouldn't they get the report signed by a responsible doctor before sending it?'

'No. The report is fed into the computer, which has an app for recording the autopsy data. The app then generates a report which can be printed. I remember filling in the data and generating the report. Next, it must have gone to a clerk who prints it, files one copy and sends another to the requesting agency.'

'There's a flaw in the system which allows tampering with the content of the report. My hunch is someone from my police station took an old autopsy report—he must've requested someone from your lab to email it to him—tampered with it by entering this boy's details and the data that made it look like a normal report. Then he printed it and gave it to our clerk, making it look like it came from your lab.'

There was another long pause, after which he asked, 'How can you be so sure?'

'Because the prints are surely from our printer. Whether or not it was fake can be determined by cross-checking it with the report you generated.'

'And why do you think our guy may be involved in this?' The man again sounded defensive. Nobody liked a finger pointed at them.

'Because our guy—who faked the report—must've made sure that the actual report wouldn't reach us, and that a copy of the fake report goes into your file. Suppose someone tries to check your copy to make sure the contents of our copy tally with those of yours. Our guy made sure our copy of the report and yours—both the hard copy and the soft one—are identical. Hafeez Sahib, I want to see your report if you can help me. If I'm correct, the report in your file must be different from the one on your computer, which I guess is still the original one.'

'Now? It's late in the evening.'

'Is there someone in the lab whom you can instruct to help me see the documents? You don't have to come to the lab.'

Another agonizing pause, as he talked to someone, probably his wife. 'Hmm. I can do it. We have at least one staff member in the lab on each shift. I'll call the guy in the lab and instruct him to help you.'

'Thank you, Hafeez Sahib. I'm setting off for your lab at this very moment.'

21

Waqas

Present day

'Sir, he deserves to be charged with disobedience,' Shakir said to DSP Abdul Khaliq, pointing towards me, only his immense respect for his boss restraining him from shouting.

Shakir and I were on the edge of our seats while Khaliq rocked in his swivel chair, with his belly pointing towards the ceiling fan.

Shakir continued, 'Sir, you decided there would be no autopsy, and I categorically told him not to meddle with this Deen business. But he didn't listen.'

Elbows on the table, Khaliq leaned forward and regarded me, not accusingly but as if he expected another interesting story.

Shakir grabbed the chance to bash me some more. 'Sir, I've talked to his previous bosses. All of them agreed he was no good. All he has ever done was argue about tried and tested methods. Sir, do you know he was chosen to represent the police on TV and he messed it up big time? He didn't even try to defend the police.'

Khaliq looked amused. 'Oh yes, I remember the TV show. But he was impressive. Just a wee bit too honest.'

Shakir looked taken aback but he was not done. 'Sir, he has never solved a case successfully. He just preaches human rights and all that nonsense.'

Both of my bosses now looked at me. I hadn't slept all night. The lab guy worked his shift from home and sounded irritated when I reached out to him. He took his time coming to the lab. He spent another hour finding his way around the computer stuff, the files and folders, the passwords and everything that stood between me and the report. The guy had to phone dozens of his colleagues to overcome each obstacle. Finally, when I grabbed the report and returned home, I found Fareeha sulking. Despite my attempts to appease her, she didn't respond to me—she lay in bed with her eyes shielded with one arm. I should've climbed into bed next to her, the way we usually apologized to each other, but my mind was on the autopsy report, the blasphemy incident and Hasan. I decided to read the articles that had provided a clue to the fakeness of the report. I slept for less than an hour and woke with a headache, which was threatening to blow my brain off when I reached the office, where there was no electricity because of a fault in the area's transformer. Despite drinking two cups of tea in the morning, my head throbbed, and I wanted to strangle Shakir.

Instead, I said, 'Sir, I wouldn't answer Shakir Sahib's allegations. All I can say is that in my career, I've tried to go by the book, something that didn't sit well with most of my superiors. About the autopsy, I had a good reason to go ahead with it, and the report has vindicated me.'

Shakir interrupted. 'Excuse me, mister. The autopsy report says there was nothing abnormal with the body, so it was certainly a suicide. The boy died by hanging himself. We discussed this yesterday, didn't we?'

'Sir, that report is a fake. Here's the original one.' I placed the report on the table, spread it out evenly, and waited a while to let my discovery sink in. The *so what* expression on both their faces said such things happened every day. Disappointed, I explained how I got hold of the report.

'How do we know that this is the correct one and that the previous one was fake?' Shakir objected, without even bothering to ask what the new report said.

'Sir, I personally went to get this copy from Suprema Lab last night. The original will reach us soon. If you want, I can take you to meet the pathologist. He will show you the report he generated himself.'

'What does this one say?' Khaliq asked.

'That the boy was administered anaesthesia—more than fifty milligrams of propofol—before he was hanged. He was most probably unconscious at the time of the hanging, so he couldn't have done it himself. This was clearly a murder, sir.'

'But how did you know it even before you saw the autopsy report?'

'Sir, I have my sources, whom I want to protect. You know this case involves the Deen. I'll disclose everything soon. What's important for now is the confirmation that Hasan was murdered.'

'Also important is to find out who faked the report.'

'Very true, sir. I have a clue, but please allow me to finish my investigation. I'll explain everything then.'

Shakir tried another angle of attack. 'Sir, we should let the Hasan family decide whether to go ahead with the investigation.

They said no to the autopsy, and the boy's father had asked me
again to discontinue the case.'

How did this behan chod find out about it? Did Hasan's
father approach him? I decided to let Khaliq handle this.

'This autopsy report means something, Shakir. The
media and the human rights organizations—not to forget my
superiors—won't spare us this time. We can't just sweep this
case under the rug.'

Shakir interrupted again. 'Sir, but he mustn't have a free
hand. Let's not delve into these mullahs' business.'

'Bhai, let him conclude. If it was a murder, the culprits must
be brought to court. Do you agree? If we must make some other
decision, we will, after the facts are revealed.'

* * *

There was only one place I could look for the men in the sketches
now. But aware of how the Deen people would react, I decided to
call Furqan first. There was no reply. Alarm bells started ringing
in my head because he always answered his calls promptly. I
phoned Ram, but there was no reply from him either. I steered
my jeep towards Furqan's house. A lean man, perhaps in his early
sixties, opened the door. He must have been Furqan's father.

'Is Furqan home?' I asked.

'No. He's been gone for more than three hours and he's not
responding on his phone.'

My doubt morphed into fear.

'Have you contacted any of his friends?'

'Yes, but no one knows anything.'

The man's furrowed brow and pained eyes betrayed the
pressure cooker of myriad emotions he was trying to contain.

'Did you talk to Ram?'

'Ram said he met him this morning, but since then, he has not seen him. Is he alright, Inspector Sahib? I beseeched him to stay away from this business.'

I told him everything was fine though I felt it wasn't. Maybe there was nothing to worry about. The Deen were only talking to him, the way they did to Ram. But why was he not answering phone calls? I called Maulana Saleem who said I was free to search his madrasah. I decided it would be futile.

'Furqan's missing, and I need your help in finding him.' I was at Ram's door. Made of stiff wood, it had wrinkles all over it, like an old man's face. It reminded me of all the stories I had heard about it from Lubna and Furqan and their account of Mohan's lynching. How could things I hadn't seen become so vivid in my head?

Ram took a long time to reply. 'I don't think I can help you, sir.'

'Listen, your friend's life is in danger, and only you can help me find him.'

'How?' Behind him, the door was ajar. He stepped out and closed the door.

'First, do you know these people?' I pulled out the sketches from my bag and handed them to him.

'Hmm. They look like Faisal and Akbar. Both are from our college. I haven't seen Akbar for many weeks, but Faisal was there in college just before it closed.'

'You're sure?'

'Yes, I'm sure. These are very good sketches. Who made them?'

'Sadia, Hasan's younger sister.'

'But how would these sketches help in tracing Furqan?'

'I believe these men are behind Hasan's murder and behind your brother's murder too. They must be behind Furqan's disappearance as well. Do you know where either of these two lives?'

Ram looked down and appeared to be thinking. 'No, but there was a boy in our college. Yasir. I guess he must have some information.'

'Why do you think he might be of help?'

'Yasir had a brush with the Talaba or the Deen men. He stayed away from college for a few days—didn't even answer phone calls. When he returned, he didn't say much, but he confided a few things to me. I gathered he wanted to get even with his kidnappers.'

'Can you take me to him?'

Ram pondered a while and said, 'Let me see if he's home.' He called a number.

'Look, the police need your help. Can we meet?' Ram spoke on the phone while I looked at the kids playing cricket with a makeshift bat and tennis ball. As soon as the call ended, I took Ram along in my jeep, and after about half an hour, we were in front of an elegant house with a chocolate brown façade in a posh locality.

A short but imposing looking man dressed in a shalwar-kameez opened the door. His brows knitted together on seeing a policeman. He looked at Ram too, but I couldn't tell if he recognized him.

'I need to talk to Yasir. He's your son, I guess. It's about the death of his classmate, Hasan.' I thought it was appropriate to explain everything at the outset.

'The one that happened a few days ago? What does Yasir have to do with it?'

'Nothing, I assure you, but I believe he might have some information about those who are responsible for it. The police have reasons to think they were his college mates.'

'Look, we don't want any involvement in this. Unless you have a proper warrant, I can't allow you to talk to my family.'

'A warrant is for a search or an arrest. I can arrange for it in a minute. But then it will be a lot of fun for your neighbors to watch. I'm sure you don't want it.'

The man scanned the street, which was empty except for cars parked outside some houses. Relieved, he opened the door and led us through a neatly trimmed lawn to a well-decorated drawing room and went inside the house. 'Please sit here. I'll call him.'

Yasir entered in a while, followed by his father. He was short but well built. Crew-cut hair, sports shorts and a sleeveless T-shirt gave him an upper-class look. As we sat down, Ram asked him, 'Do you know Hasan has died?'

'Yes, I heard. It's so sad. So how can I help in this matter?' He looked at me after a glance at his father.

'There's another issue. You know Furqan, right?' I asked Yasir. 'He has disappeared, maybe abducted.'

'Oh!'

'Ram told me you had an encounter with the mullahs a few months back. Can you tell me about it? Did they take you somewhere?'

The boy's father scowled at him. Yasir might not have told him about the episode. Or perhaps he did, but his father might've instructed him not to tell anyone in college.

Yasir said, 'Well, I had a habit of annoying them, which they didn't mind initially, but I happened to befriend a guy who I later found out was from the Red Brigade . . .'

The boy appeared to be relishing the opportunity to narrate his story, which he did in a theatrical style, introducing pauses in his speech, which I would've found impressive had I not been worried about Furqan.

He continued, 'That's another student body. They're a rival of the Talaba, which is the student body of the Deen-e-Kamil. But the Red Brigade remains underground. Kind of secular. Most of them are inspired by the socialist ideology.'

I said, 'I think they are inspired by another Marxist student body that was formed in 1949 but was banned soon after because of its association with Pakistan's Communist party. This Red Brigade was formed in the 1980s—a kind of regrouping of the parent party. I did not know it had a presence in your college. Anyway, go on.'

'The guy I befriended was from the Red Brigade, although I didn't know it at that time. He could talk about several things— philosophies, ideas, books and similar stuff. I was impressed, and we often talked. Ram also enjoyed his company. Didn't you, Ram?' He looked at Ram, who nodded. 'The Talaba knew he was from the Red Brigade, but they let him be there. Maybe they were observing him. Then something happened. He probably reached out to Akbar, the guy who was always with the nazim. Kind of a goon,' Yasir said this more to Ram than to me. 'The Reds probably wanted Akbar to join their party, which was strange. I'm not sure what happened because the Red Brigade guy disappeared. Stopped coming to college. The Talaba guys asked me a few questions. I had no idea why they were so serious about a nerdy guy, so I gave them some annoying answers, like *Do you want to learn Marxism?*' Yasir scoffed. 'They thought I was one of the Reds and that I was hiding something. Probably that's why they took me aside to question me.'

'Tell me in detail what happened.'

'I was on my way home from college when they approached me. There were two men. They said they wanted to talk. I said, "Alright, go ahead." They said they needed to go to a quieter place. I agreed.'

'You didn't resist?' I asked. The father seemed more interested in Yasir's answer. The boy ignored his father. Quite a cocky boy he was.

'I didn't have an option, so I went along. They took me to a nearby park and questioned me. Pretty soon they realized I didn't have much to offer, so they let me go.'

'It doesn't help me to reach Furqan,' I said.

Yasir pushed back his hair with his fingers and said, 'Wait. I think I might have something more. One of them mentioned Murshidabad. It's a town on the outskirts of the city. I think they have a madrasah there. You can check it. The Red guy told me the Deen kept their prisoners in some part of the madrasah, maybe a basement. As the police hesitate to raid madrasahs, the Deen get away with such crimes. One of the Talaba guys threatened to detain me in Murshidabad. He said something like: "The boy"—meaning me—"wants a joyride to Murshidabad". The other guy said, "Maybe later".'

I phoned a constable and asked him about the location of the Deen's madrasah in Murshidabad. After a while, the constable called and said Shakir wanted to talk to me. I called Shakir. 'Sir, I need a search warrant for Deen's Murshidabad madrasah.'

Shakir's short fuse blew at once. 'Waqas, are you out of your mind? It's a dangerous place to poke your finger in!'

'Sir, it's important. They've abducted a prime witness in my case.'

'Which case?'

'Sir, the boy whose body was found in Shanti Nagar.' My anger rose. The boys and the man watched in silence. I walked to a corner of the room where a beautiful floor lamp stood. It reminded me of Fareeha's plan to decorate our new home. She would be waiting for me at dinner and would ask me if I was still working on the blasphemy case.

'Waqas, I won't allow you to disturb the city's peace in your schizophrenic pursuits.'

'Sir, then I'm going to raid the madrasah without a warrant.'

'Waqas, wait!'

I hung up and said to the boys, who must have heard the other party screaming before I ended the call, 'Thanks, gentlemen. I've got to go. Come, Ram. I'll drop you home. It's on my way to Murshidabad.'

* * *

Murshidabad was a long way off, and the journey gave me a lot of time to think, among other things, about how Shakir would react after our latest spat. Shakir rang me, but I didn't respond. I was worried about Furqan. The poor boy was not the kind who would be able to face any manhandling. Yasir sounded more street-smart and tough.

As I neared the neighborhood of Murshidabad, my phone rang again. But it was no time for phone calls. I started searching for the exact location of the madrasah, but I found I was clueless. With hardly any working streetlamps, the place was almost pitch-dark. Have I reached the right place? I scanned the roadside for milestones—I had to turn my jeep so its headlights would illuminate them—which indicated I was already there. But where was the madrasah?

A horrifying face pounced at the left window from the darkness. Then I heard a growl, so close I felt it came from the rear seat.

'Behan chod!' I shouted in panic, as I realized it was a dog. There were two in fact, one on each side of the jeep. Oh, God! They didn't sound like ordinary dogs. They were wild dogs. Wolves, perhaps. I made sure the window was pulled all the way up. I leaned across to the passenger side to work the other window up. The jeep swerved as my eyes left the road ahead and ran into a series of bumps and potholes on the road, making me jounce in my seat. The wretched creatures followed me for some distance, growling and barking, and then disappeared into the darkness, although the bloodshot eyes of one of them stayed with me for some time.

When my heartbeat had returned to normal, I resumed my search for the madrasah, but there was no building in sight. Nothing was visible at all. From the dust clouds and the stench, I could guess the road was flanked on both sides by dusty plots of land, swamps and fields. I couldn't see anyone I could ask for directions.

Damn! I should've taken along an ASI or a constable who had been to the place. Going back to the police station, though, was a bad idea because Shakir wouldn't have allowed me to go. Close to tears and mind numb, I shut down the jeep and climbed out, still wary of the dogs. I had a pistol, but opening another battlefront was the last thing I wanted, so I stayed close to the jeep. Except for the incessant chirping of the crickets and the occasional barks of distant dogs, the place was quiet, like a graveyard. A foetid combination of vegetables and rotten smells was the only other sensation. It suggested there were marshes and cornfields nearby. I stood near the jeep, smarting from the jolts to my back and figuring out what to do.

Was the tractor-like sound I heard real or only a figment of my imagination? Who could be running a tractor at this hour? The rumble grew louder and sounded less like a tractor and more like a jeep. It was Shakir's, I realized. The headlight of the jeep swung in a big arc, illuminating the wilderness. Did I see the spooky outlines of an unpainted building, perhaps the madrasah I was looking for? The jeep approached slowly and stopped.

'What are you doing here?' Shakir asked, still seated with the jeep's engine running.

Not wanting to admit my helplessness, I remained silent and looked at the broken road under my feet.

'Let's go back. Come on! It's not a good idea raiding them at this hour.' He paused, sitting at the steering wheel, and stared at me. Then he added, 'Nothing will come out of it. It will only spoil the situation. We'll find a solution in the morning. Your wife is worried. She called me.'

I looked at my mobile phone, which sat on the passenger seat. The last few calls had been Fareeha's. Suddenly, another fear gripped me. In my worry for Furqan, I had forgotten about my own family. I called her on the phone and told her I was coming home, as I drove behind Shakir's jeep in almost pitch-dark surroundings.

The realization that I was utterly helpless in rescuing Furqan, who was in danger thanks to my obsession with the case, gnawed at me from inside. And outside, the bloodhounds

of my failures—my failure to speak out for Abba, my failure
to stand up for the woman I loved as I succumbed to financial
pressure, my failure to voice my principles in the police service—
haunted me, snarling and growling.

I should've listened to Fari and Bhai Jaan. I can't do this.

22

Furqan

Present day

Someone removed my blindfold and pushed me from behind. My eyes took some time to get used to the light. A chain latch clanked behind me as someone bolted the door from outside. I stood still for a long time, contemplating the situation and the room I was in. I was more surprised than scared—was this how an abductee felt? The thought that Ammi and Abba would be worried to death in my absence gnawed me. *I told him to be careful but he didn't listen,* Abba would say. Ammi would surely be crying. But what could I do? Inspector Waqas needed my help.

I tried to recall the journey from the road near my home to this strange place—being grabbed and thrown into the green van, blindfolded. The bumpy and seemingly endless journey. Then being led down a flight of stairs. One thing this episode revealed was that I was claustrophobic—being blindfolded did not hurt me as much as it threw me into a panic. I felt suffocated. Maybe everyone felt like this when blindfolded.

I tried to gauge where I was. Perhaps in a basement. A strong smell of cement and sand had invaded my nostrils as soon as I entered. It was a partially constructed room. Probably the construction budget ran out before it was finished. Part of the floor was cemented chip style while the other part was soil and sand. Surprisingly, it reminded me of Mohan's room. The only light and air in the room came through a small opening at the top of one wall. Through it, I could see it was daytime. I could see people walking across the ventilator-like hole. After a little while, I heard voices too. I strained my ears and tried to listen closely. Most of them were children's voices. Was I in a madrasah? Which one? The one near my home, which I had visited a few times with Hasan, or some other one? I tried to picture this place based on what I had seen during those visits: children sitting on mats and reciting the Quran, their torsos swinging rhythmically as they shouted out the Quranic verses, groups of students sitting around a teacher and discussing things.

Nothing was happening. No one turned up. I considered shouting for help but decided against it. I tried to push open the door. It creaked and moved but didn't open. It was locked from the outside. I was tired and probably injured. I didn't know how it happened, but a lot of places in my body ached. On top of that, the place was hot and suffocating. What could I do? Would Abba go to the police? When? And could Inspector Waqas help?

I sat down on the floor and tried to guess the time. I didn't wear a wristwatch, and they had taken away my phone so I could only guess from the fading light outside the ventilator. It must have been several hours since I had come to the room.

Suddenly, I realized my glasses were missing too. How could they have survived the blindfolding?

It was dark now. Someone had opened the door and left me a glass of water and food, two rotis and a plateful of lentils, which was surprisingly tasty—or was it my hunger that made them so? No one had bothered to talk to me, though.

Hours later, I heard the door being unlatched. Someone would push in a tray of food and leave. Wasn't it too early for it? I wasn't hungry yet. But this time, the entrant closed the door behind him. It was dark, so I could only trace the person's silhouette. My heart missed a beat as the shadow-like person stepped forward and uttered my name. Who could it be? What was more astonishing was that the man whispered as if he was afraid of being heard. He stepped closer and repeated my name.

23

Waqas

Present day

Back home, I was ready for Fareeha's onslaught—yesterday's spat and tonight's missed calls warranted it. But there must have been something in my face that made her change her mind. I took a quick shower and sat on the bed, thinking. Fareeha brought dinner in a tray, which she placed on the bed in front of me, and sat down. Both of us sat with one leg folded and the other along the bedside.

'The smell of whitewash is still around,' I said, surveying the walls. 'The low-quality paint they use comes off fast. I hope it will stick.'

'You don't like the food? It's your favourite, spinach.'

'No, it's good. But I'm tired.'

'You're more worried than tired.'

I smiled. 'No, there's nothing to worry about.' Then, after a pause, I said, 'Listen Fari, why don't you go to your Abba's in Lahore? The landlord's taking too long to do the electrical and plumbing repair. While you and the kids are away, it will be easy for him to arrange the necessary works.'

Fareeha nodded. 'The case is still open?' She waved away a housefly and asked. 'Last night, you were running around for a report. You can't let go of it?'

'You mean the blasphemy case? I don't know. It's neither here nor there. But I'm working on another case.'

'So why are you so anxious? You're sending me away because of it?'

'Just tired. Nothing else.' I smiled, pushed the tray aside, and holding her hands in mine, pulled her closer. 'And only you are the therapy for my fatigue. I'm sorry about yesterday.'

'Don't worry about it.'

I pressed her to my chest. She had to bend her torso because of the hug but she didn't resist. When she sat back, she said, 'Please tell me about the case, Vickie.'

I thought a great deal, summarizing the facts in my head. 'I guess the two cases are connected. In both, a religious party, the Deen-e-Kamil, is involved. They can do anything in the name of religion. Today, they abducted a young boy who was my key source of information.'

'Are you worried about the boy?'

'Yes. He's a well-meaning, sweet boy. He wants to help find his friends' killers.'

'Can you arrest the culprits?'

'I think I can. It's a straightforward case. I even have sketches of the guys' faces. It's our fear that's holding us back. I'm worried about the boy. I'm worried about you too, although I'm certain they wouldn't hurt a policeman's family. But . . .'

She asked me to finish the meal, which I did. She sat watching me, and when I had finished, she said, 'You want to crack the case because of your Abba Jaan? This case gives you an opportunity to talk about him. Right?'

'That too. But it's more than that, Fari. If it hadn't been for Abba, I might have brushed aside this case and closed it. Call me selfish, but that's the truth. But there's another thing. Because of Abba's death, I can empathize with the victims of blasphemy accusations and their families. While they suffer, the rest of us just keep mum about it. We are too afraid of the mullahs to speak out. This man Mohan didn't say or do anything to malign Islam, but he was lynched without any opportunity to defend himself. Even if he was guilty of blasphemy, he had the right to a trial. These mullahs will have none of it. They instigated the public to the most brutal lynching. How can we allow it to happen without a word of protest? I know now that I'll become a party to this crime if I don't do my job.'

'Then do it. Don't hold back. Go for it.' She paused, waiting for me to say something, but I was speechless. She added, 'You were right when you said that our fear is holding us back.'

'But the boy? And you? You cried last time we talked about it.'

'I won't, now that I know you want to crack this case so badly.'

I was still in disbelief. She snuggled into me and kissed me, perhaps the only time she had kissed me when we weren't in bed. 'Our fears hold us back, that's the truth. If you know you should go after the culprits, then don't worry about the boy or your family.'

I pulled her to me and kissed her passionately. She whispered, 'Let me give you a good shower.'

The look of utter astonishment on my face made her laugh. 'Look, my grown-up police sub-inspector doesn't know how to wash himself. There's soap in your ear. And after all, it will be many days before I return from Abba's. Come on, get up. Let me take you to the bathroom.'

24

Furqan

Present day

'Who is it?' I managed to speak.

'Zameer.'

Oh yes, why hadn't I recognized his voice earlier? We had met only two days ago at Hasan's. For a while, I didn't know what to say. Zameer had now come closer. In the dim light of a streetlamp outside, I could see it *was* Zameer, dressed in a blue shalwar-kameez, his posture stiff as always and his forehead creased.

'Why have they imprisoned you?' he asked. 'I saw you being brought in.'

'I guess it's because I talked to a police officer about Hasan's murder.'

After his eyes had adjusted to the low light, he asked, 'Murder? Wasn't it a suicide?'

'The police officer is sure it's a murder. He's a good man, that officer. Not the usual policeman.'

For a while, we stood in the dark. Had I told Zameer too much?

I said, 'So this *is* a Deen madrasah. I could guess. Do you work for the Deen? You must be an inside man; else they won't let you see me.'

'No. They didn't share any information about your capture with me. I only chanced upon it when they brought you in.'

'But how did you get in?'

'They have given a key to the cook. I got it from him, telling him I would be taking your meal to you. But they don't know I'm here.'

'It must be risky for you. What brought you here?'

'Well, I wanted to know why you're in trouble with them.'

'Do you know what they'll do to me?'

'I'm not sure.'

'Will they kill me?'

'I don't think they kill people.'

'I'm not so sure about it.'

'Anyway, you should eat. I'm worried about you.' Zameer placed the food in front of me on the floor. 'Let's sit.'

We sat on the sandy floor, and I began to eat. 'You want to join me?' I asked Zameer as I made a morsel of a roti wrapped around dal.

'Even in custody, you can't forget courtesy. You're a sweet boy.' Zameer laughed as he squatted on the floor. 'This is your food, and you must eat as much as you can. Aren't you scared? I thought you might be crying, to be honest. I'm not insulting you, but anyone in your situation would cry.'

'I'm surprised too,' I said, between morsels. 'I'm not very scared. I feel like I'm doing something for Mohan and Hasan. I'm worried, though.'

'Is there anything I can do for you?'

'No, thank you,' I said. I thought of asking him to let me use his phone. I could text Inspector Waqas if Zameer would allow me. But he might refuse. His sympathies must be with the Deen people, and it's not a good idea to endanger him. On second thoughts, I said, 'In fact, yes. Can you please tell my family I'm fine?'

I continued after a pause, 'Tell them I went to see a sick friend in a village. Mansehra. Yes, tell them I'm in Mansehra, where the signal is bad.'

'Clever idea. Give me your brother's number. I'll see what I can do. But I have to go now or they might find me here.'

What if Zameer snitches on me to the Deen? I wondered as he left.

25

Waqas

Present day

After dropping Fareeha and the kids at the bus station—the little ones were excited about the visit to their grandma in an air-conditioned bus, rushing in and out of it and climbing on the cushioned seats—and briefing the sepoy, who was traveling in the same bus, to keep an eye on my family from a safe distance, I texted Amber to send me Rehan's number. She did, and I called. No answer. On my way to the police station, I called him again. Still no reply. Maybe these intelligence people were hard to reach. I wrote a long text message reminding him of our time together in the university and requesting help in handling the Deen party, which had most probably kidnapped one of my key witnesses. What an awkward sounding message!

When I reached the police station, I found Furqan's father in the bare investigation room. The man was of slight build and looked thinner than when I had seen him last.

'Ashraf, who called this man to the police station?'

'Shakir Sahib, sir.'

Exasperated, I first contemplated confronting Shakir, but then decided to first find out how the poor man was doing.

'I'm sorry. This is a mistake. But while you're here, do you want to file a missing person report?'

The old man appeared to be in disbelief. One did not hear an apology from a policeman every day. He sat facing the door, in anticipation of someone coming to end his ordeal, while the chair he sat in faced another direction. He was visibly afraid to mess with the thana furniture.

I continued, 'Did you come here of your own free will or were you summoned?' He had the same small eyes as Furqan, and a nicely trimmed moustache.

'A police constable brought me here,' the man finally said, with a newly acquired courage.

'I'll have you dropped home soon. Don't worry. By the way, any contact with Furqan?'

'Yes. Someone called my son—the elder one—and said that Furqan had gone to a friend in Mansehra, from where he couldn't contact us because the signal was bad.'

'Someone? Who was he? You don't know him?'

'No. I'm not sure whether to trust him. Why would Furqan go to a friend's after what had happened recently?'

The way the message was relayed to Furqan's father worried me too. But I didn't show my worry, for fear that it might crush the old man.

'I'm sure he's alright. He'll be back soon. I'll arrange for you to be dropped home.'

The old man still looked unsure about which policeman to believe, me or the one who had brought him here.

'Can you retrieve the number you received the call from? Please give it to me.'

'Yes. We tried to return the call but there was no reply.'

I strode into Shakir's office. His face showed that he felt he had one-upped me last night. How wrong he was!

'Sir, why is this man in the police station?'

'When did you acquire the right to talk to me like this?' He set aside the file he was working on. Surely to prepare for a battle with me.

'I was assigned this case, and I have a right to handle it the way I deem fit.' Not wanting to display any camaraderie, I remained standing.

'Not if your way is posing problems for the police. Come with me. I'll take you to DSP Sahib.'

Shakir was a clever man. Aware he couldn't win a war of words with me, he left it to DSP Sahib to settle the case. He called Khaliq on the intercom, seeking permission to come to his office. He then told me to come along with him. I didn't mind.

'Sir, his wife called me last night, requesting me to take him off the case,' Shakir said, as soon as the two of us had taken seats.

'What? That's a lie! She just wanted to know where I was.'

'Ask your wife before you label me a liar.'

I was speechless for a while. I tried to recall Fareeha's behaviour the previous night.

Khaliq asked, amused, 'Do we make decisions based on our wives' inputs, Shakir?'

'Sir, as I've told you, he's not competent enough to handle the case. I had already taken him off the case before his wife

called. He would've raided a madrasah had I not stopped him.'
Shakir was his obsequious best when talking to his boss.

'Excuse me, sir. Shakir Sahib didn't even inform me I'm off
the case, and he has been meddling in my work. He has called
an innocent man for interrogation. That's completely unfair—
and useless.'

'Sir, he told me last night that one of his prime witnesses is
missing and that he thinks the Deen are behind his abduction,
without any evidence. He tried to search the Deen's madrasah,
again without any evidence. Today, I called the witness's
father to find out about him. Sir, we're not even sure if the
boy's really missing. His family hasn't filed a missing person
complaint.'

Khaliq silently looked from one face to the other, the
fingertips of one hand tapping those on the other.

I said, 'Sir, it's true the family hasn't reported their son
missing. But we know how people fear these religious parties,
and when the case involves blasphemy, no one wants to be on
the other side of the fence. Reason, logic, evidence and rationale
all go out the window. Don't they, sir?' I paused and looked at
Khaliq to find out if he was convinced. Realizing I still had
the opportunity to talk, I continued. 'Sir, I understand this is a
delicate case, and I respect Shakir Sahib's reason for not delving
into the religious business. But sir, for the same reason, I feel
it's important to dig into the facts, bring them to the fore, and
catch the culprit. And I'm close to cracking it. Give me a few
more days, please. Let me handle it my way.'

Khaliq looked at Shakir in his characteristic languid way—
he was never in a hurry. Shakir said, 'Sir, there's another issue
here. Only one paper is linking this case to the blasphemy riot
of two months ago. And guess which one? *The Breaking News*.

Why? Because our Waqas has been leaking information to his girlfriend who works for that paper.'

'Waqas, is that correct?' Khaliq eyed me.

I realized I had underestimated Shakir. He had been spying on me. I quickly recovered. 'Sir, I knew the woman in college, but she's not my girlfriend. And why would I leak anything to her? Will Shakir Sahib explain what's in the news he thinks I've reported to her?'

'But why is she the only one so keen on this case?' Shakir rebutted.

'That's enough, boys! Enough! Waqas, take a day or two but wind it up quickly. Shakir, please let him do it his way. If he bungles it up, we'll see. *Oye*, I need something cold. Behan chod, how humid!' Khaliq cursed the heat and ended with a loud shout to the peon.

'Sir, I'll order it for you,' Shakir said as he rose. I, too, rushed out.

Nearly an hour later, I was in the madrasah again. Initially, I thought of going to the Murshidabad madrasah first, hoping to free Furqan. But knowing that it could lead to fruitless confrontation, I decided to enquire about Faisal and Akbar in the Shanti Nagar madrasah. A teenage boy asked me to sit and wait for Maulana Sahib. I found time to look at my phone. Rehan had replied, saying he was so glad to receive a message from me and would appreciate meeting with me over a big lunch of chicken *karahi*, although he wondered how he could help with the issue I talked about. How thoroughly departmental! I recalled the last time we had met. It was during the 2008 elections when we happened to be at the same polling station. Either 'The army will take care of everything' or 'The police are not equipped to handle this' was perpetually on his lips.

Eventually, Saleem entered the office through the inner door and shook my hand warmly.

'What brings you to our poor madrasah again, Inspector Sahib?'

'The murder—the apparent suicide—of the boy Hasan. We have reasons to believe it was a murder, and I need to talk to some people who had visited him in his last few days. I have sketches of two of them. Can you look at them and give me some information?' I handed him the two sketches Hasan's sisters had made.

'I don't think I know them, Inspector Sahib,' Saleem looked at them cursorily and said what I expected him to. A boy came with two teacups and placed one each in front of Saleem and me.

'Really? My investigation has revealed they're linked to your madrasah. This one—I've come to know his name is Faisal—knew Hasan in his college. Hasan's family confirmed he had been visiting their house days before Hasan's death. It was because of him that Hasan was "beginning to learn the deen", to use your words.'

'You see, Inspector Sahib, Islam has a universal appeal.'

Saleem was a master of prevarication. *Not another sermon, please.*

He continued, 'There are many who are spreading the light of Islam—I hope you'll also join our ranks soon, as will the entire world. The scientific community will testify to the veracity of the Quran, *Insha Allah.* Waqas Sahib, a few days ago, my son was reading about how the universe was created. I realized scientists have recently discovered that all heavenly bodies were just one mass a long time ago. The Holy Quran said this fourteen hundred years ago: "Do not the non-believers see that the heavens and the earth were joined together before we separated them, and that we brought all living things into existence from water?" *Subhanullah*! There are numerous such passages in the Quran. Science has verified the message of Islam, which is going to spread to all corners of the universe.'

'Can you get to the point, Maulana Sahib?'

'That's what I'm about to do. As I was saying, due to the universality of our message, many people who are not our members but who are in search of the truth tend to speak our language. It appears to people like you that they're our members. You see, we have formal members and some are impressed by our message. This man whose photo you showed me may have friends in my madrasah, but he's not our formal member. Please drink the tea. Or would you rather have a cold drink to cool you down?'

'Thank you, Maulana Sahib. Tea will do.'

I was not a fan of the tea served in most places, where people drank it as a dessert. Who the hell would want it in this temperature, anyway? But there were more important matters at stake.

I asked, 'So this man *has* friends in your madrasah? Can you ask some of them to help me find this man?'

'You see, Inspector Sahib, I don't want my madrasah embroiled in any needless police controversy. Religious parties get the flak and earn a bad name for no fault of theirs—even a small blemish becomes conspicuous on a white cloth'—oh yeah, I've heard of these metaphors, which even Mirza Ghalib would be proud of—'But I'll see what I can do for you. Despite what I said, we would also like to help the police.'

'Thank you, Maulana Sahib.'

Saleem took the two sketches and went inside the madrasah. I sipped the tea and found it expectedly cold and sweet. I didn't take another sip and placed it on the table. After only a little while, Saleem returned with the sketches.

'I've talked to my boys. One or two of them know this one you called Faisal, but they say they haven't seen him for many days. If I get any information about him, I'll share it with you.' Saleem turned to the inner door, as if the meeting was over.

I knew the time for courtesies was over—perhaps Saleem's tone of finality convinced me. I sprang to my feet and said, 'Maulana Sahib, I'd like to speak with your boys.'

Saleem appeared to have noticed the change in my demeanour. He turned around to face me again and responded in kind, 'I'm afraid it's not possible. I told you I don't want to malign my madrasah. A police officer barging into the madrasah and interrogating the boys—you know what message the students, their parents and the public are going to get, right?'

'If you're so worried about your madrasah's reputation, you should make sure your madrasah doesn't host murderers or that your students don't make friends with them.'

'Murderers? I thought you said these men were visiting the boy. That doesn't make anyone a murderer, does it?'

'Yes, but then disappearing at about the same time as when the murder took place makes one a prime suspect. And I have reasons to believe this guy is hiding inside your madrasah or someone from among your boys is sheltering him.'

'Now that's a mouthful, Inspector Sahib. You would need a search warrant to step inside my madrasah. And let's see how quickly you can obtain one.'

'That's what makes your madrasah a good hiding place. It may not be just a search warrant, Maulana Sahib; don't be surprised if there's going to be an arrest warrant as well. It would be good for us if we could find out about this boy now. Can you call those boys who know Faisal?'

There was a fire in Saleem's eyes, but he remained patient. He went inside and returned after a while. 'Luckily, one of our boys has this man Faisal's phone number.' A boy in his early teens stood at the door. 'He has called Faisal, who will be here soon. Would you like to come back later?'

'Thanks, Maulana Sahib. I'll wait for him. Would you keep me company till he arrives?' Surely, Saleem was hiding something about Faisal. If Faisal was at the forefront of the student wing, the Talaba, he must be well known in the Deen party. How could Saleem not have known him? So I didn't want to give Saleem any private time to tutor Faisal before I interviewed him. It was important for me to get hold of Faisal as soon as he arrived.

Nearly an hour later, Faisal stood at the door, looking from me to Saleem and back at me. After his soft-spoken introduction, as if Faisal had been invited to meet a friend at a wedding reception, Saleem looked at me, giving me a signal to begin. I politely requested him to vacate the room and asked Faisal to take a seat. The baby-faced boy with dark eyes and a small beard looked ready to cry at any moment.

'Did you meet Hasan at his residence?'

'Yes,' came the meek reply.

'What was the purpose of your visits?'

'He was a good friend. We studied in Islamia College and the madrasah.'

The boy was reading from a script. *Well done, behan chod!*

'Do you often visit friends' homes? I don't think disturbing a household, especially the ladies, is appropriate.' When Faisal didn't reply, I asked, 'Did Hasan return your visits? Did he come to your house too?' Again, no answer. 'Why did you have to visit him? You could've phoned him.' After a pause, I added, 'Okay. Let me help you. Did you visit him because he wouldn't come to your madrasah?'

His eyeballs jumping like mercury, Faisal spoke after a long pause, 'Yes. We were worried as he wasn't coming. We thought he might be sick.'

'Did he stop answering your phone calls?'

'Yes. No . . .' Faisal was speechless. The boy was clueless about what each answer would lead to. His script didn't help.

'Did you think he was slipping away from your hands? Why did you befriend him? Because you wanted to turn him against Mohan?'

'Mohan was a bad influence. He was teaching un-Islamic things.'

'So, the answer to my question is yes.'

'Yes . . . No . . .'

'How did you begin to work on Hasan?'

'Work? We wanted him to return to Islam. We knew he was a good boy, God-fearing. He needed some guidance.' He looked more comfortable with the stuff he usually talked about, his eyeballs steadier. He wriggled in his chair.

I leaned towards him. 'So how did you start?'

'The usual way. He went to a few Shab-e-Juma with us— Thursday nights at a mosque. He listened intently. Seemed genuinely interested. He wanted to understand why Muslims, as a community, were declining, why they were morally bankrupt.'

'But he was a peculiar case too, was he not? He was fond of Mohan, a Hindu.'

'Yes. We told him Mohan was teaching filth. Art and poetry are outside Islam. Mohan liked Meeraji. I told Hasan that Meeraji wrote obscene poetry.'

'Where did you learn all this? Have you read Meeraji's poetry?'

'He has written poems about sexual freedom and masturbation, and about freedom from clothes.' The boy's face grimaced as he uttered these words. 'So I thought I should tell Hasan what Mohan was luring him into.'

'You read them yourself? You don't usually read Meeraji, do you? Or did someone coach you about it? Maulana Saleem?' I recalled the Meeraji book on Saleem's shelf.

'Yes. It doesn't matter who read it. It's so dirty.' So Saleem had been lying about not knowing Faisal. *You're a bad liar, Maulana.*

'What else did you tell him? Did you tell him about what Mohan taught his sister?'

'Yes.'

The madrasah sounded unusually quiet. There were no voices of children playing or reciting. Had the maulana told everyone to be quiet so he could eavesdrop on us? I paused, took some notes, and asked. 'Okay. Why was Hasan killed?'

'Killed? I heard he committed suicide.' The boy looked at the glass of water on the table and then at me. I nodded. He drank the water in one gulp, ending with a vociferous sigh, as if he had finished a marathon. 'Thank you.'

'He was drugged less than half an hour before he died. This means it's a murder. Who could've killed him?'

'I don't know.'

'Alright. Why do you think he would commit suicide?'

'He was depressed after Mohan died when he committed blasphemy. That probably would've caused Hasan to . . .'

'Two months—three months nearly—after the incident? When he had recovered sufficiently from the initial trauma? Doesn't it sound strange?'

When Faisal didn't say anything, I pulled the two sketches out of my pocket and placed Akbar's photo on the table, ironing out the creases. 'Who's he? Do you know him?' I scrutinized his face. He was probably thinking of what he should say. I added, 'He's Akbar, your friend, a member of both the Deen and the Talaba. Everyone in the college knows him, right? I got this sketch from a member of Hasan's family. They recognize you very well. Here's your sketch.' I spread out the second paper— Faisal's sketch—beside the first one. 'See? Someone has done a decent job providing this evidence. Now, the police know that you and this guy were visiting Hasan only days before he died. And maybe you two visited him on the night he died. You two are my prime suspects . . .'

'But sir, I didn't see him that night. I swear I didn't.' Faisal was close to tears, his voice choking with emotions.

'I could arrest you now, but if you tell me where I could find this other guy, I might believe you.'

'Sir, I don't know. I swear I don't. I haven't seen him for many days.'

'Ever since Hasan was murdered, right?'

'I can't say. But at least not in the last week.'

'I want Akbar's address and phone number.'

'Sir, I don't have them. He's not my friend.'

'Behan chod! You went on a brainwashing mission with him, and you don't have his details. Do you think I'll believe

you, you sissy?' Faisal cowered in his chair, even though I sat
at least five feet away from him. 'You won't talk here, will you?
Let's go to the thana.' I wanted to let the boy surmise what a
police station interview would be like.

'No, sir! I'll talk.'

The door leading inward opened, and Saleem's head
appeared. 'Just want to check if you need anything else.'

'No, thank you, Maulana Sahib. We're enjoying this
conversation, aren't we, Faisal?'

I had already made up my mind. Saleem wouldn't let Faisal
talk. In less than fifteen minutes, Faisal and I sat on either side
of a metal table in a bare investigation room, the same one
where Furqan's father had sat a few hours ago. I had discovered
that its emptiness made the suspect feel lonely and vulnerable.
Faisal's face signalled he was going to piss in his shalwar.

After a brief lecture on how the police conducted
interrogations—I told him that the police learnt a lot from how
US agencies did so in Guantanamo Bay and Abu Ghraib—I
asked him to hand over his phone to me after unlocking it.
I scrolled through the contacts list but couldn't find Akbar's
name in it. 'Any other name he goes by?'

'Sir, I have his number. I remember it now. And I think I
know where he lives. But let me go, please.'

'That's a good boy.' Fear made his face look cuter.

Faisal wrote something on a piece of paper I gave him along
with a ballpoint pen. The table wobbled as he wrote on the
paper, making Faisal more jittery. I looked at the paper and
put it in my pocket. 'Now, tell me about your visits to Hasan's.
Everything . . . nothing left out.'

'Sir, I went to his place with another boy—his name is
Zameer. Hasan had been away from the madrasah for nearly

a month—that was a long hiatus. He wouldn't stay away that long. He didn't even return my phone calls.'

'Where did you sit?'

'First, in his drawing room. Then he took us to his room.'

'Was he friendly or angry?'

'I can't say. He was courteous. His little sister brought us cold drinks. He said he would visit us soon. We stayed only a while.'

'Then?'

'He came to the madrasah a couple of days later. I didn't meet him then; I just saw him. Saleem Sahib took him to a room, where they had a long discussion. I don't know what they talked about.'

'Who else was with them?'

'There were other men, but I don't know them.'

'Okay. Did you visit again?'

'Yes. Hasan didn't come again to the madrasah so Saleem Sahib asked me to go visit him again. I didn't want to, but I went anyway. At that time, he asked me to take Akbar along.'

I kicked the metal table away; it screeched. 'Why Akbar? You know, of course, that he and Hasan had a fight? They weren't on good terms.'

With the table no longer between us, Faisal cringed and whimpered, 'I don't know anything about a fight, but I think they were alright. I mean, they were quite friendly in the madrasah.'

'Okay. What happened?'

'Nearly the same as before. Hasan took us to his room and served us cold drinks. We asked him why he was no longer coming to the madrasah. He said he would. We left.' I pondered over it for a long while. Faisal pleaded, 'Sir, I swear it's the truth. I haven't hidden anything. Sir, please let me go. My parents will be worried to death.'

'Okay, Mr Faisal. You will remain in the city until I allow you to leave. If you disappear or try to take refuge under the wing of the Deen, I will get hold of your family and arrest them, including your mother and sisters—yes, I can do it. Don't you look at me like this.'

Despite the look of disbelief on his face, he was too scared to challenge my hyperbole.

'Your only option is to cooperate. If you get any information about Akbar, you'll convey it to me, do you understand? Here's my number, and I want yours.'

26

Waqas

Present day

The Red Brigade guy owned a shop in a middle-class locality. With Yasir's knowledge of the place, we found the shop easily after another boy guided Yasir on the phone. It was on the first floor of a building that housed several shops and estate agencies in a narrow and busy bazaar. The man, Fazal, who welcomed us at the top of a dark staircase strewn with *paan* spit stains, was probably in his early thirties. He was short and overweight, wore jeans and a sweaty T-shirt, and had a French beard. Although Yasir had informed him about my arrival, he dragged his feet and wore a sheepish grin. His shop, which bore a dark and unkempt look, was stacked with opened and closed computer casings, monitors and spares. On the walls were posters of tech stuff and logos of various computer-related terms, most of which were Greek to me. Two of them read NetBeans and Ubuntu, terms I had heard from a programmer friend.

He asked, as he chewed paan, 'How can I help you, sir? We have had a frictional relationship with the police through no fault of ours. It's good to know we can be of assistance to the police.'

I laughed. 'Through no fault of yours? I doubt it. But let's leave it for another day. Let me get to the point right away.'

I showed Fazal the sketches. 'This one's named Akbar, Akbar Mughal.'

He looked at the sketches, but no sign of familiarity appeared on his face. Then he went to his table, sat down in a chair, and switched on an LCD. For a while, he slid the mouse around and kept his eyes glued to the LCD screen, which wasn't visible to me.

'Yes. I've got something on this guy, Akbar. Please come over and sit here.'

He dragged a chair for me beside him. Arms crossed on his chest, Yasir stood behind us. I spotted an air conditioner installed next to the computer to keep it cool, but cooling the room was not within its capability. The LCD screen showed rows and rows of data arranged in a table. A closer look revealed that the table had fields of names and particulars of several men. There was also a small icon at the end of each record carrying a small, hardly visible photo.

'Yes, his name is Akbar Mughal. But he goes by a lot of other names. Nadeem, Qadir and probably a few more.'

Fazal clicked on the photo, enlarging it. It was a casual snap—probably taken without the man's knowledge—and showed a partial view. Short hair, a large beard covering most of his face and beady eyes. I could see he was the same guy, the one whose face had looked familiar to me in the sketches Sadia made.

'You guys keep a computerized record of these men?' I asked, amazed.

'Yes, you can see for yourself.' Fazal smiled, keeping his eyes on the screen and patting his enormous belly. He was surely enjoying the impression he made on his visitors. 'Would you like me to order a cold drink for you, sir?'

'No, thank you. What else do you have on this man?'

'He's been changing parties. He was once with the Red Brigade.'

'Yes, some of your friends in Islamia College told me about him,' Yasir said, looking interested. When he agreed to take me to the Reds, obviously without informing his father, I knew he wanted to settle a score with the Talaba.

Fazal nodded and stroked the goatee on his chin. Then he sat back and turned towards me. 'I recall something about him. We wanted him back, but the Deen wouldn't let him go. He has a history of violence, mostly related to sectarian rifts in Jhung and adjoining areas. Sir, I'm sure you know what we call a sectarian rift started as a class and land dispute in this region. They say faith can move mountains. Unfortunately, it can also drive a wedge between people.'

'Yeah, I know a bit about the sectarian rifts.'

'This guy, Akbar, is pretty good at what he does, which is to scare people. Fear and religion are a great combination. Most religious parties need men like Akbar.' He looked at the LCD again. 'We have some phone numbers associated with him. I hope one of them can lead you to him.' He scribbled a few mobile numbers on a piece of paper. 'And here's an interesting piece of information. Here, look.' Fazal scrolled the mouse on Akbar's record again. 'We also try to record any additional info on these men. Look, the record says that this man—Nadeem or Akbar, whoever he is—has someone—a brother or someone close to him—in the police force. That's why he has never gotten into the police's wanted list even though he has a criminal record.'

I stared at Fazal in disbelief. His smile told me how much he enjoyed my amazement. Outside, the constant croaking sound of rickshaws and motorcycles provided an interesting contrast to the air-conditioned IT shop. 'Are you sure about this?'

'One can never be sure of these things, sir. The data is on a take-it-or-leave-it basis. But we collect even small nuggets of information, and if this info found its way here, there must be some truth to it. What's more, the police guy is in your backyard. You're in the Ferozepur thana, you said?'

'Yes.' I was still in disbelief.

'Then this man's very close to someone in your thana. I don't think you have to look far, sir.'

'Thanks, Fazal. This was helpful.' Pensive, I stood up. Then as an afterthought, I asked him, 'What do I owe you?'

'Don't mention it, sir.' Fazal stood too. 'Perhaps my friends or I might ask for a favour in return someday.'

I could sense it coming. The man was street-smart. I handed him my card. 'Sure. Here's my number. I'm not sure what I can do to help you, but don't hesitate to call me when you need me.' I turned towards Yasir and patted his shoulder. 'Thanks to you too, young man, for helping me on this. I hope, for your sake, your father does not come to know about it.'

'He won't, sir. Don't worry about it.' He paused and added as we walked to the stairs. 'I knew little about Mohan—poor man— but I know Ram very well, a golden boy.' He raised two thumbs. 'I'm helping you for him mainly. Please do your best to bring these fanatics to book. Do you think you can?'

The boy's concern shone through his usually insouciant attitude. 'You have been a great help, Yasir. I'll do the best I can.'

27

Furqan

Present day

Zameer came again the next morning with my breakfast, the same dal and rotis but this time with a cup of tea.

'Did you sleep well?' he asked. 'As well as anyone can sleep here?'

I had had a terrible night in the suffocating prison, imagining all kinds of insects—particularly lizards, which reminded me again of Mohan's room—crawling over my body. I couldn't sift the dreams from reality. The worst part was the stench resulting from my urine and stool. Before sleeping, I managed to control my bladder. But in the middle of the night, I woke and had to relieve myself. A corner of the room was the best place for it, I decided.

I said I slept fine. 'Did you convey my message to my family?'

'I did, although I didn't disclose my identity. Your brother had a lot of questions, but I dropped the call as I didn't want the

police to reach me. If the police raid this place, I'll be in trouble
with the Deen people.'

He sat on the sandy floor beside me, his back against the
wall. His sniffing told me he had sensed the smell, which I
had tried to mask with layers of sand. Thankfully, he didn't
comment on it.

'Do you believe it wasn't a suicide—Hasan's, I mean?'
Zameer asked, after we had talked a little about how Ram had
changed since his brother's death.

'No. Do you? I mean do you believe he was depressed
because of Mohan's death and that he took his life because
of it?'

Zameer nodded. I continued, 'Think about it. If he had to
kill himself because of guilt or depression over what happened
to Mohan, why would he do it more than two months after it
happened—three months actually? I knew him very well, and I
believe his initial depression was over by then. You must've seen
him in the last few days before his death. Didn't you?'

'I didn't see him a lot. I mean, only a few times, so I can't
comment. But are you suggesting that the Deen people killed
him? Why would they? They don't do such things.'

'How can you say that? Didn't they kidnap me? As for why
they would kill Hasan, I'm not sure.'

'Look, they are good people. I told you the other day I
wouldn't have survived in this city without the help of three of
you. I didn't mention that Maulana Saleem and his madrasah
was another factor. They were even willing to aid me financially.'

'I know these madrasahs succour so many poor households.
But . . .' I paused. Not wanting to sound belligerent, I asked, 'I
hope you're being careful. They won't spot you coming to see
me, will they?'

'Don't worry. I come here when no one's around.'

I could sense Zameer's ambivalence. What I had said had shaken his allegiance to his madrasah. Could I win him over and make him help me? No, it would be mean to take advantage of him or to manipulate him.

Instead, I said, 'Hasan didn't take the first-year exams. I asked him why and he said he wasn't prepared. When was the last time you saw him? You must've met him at the madrasah.'

'I don't remember exactly. Maybe a week or ten days ago. I wasn't going to the madrasah at that time because of the exam.'

'How was the meeting?'

'Nothing remarkable. But why are you asking about it?'

'I'm trying to figure out if he did fall out with the Deen guys. Not that I'm suggesting they killed him, but whatever happened in the few days before he died might provide a clue.'

'There's something I need to tell you. Remember that incident with Mr Abid? When we went to seek the Talaba's help?'

'Yes.'

'Ram told me later Mohan was not happy that we complained against a teacher. I mentioned Mohan's opinion to the nazim. He didn't look pleased. I guess the Talaba never liked Mohan.'

'I knew that. And that Ram told you about Mohan's opinion of the incident. All of us knew. Ram, Mohan and Hasan.'

'Weren't you guys mad at me?'

'At that time, we didn't know what would happen to Mohan. And we knew you didn't really have bad intentions.'

'Thank you for understanding. But I have some qualms about what I did. Could it have led to Mohan's lynching?'

'Who knows?'

'There's more. Maulana Saleem had told me to keep an eye on Hasan.'

He looked sheepish at this admission of the wrongdoing of the Deen people. He eyed the floor and then the area in front of him, but not at me, as he continued, 'When I tried to do it, I found it wasn't an easy job. I had to act like a film actor, which I wasn't good at. One day, I went with him to a bookshop, where he was going to return some books. *Wouldn't he wonder why I'm interested in his books?* I thought. He was probably surprised, but he didn't show it. In the last few months, he had grown so quiet it was difficult to gauge what he was thinking. I did a bad job asking him what he was reading. He pulled out two books from a plastic bag, which he handed over to me. One of them was a poetry collection of a certain Noon Meem Rashid—that's a unique way of writing initials; you don't see that in Urdu—and another was a history book by another name I didn't know— Sibte Hasan, I guess. We walked a few streets till we came to a small bazaar where Hasan entered a shop. There was a decrepit looking blue board on its front. It read *Karamat Ali, Homoeopath* written in unprofessional looking white paint. The man who came out, probably Karamat Ali, must not be filling his patients with lots of confidence. He looked unhealthy.'

I laughed. I had found Karamat healthy enough.

Zameer continued, 'Hasan introduced us to each other and gave him the books and some money. Karamat showed him an Urdu book. He told Hasan it was a splendid work on Meeraji. Hasan thought for a while and was about to leave when Karamat said Mohan loved it and even added notes and comments of his own to it. Karamat said he loved reading those notes on the margins of the pages. At this, Hasan turned back. Karamat handed him the book. Hasan took it, and we left.'

'Did you tell Saleem about it?'

'Yes.'

'Did you ever go to Hasan's house?'

'Yes. Once. With Faisal. He said Hasan was not coming to the madrasah and we should go and find out why.'

'Can you tell me more about your visit?'

'We sat in his room and talked for a while. Hasan was quiet, saying little. He said people didn't like it when he talked. Faisal said he asked too many questions about something bygone. Let bygones be bygones, Faisal said. He was good with clichés, I thought as I watched them converse. We asked him to come back to the madrasah.'

'Did he come?'

'He did. Two days later. I saw him when I went to a room generally used by Maulana Saleem for discussions with his senior cohort. With them were Akbar and a few men I hadn't seen before. They discussed something but stopped when I entered. I felt I wasn't wanted there. I even forgot what I had gone there for. Maulana Saleem asked me to join them. I found a place on the prayer mats where everyone was sitting. They were talking about how Mohan died. Hasan sounded angry—he was loud— and Saleem tried to placate him, to make him understand that the townsfolk killed Mohan, not the Deen party, because they were angry with Mohan for having defiled Islam.'

'Anything more?'

'Akbar said—it sounded like he was complaining—Hasan was still reading Meeraji.'

'Saleem knew about it of course. You told him, right?'

'Don't keep blaming me for it. Saleem told me to. I believed it was all for Hasan's own good.' He raised his bottom for a while and sat down again.

'Hurts sitting on the hard floor?' I asked and he nodded. 'But I've gotten used to it. And no, I'm not blaming you. I'm just getting the facts straight. So you knew there were differences between Hasan and the party. What next?'

'Not much. But wait a minute. Let me think. Ah yes, Hasan held the book in his hand—I think it was the one Karamat had given him. He read something out of it . . . I don't know what exactly. All the people looked at each other, wondering what he was up to, because I'm sure no one paid attention to the book or whatever was in it.'

'What was he reading?'

'Some poetry—you know I'm not a poetry person—and something about what Mohan and Lubna had said. He appeared strange that day. He recited poetry a few times, complete poems I think, without bothering to find out if people were listening. When Maulana Saleem intervened and asked why he was reciting poetry to them, Hasan said something like, "Didn't the Meccans say the same thing about Muhammad when he recited the Quran?" Maulana Saleem became furious, but Hasan was probably in another space and time. He continued to recite poetry—not reading it from any book. The book lay there in front of us. Hasan spoke from memory. Eventually, Maulana Saleem stopped arguing, and everyone left. Hasan went home too. That was the last I saw of him.'

We sat quietly for a long time. Some sounds were coming from another part of the madrasah, but Zameer didn't look bothered. He said, 'Did they love each other, Mohan and Lubna? I think that was one of the reasons Mohan was killed.'

'Who said that?'

'Well . . . Maulana Saleem mentioned it once. He said that Hindus were trying to seduce Muslim women and that Islam was under threat. He didn't mention Lubna, but whispers were going around about Hasan's sister. Hasan mentioned her name that last day. It disconcerted me. Imagine talking about your sister amid strangers.'

He looked sideways at me. 'Did they love each other?'

'How can you tell if two people love each other unless they announce it themselves? Love is like faith, don't you think? I mean, no one should try to guess it. It's proclaimed, else it remains between the individual and Allah. I never came to know if Mohan and Lubna loved each other.' I paused as something occurred to me. Was I jealous of Mohan? Was I relieved to see him die? Zameer looked at me blank-faced. I asked, 'Why should anyone try to guess what was going on between them?'

28

Waqas

Present day

'Amber, I need Rehan's help.'

I rang up Amber as soon as I left Fazal's den of declared computer repairs and undeclared computer data. Yasir said he could return to his home by himself. I took a taxi back to the office while I talked on the phone. 'His office isn't far, you said?'

'Yes, about two hours' drive. What about him?'

I could not hear Amber's voice clearly in the backdrop of the Bollywood song playing on the taxi's radio. With a twist of my right hand, I signalled to the taxi driver, an unshaven young man, in the rear-view mirror to lower the volume. He made a face but did as he was told.

I said to Amber, 'I need you to help me contact him.'

'I can send you his number.'

'You already did, but I want to meet him in person. He didn't sound keen to help me when I contacted him. You see, I haven't seen him in ages. You're going to renew my acquaintance with him. I know you meet him often—regarding professional matters, of course.'

But what if Rehan brought his red tape or tried to degrade me one more time? Let him. With Amber making the request, there was some hope.

'What do you want from him?'

'I'll tell you when we meet. Another thing. I need you to take me in your car. I don't want my boss to know I'm going there. He will shit his pants if he comes to know. I hope you're free. I'll pay for the fuel.'

'Shut up! But I won't be free before lunch. I can pick you up at around two. That is, if Rehan is available for a meeting.'

'Yes, of course.'

'Oh, Waqas, I've something on Arshad Karim. I went to see him. I've met him before at various press conferences, but I had never been to his place.'

'Oh, good. Anything useful you learnt?'

'He lives near the boy's home. He said the boy and Mohan were his friends. The boy visited him a few times in the last month or so. I told you he runs a bookshop. In fact, Hasan and Mohan borrowed books from him.'

'Wait a minute. Is Arshad Karim his real name? Is he known by any other name?'

'Ah, yes. He uses the pen name Arshad Karim. His real name is Karamat Ali. How did you know?'

'I talked to a few people. One of them told me about Karamat Ali. I didn't know he was Arshad Karim. Anyway, what did you find out?'

'Hasan—that's his name, right?—talked to him about the Blasphemy Law. Mr Karamat Ali aka Karim has written a series of articles on why religious parties don't want to let the nation know the truth about the blasphemy issue. This boy read those articles and discussed them with Mr Karim.'

'Interesting. I guess I'll go and see Karamat before we meet.'

* * *

In the daylight, Karamat Ali had ennui on his face, an I-know-all-and-I've-seen-all kind of look.

'Am I a suspect?' he asked, when I showed him my ID, which was necessary as I was in plain clothes. His eyes pierced through his glasses and through me, as we sat in front of his homoeopathy shop. There were several shops in the neighborhood, but the place was quiet. What a treasure trove of knowledge, next to a kebab seller, a fruit merchant and a cobbler, who were discussing a recently released Q mobile phone.

'No, but you knew both the men who were killed in the last three months. We know how Mohan died . . .'

'Do we?' He picked up a teacup from a wooden stool and tapped his cigarette into it, using it as an ashtray.

'What do you mean?'

'Forget it. How can I help you?'

I started with something I was curious about. 'You moved from Islampura to Shanti Nagar months after Mohan and his family did. Why? I'm just curious. You don't have to answer though.'

Once again Karamat took a long time to reply. He appeared to be gauging me. Then he lit another cigarette, took a puff from it, and sat back in his chair, one leg over the other. 'I missed him,' he replied.

The puzzled expression on my face prompted him to explain. 'I had a nice little library in Islampura. Anyone was

free to sit and read. That's all I did most of my life: library and
homoeopathy.'

'You don't count freelance journalism as work?'

'So you know?'

'I'm a policeman.'

'Am I a suspect?'

'I said no. But why are you hiding—why use a pen name?
For safety reasons?'

'Yes. You'll probably understand when I tell you why I
moved.' Once he had seen you meant him no harm, the guy
was good to talk to.

'Go on.'

He issued instructions to the next-door kebab wallah about
his lunch. 'Would you like to join me? His kebabs are the best
I've tried.'

The aroma tempted me, but I declined with a thank you.

He continued, 'About the library. It was close to the local
mosque. Mohan was one of those who visited the library
regularly. I'm not sure what exactly didn't sit well with the
neighbours—my books, Mohan's presence, the way we smoked
till late at night because he said he didn't want his parents to
know or our friendship.'

The electric power returned. Karamat suggested we could
go inside his shop. As he walked to his shop, I noticed he
limped; I remembered Furqan had told me about it. Now, we
sat in the front room, whose two opposite walls were lined
with wooden cupboards crammed with small homoeopathic
medicine bottles from Willmar Schwabe and Masood, with
white or green caps. I could see a bigger room, which housed
shelves and shelves of books like a badly kept second-hand
bookshop.

'The local mullah convinced people that I offered obscene literature to young minds. They asked me to close the library. I refused. Then some people visited me and said we—Mohan and I—were homosexuals. I told them to fuck off and that it was none of their business. But eventually, we had to leave that place. It was unsafe.'

He puffed on his cigarette, exhaled smoke, and continued, 'Do you know what anamorphosis is?'

'No clue. What is it?'

Karamat sat back in his chair and seemed to gather his thoughts. 'It's an art term. I didn't know about it until Mohan introduced me to it. Look it up on Google, Inspector Sahib, and you'll know it's not just an art term. It's a universal reality. You have to view certain things from a specific angle—in a distinct way—to recognize them. Without that, you might see an entirely different reality. Do check it out.'

Everything about Karamat was rough: his unshaven face, his dishevelled hair, his almost croaking voice. But a few minutes with him and the rough edges smoothened into likeability.

'Hmm. I will. Good for this town that you moved here as it can use some bookshops. All I see here are eateries.'

Karamat smirked. 'True. Gluttony is not a sin for mullahs; reading is.'

'It must've been tough, being uprooted from your home.'

'Mohan and his family had to do that a few times.'

'When he was killed, you must have . . .'

'Anything else you want to know?'

His eyes and the tone of his voice told me he didn't want to talk about it. Behind the apparent boredom and aloofness, there was a passionate man.

I asked, 'Do you know that I came to your shop a few days ago?'

He looked at me closely, his interest in me visibly rising a few notches. 'You were investigating me that day?'

'No. I looked for a Meeraji book—any Meeraji book. I knew you were a friend of Hasan and Mohan. By the way, why did you ask me that night if I was from a religious party?'

'A few days before Hasan died, someone—obviously, a mullah—came looking for Meeraji books. He also asked me if I knew Hasan. I brushed him aside.'

'Please tell me about the last few days of Hasan's life. He came to see you, didn't he? Did he discuss any articles you wrote?'

'Yes, the ones on the Blasphemy Law, section 295. I gave the articles to him after Mohan's death. I hoped they would open his eyes.'

'Did he know you're Arshad Karim?'

'I didn't tell him, but I think he guessed.'

'So, did the articles help him?'

'I think so. Maybe they helped him realize that ever since this Blasphemy Law was passed in the 1980s, it has done more damage than service to Islam, that religious parties and individuals have exploited it to settle scores, to target non-Muslims and to gain political mileage. Nothing else.'

Visions of an animal swallowing Abba revisited my head.

He continued, 'I hoped Hasan understood that the Blasphemy Law was part of the obscurantism the religious parties wanted to put in place. An attempt to instil fear in people, so no one would question the issue or the religion. They want to restrict people's vision to the view they see. That's why I titled my articles *Blasphear*, from *blasphemy* and *fear*.'

'Yes. An interesting term you coined. By the way, I saw a book on madrasahs in Hasan's room. Did you give it to him?'

'No. I did not give him that one. He may have got it from somewhere else. Maybe from his college library. Looks like he was carrying out some study.'

'So he *did* borrow other books from you, did he?'

'Yes.'

'I want to understand what he was going through. I believe he was killed because he fell out with the Deen party. Any clue to his state of mind might help. What was he reading?'

Karamat looked at me for a long time. Maybe he was deciding if he could trust me. He limped to the inner room of his shop—I now saw a swagger in his gait—and returned with a book in his hand. 'This is the last book I gave him.'

I leafed through the book and said, 'This is a criticism of Meeraji's poetry. Did he choose it for himself or did you recommend it?'

Karamat put a cigarette in his mouth, where it stayed as he took the book from me, opened it to a certain page, and returned it to me. 'I gave it to him. See the comments on the sidelines of many pages? Those are Mohan's. It's his handwriting. Very neat and respectful. Like he didn't want to defile the book. I wanted Hasan to read these comments.'

'What were they about?'

He flipped a few pages as the book rested on my right palm. 'He has highlighted parts of the book. See this thing he has highlighted in green and commented on? The author wrote: *Meeraji's so-called obscene poetry is quite ordinary, not his best.* His comments on the sides say *True. It's unfair to judge him based on such poetry.*'

'There are other comments from someone else. I don't think this handwriting is Mohan's.' I looked at Karamat.

'Correct. They're comments on Mohan's comments. See?'

'Oh, yes.' They, too, were in a very neat handwriting, and together with Mohan's comments, they made an interesting visual combination.

'Do you know whose comments these are?'

'No.'

'Lubna's. Hasan's sister. Read some of them. Lubna's comments—mostly questions—are on yellow sticky notes pasted inside the book. Mohan's are on green ones. Go on, read.'

I flipped the pages and read the comments.

Yellow: Eroticism is part of Hindu culture. Some say it's a path to divine love. Meeraji's poetry has that element too. You don't have to hide your work.

Green: I don't think this aspect of Meeraji's poetry is particularly important; his erotic poetry isn't his best.

Yellow: Duality or even multiplicity is everywhere in his poetry, especially in this poem about the boat.

Green: Yes. Meeraji perhaps wanted to depict the multiplicity of sentiments and ideas that modern man encounters. Modern man is like a single piece of paper layered repeatedly into a child's boat—fragile and vulnerable. He sails aimlessly on the ocean, only to realize that the whole sojourn was probably a child's game.

Yellow: What is *khala*?

Green: The spiritual void the modern man faces owing to a new awakening, perhaps due to distance from religion or because religion fails to answer all his questions, or owing to the colonial experience.

Yellow: The graves mean a burial of the past?

Green: Well said. The void results from a refusal to accept death or perhaps from waiting for a saviour—who tells people

what to do. The saviour tells the people to accept death and
move on. The acceptance of the void begets its remedy; the void
becomes a kind of womb—it gives birth.

Something happened. Something strange. The conversation I
read took me back decades.

*'Come, look at this magazine, Waqas,' Abba says with a subtle
smile but one that's enough to light up his bearded face.*

*I'm drawing one of my favourite landscapes, an idyllic cottage
near majestic mountains whose peaks are engulfed by clouds. I put
aside my drawing pad and run towards him. His attention is special
to me. He opens the magazine and rolls back the front pages.*

*'Look. These are the questions you asked. Read. They've been
published. They're in print, the things you said. Amazing, isn't it?'*

*Yes, those are the things I had asked Abba: Where does Allah
live? Why did He create pain? Where is paradise? Why was Satan
punished? And his answers to them are there as well, all set down
neatly. We look at each other in amazement. I hug him, hanging
from his neck. He kisses me on the forehead. I take the magazine
from him and sit down to read . . .*

'What happened, Inspector Sahib? You look lost.' Karamat's
voice shook me.

I looked at Karamat, who peered into my eyes. Did he
figure out I was in a trance?

See? his eyes asked, with the glint of a smile.

I said, 'They were communicating through this book.'

'Yes. And I wanted Hasan to read this communication.
I wanted him to understand that theirs was an intellectual
relationship, a profound bond. Questions that were not meant
to challenge but to understand. Mohan and Lubna were not
the way the Deen party told Hasan they were. Mohan was

not a seducer. And I guess Hasan finally understood it. There was a void in him too, a Jungian void that he found religion couldn't fill. And I bet he could relate to Meeraji's *khala*. But by then, he had begun to ask questions, which no religious party likes.'

* * *

'What do you want from Rehan?' Amber asked, when I took the passenger seat, still thinking of Karamat's book, Mohan and Lubna.

'I have the phone numbers of the prime suspect, but he's not answering calls. I'm sure he'll use one of the SIM cards—he's got a few—sooner or later. The intelligence agencies have recently acquired this computerized system that can help them locate a phone in the cellular network, but the police have yet to get hold of it. It's still in its infancy. I'm sure Rehan's department already has one.'

'I guess they do. It's been in Hollywood movies for some time now. When's your police force going to come out of the Stone Age?' She was manoeuvring her car past rickshaws, donkey carts and bicycles, and spoke between pauses.

'Don't get me started on that one.'

'Never mind. Can't your police force arrange transport for an official job? Why aren't you using the police jeep?'

'Because yours is better. It's nice, by the way. Which year?'

Amber didn't enjoy the joke. She never enjoyed anyone's jokes.

'I'm reasonably sure there's a mole in my department—maybe my boss himself. I don't want him to know that I'm seeking the help of the intelligence people.'

'Who's your boss? That asshole Shakir? . . . Behan chod!' Amber let one out for the bicycle that had suddenly swerved in front of her Toyota Vitz—for a moment I thought the expletive was for Shakir, something I would've loved. I recalled how I had cautioned her to mind her language on the few occasions she had visited my family.

'Indeed. You know these police wallahs well by now.'

'Not this one, I confess.' She pointed her thumb at me.

'Was it a joke? I didn't get it.'

'Simple. I underestimated you. You've done well in this case.'

'How generous of you!'

We had left the city and were now on the M-2 motorway. With the heat and the resulting mirage, the highway was like a large frying pan.

'Really. In case you think that's another of my jokes.'

I looked askance at Amber. What was with her? I opened two cans of Coke and handed her one. She continued, 'Thank you. You see, ever since I came to know you . . . hmm . . . I've seen you as an introvert. A rebel too timid to come out. I loved the rebel, not so much the coward. I hoped the rebel was stronger than the coward—when we considered marriage.'

Amber's face was expressionless as she focused on the road ahead and glanced at me occasionally. My eyes turned towards her profile, her neck, her bosom covered in a light-blue kurta, the slight bulge of her belly, and the wrinkles of her trousers, which converged between her thighs. This woman meant so much to me. Everything about her was special—every inch of her body, her manner of speaking, all her expletives and her egoism and obduracy. But now she looked so distant despite being so close.

I said, 'Don't start that again.'

'Oh, goof. I'm not going there. I meant to say I expected something brave from you—whether I was right or wrong to expect is another matter. You didn't meet those expectations. I know, I know. Just listen. Here's what I want to say. In this murder case, I see a new Waqas. Perhaps I never knew the real Waqas—I admit it. But I'm glad to meet the new Waqas.'

'Nice to meet you too.' I tried to play down the solemnity, though it was rare to win admiration from Amber, so I might as well have enjoyed it. 'The new Waqas may not have come out but for some people's help, I guess. There's this boy who's shy but somehow mustered enough conviction to approach me. Not everyone fears religion—I mean, not everyone's scared of being judged by the religious bigots. There's this girl too, Lubna, who loved Mohan, the man who was lynched. I discovered the most amazing story about them. Karamat showed me something fascinating.'

'Oh, really?! Tell me more. I'm a sucker for rebel love stories. We have enough time for long ones.'

'Sure. But let me call Fareeha and update her on my well-being. She's been wanting to talk since this morning. It's good I've been too busy to miss the family.'

29

Furqan

Present day

I had tried to listen to Zameer's instructions carefully because my attention span had always been short. A few minutes in the classroom lecture and my mind would wander off. I usually forgot even the last part of Ammi's shopping list if I chose not to put it in my phone. So I had prodded myself to pay extra attention to Zameer's whispered instructions. Despite that, as I exited from the back door of the madrasah, the place looked nowhere close to what Zameer had described—or what I had in mind. I panicked. I had no idea where to go.

Luckily, Zameer appeared again at the door and whispered a rebuke, 'This way, idiot. I told you to go through the marshy path, in the direction of the sunset. Don't walk on the road or they'll see you.'

Oh yes! There it was! I ran towards the path Zameer had indicated. It descended sharply, and I stumbled down the slope. When I turned around, Zameer had disappeared, and the door was shut. From outside, the madrasah could have been a big barnyard, green moss climbing up its unpainted red-brick wall. I suddenly felt vulnerable and scared. I looked ahead. The place was swampy and stinking. On my right, the dusty land rose to meet the road while ahead and towards the left, the swampland stretched as far as the eyes could reach. Zameer had advised me to disappear in the bushes as quickly as possible so that no one from the road or the madrasah could spot me. In the fading light, I began to wade through wet and green patches of mud, waving aside swarms of mosquitoes.

Not many of them are around. They've gone to the Shab-e-Juma. They seem to have forgotten about you, I recalled Zameer saying.

'Won't they know you helped me escape,' I asked him. 'What will you do?'

He said, 'Don't worry. I have it all worked out. I'll lock the room they imprisoned you in and then go to the mosque where they are congregating for the Shab-e-Juma. I'll stay there for a while before catching a bus to my village. But first, we need to sort out how you're going to escape from this area. This place is miles away from the city. You'll have to walk or run a lot. But they might get you before you go too far.'

Zameer had suggested that my brother could arrange for a car or taxi to fetch me, but Bhai didn't know anyone with a car and, on second thoughts, Zameer also rejected the taxi idea. I told him to text or call Waqas. I thanked Allah for retaining Waqas's phone number in my head. This ability came with my aptitude for storing number patterns in my mind, something I learnt from Ram, who was a great fan of Shakuntala Devi, the so-called human computer. He had explained to me how identifying patterns in number sequences could help one to remember phone numbers: break them up into smaller groups and look for images and associations. For example, 47 should remind me of Pakistan and 442 was my enrolment number in college. Before leaving, I texted Waqas using Zameer's phone, but I received no reply. Zameer said he would call him later and tell him to reach where I was headed. But would Waqas be there? He had so many other things to take care of.

Don't look down, don't look down, I kept telling myself for the sight of green and black excrement, moss and growth was enough to make me retch. I kept my chin tilted up so I wouldn't see the ground. All I was seeing now were the tops of the bushes and through them the evening sky. Sometimes swarms of mosquitoes came buzzing in and cluttered the view. How to escape the stench was an insoluble problem. *You'll get used to it . . . you will . . . you will*. But the spectrum of the odour was so broad—the smell ranged from foul to extremely foul to unbearably foul—that it was hard to get used to. The toilets in my school many years ago were perfumed gardens of paradise in comparison.

What's rising inside my tummy? The dal and the rubbery rotis I had been eating? Will the excrement I had kept inside me because my makeshift toilet was so repulsive now make me throw up? Oh God, my head was spinning. I needed to sit, but where? I couldn't. I threw up, my vomit mixing with the festering green and black marsh. As a sharp pain clasped my innards, the fear of what would ensue gripped me. Dizziness always followed when I vomited. I was going to black out. The bog would swallow me.

30

Waqas

Present day

After more than an hour at the military intelligence people's guardroom, where they sniffed our identities—the well built sergeant's face told me that neither policemen nor journalists were popular with the army people—Amber and I had to sit in their waiting room for a long time because Rehan was in a meeting that took longer than expected, the sergeant informed us. There was no way Amber could reach out to Rehan, so we just sat and fretted.

After a wait of nearly two hours, a Suzuki van drove us for nearly a mile on well laid roads, flanked on both sides by military offices, and took us to Rehan's office. I was meeting him nearly ten years after we had left the university and three years since I had last met him, which was during the 2008 polls. He had developed an ungainly paunch. Like most intelligence officers, he was wearing plain grey trousers and a white shirt, instead of the army uniform. Below the army chief's portrait that adorned the wall behind Rehan was an honour board listing the names of people who had held the post of sector commander of the region. Lieutenant Colonel Rehan Aziz was of course the most recent name. Amber and I sat facing him at his table.

'How can I help you, Waqas?' He asked, after a perfunctory apology for keeping us waiting. A neatly dressed waiter entered and served us tea in beautiful cups and saucers. The tea was a welcome sight because the air conditioner in Rehan's office was freezing me. No load-shedding for the military people, I was sure.

'I've heard the army intelligence has a computerized system for tracking people through their mobile numbers. I hope I can use it for tracking a suspect.'

'We do, but it's for anti-terrorism operations.' He turned a crystal paperweight on its rounded side and spun it on the table.

'Will it groan if you use it to help the police?' Amber quipped, as she placed a hand on the paperweight, halting its spin. 'It's annoying, I'm sorry. The spinning, I mean.'

Rehan and I laughed. Amber's face was expressionless, as she untied and tied her hair. Sitting on her side of the table felt good.

Rehan replied, 'I mentioned it to let you know the rules. But I'd do anything for an old friend.' He phoned someone and issued some instructions. 'My team will ready it in half an hour. I can't allow you inside our lab, for security reasons. But I can have the user interface installed in an area where you're allowed. Who's the guy?'

'A Deen-e-Kamil guy. Wanted for the murder of a boy. He's missing; I've checked the address that I could dig out. In a way, this case fits into your terrorism domain—in case your bosses ask, I mean.'

'Don't worry about my bosses. I've heard of the case. Are you sure he's the one, the Deen guy?' He leaned back in his swivel chair and stretched, resting his head on the palms of his intertwined hands.

'Reasonably sure.'

When the system was ready, Rehan led us to another room, a big hall with young men and women sitting in front of computer screens, the whole place looking like a high-tech software house. He took us to a big screen on a wall on the right.

'We call it the LIAS, which means location information and analysis system. Do you have the phone number, Waqas?'

I gave him a piece of paper with Akbar's contact numbers. Rehan handed it to a man sitting in front of the big screen—a young man in neat trousers, a shirt and a necktie. He entered the numbers one by one using a keyboard. The screen showed an aerial view of some place. As the computer guy tapped some keys on the keyboard, the view changed slowly and the screen zoomed out to show the country's map. Then the view travelled southward and zoomed in on a place south-east of Multan.

'Your man is or was in Bahawalpur,' Rehan announced.

'Was?' I asked.

'It's his last recorded location—the last time his phone was connected—which may be fairly recent or whenever he shut down his phone.'

'Wow! I hadn't believed it when I first heard about this software, but it's working. Does it show the exact location?' I asked, my eyes glued to the screen.

'Unfortunately, it doesn't. It shows the base station, the cellular system tower to which your man's mobile phone is connected at that moment. This means he could be anywhere within a few kilometers of this place here. See this dot? That's the tower.'

'What do you guys do after this, after you've traced your target this far?'

'Good question. Once we've obtained this piece of info about the location, we follow it up by sending a team with some more direction-finding equipment to the cell's coverage area. They create a fake BTS—a fake cellular tower, you can say—to which the target's phone is hooked. From this fake BTS, they can find the direction and hopefully the exact location.'

'You can track any number anywhere? So nobody's hidden from you?' Amber asked, as we stood and watched.

'Yes,' Rehan smiled mischievously. Suddenly, I recalled his chutzpah of ten years ago. It was still there but it didn't go well with an unhealthy, overweight face. 'I know what you're hinting at. The privacy, the human rights issues and all that blah blah. Am I right?'

'I believe it's an important issue.'

'Maybe. But crime fighting is not fair game. If you want us to catch the bad guys, spare us these tears over human rights.'

'He's right,' I said, looking at Amber. 'But the police must also have this tool. If you'll let us have it, you guys can focus on the borders.'

'I have my doubts. But if you're so sure, go and get it. People are making such software and, with the government's nod, you can make the mobile service providers give you the data. It needs some patience, though, and lots of coordination. Sometimes the target is smart and switches off his mobile phone. You must wait till he's on air. Also, you must make sure you're not observable when you create a fake BTS. I'm not so sure if the police are capable of all this.' Rehan did not try to hide his low opinion of the police's literacy level.

'That's for another day. For now, I need help with catching this man.'

'I've reduced your search space from hundreds of thousands of kilometres to a few kilometres.'

'Yes, I think I can manage the rest. But there's another issue. He's a Deen guy. My bosses will think a thousand times before letting me have him. The army has no such problems, does it?'

'Are you asking me to authorize his arrest?'

'No. I want to know how much backing the Deen think they have from the army.'

'None. The Deen is not on our radar. We won't want to meddle in their business unnecessarily. And I guess the Deen won't throw tantrums. They're still finding their feet. The blasphemy lynching might have earned them a lot of awe from public and religious parties, but they won't find sympathizers for a murderer—if you're sure it's a murder.'

'I'm positive.'

'But if I were you, I'd stay away from this business. For obvious reasons. The public can turn into savages on the blasphemy issue. And army or no army, the Deen know how to exploit public sentiments. So I'd be very scared, to be honest.'

'Waqas is not scared,' Amber said, before I could. 'And that's what we need here. Someone who's not scared.'

I'd never thought this meeting would be a victory for me on more than one front. But as Amber and I returned to her car, something else played on my mind. I couldn't lay a hand on my target before Furqan was free. When we collected our phones and ID cards from the guardroom, I saw countless missed calls from an unknown number.

31

Furqan

Present day

No, no, no. I needed more willpower. Control it, control it. I couldn't give in to something happening inside my tummy. The enemy was inside me. I could fight it. Yes, I could. I was doing it for Mohan and Hasan. Those two lost their lives. I needed to do it for Lubna or she would continue to blame herself.

The nausea began to subside. Oh, what a relief, despite the bitter taste in my mouth!

As I pushed aside the tall bushes that scraped my face, how I wished I could walk towards the nearest road, which was sometimes visible through the grass. But Zameer had warned me: the path will be muddy, but it's better than taking the road as they will spot you there. Many a time, I slipped or my feet sank in what was perhaps a bog. Then I would pull myself up and slog on.

What a relief it was to see the other side of the swamp! But so beset was I with doubts and fears that I wondered whether I was at the right place. *When you reach the other side of the swamp, the police inspector will be there—if he is on time. Wait for him there, on the other side. Stay hidden in the bushes till you see him,* Zameer had instructed. Still hidden, I tried to look for Waqas's jeep. It was so dark now I couldn't figure out the make or shape of the few cars that passed by.

The vehicle parked on the opposite side of the road could have been Waqas's. I emerged from the bushes and crawled on all fours up the dirt track leading to the road. A street hawker pushing an empty cart after a long day's work gawked at me. My appearance was certainly like that of a convict who had just escaped from prison. I looked at the vehicle again. It was a jeep alright, but it wasn't Waqas's. It looked too good to be true anyway.

I panicked again as the headlights of the jeep showed two men walking towards me. With bearded faces, prayer caps, white kameez and shin-length shalwars, they were surely from the madrasah. I thought of running the other way, but my legs were so heavy with the sticky mud I could hardly walk. I looked back. The two men had quickened their pace after the jeep overtook them and disappeared. They were certainly after me. While I resigned myself to my fate, I hoped they had not gotten hold of Zameer, who had to catch a bus to his village. It had been more than an hour since I left the madrasah. Zameer should have already gotten away.

I turned around to look back again. Behind the two men, who were now less than twenty yards away, another vehicle appeared. Perhaps they would not grab me when the car—or whatever it was—was around. I trudged a few steps away to buy more time. Realizing they needed to be quick, the two men began to run towards me.

'Come here! Who are you?' one of them shouted as they nearly reached me—maybe ten yards away.

In desperation, I glanced towards the street hawker, who had travelled some way down the road, and shouted, 'Please help me!' My voice could hardly rise above the crickets' screeching chirps that had gelled with the surroundings.

Meanwhile, the vehicle, a Toyota Vitz—silver–grey perhaps, for the dust had camouflaged its colour and the fading light and absence of my glasses added another layer of obscurity—had neared. I feared that it, too, might be from the madrasah. Turning around, I noticed that a woman was driving it and a man was sitting in the passenger seat. It stopped behind the two men, who turned around to face the man rushing out of the car.

'Let him go!' The voice, deep and composed yet commanding, was Waqas's.

32

Waqas

Present day

'So, Mr Ashraf Mughal, will you tell me where I can find Mr Akbar Mughal?' I asked slowly, leaning back in my office chair. Ashraf sat in a chair facing me. He didn't lean backward but appeared relaxed. I continued, 'Or should I call him Nadeem or Qadir?'

When Ashraf did not say anything, I added, 'He even looks like you, only healthier. When I saw his sketch which Hasan's sister made, I immediately felt I had seen the face, but could not recall where.'

'Sir, I have no idea what you're talking about.' Ashraf's face was expressionless. He sat with his forearms on his thighs and hands clasped together. It was difficult to decide if he was amused, surprised, worried or scared. But he was always like this. Even in moments of crisis, his face remained expressionless, as if he were in a stupor.

'So you say you don't have a brother named Akbar. Let's forget it for a while. Do you even deny that, with the collusion of Mr Naveed of Suprema Lab, you faked an autopsy report to make it appear that Hasan's body was normal—pathologically speaking—at the time of hanging?'

Outside, the weather had changed within minutes. Clouds had amassed, signs of the first rain of the summer. It was eight in the evening and everyone in the police station, other than the night shift people, had packed up. Only Ashraf and I sat in my office.

I continued, 'By the way, this conversation isn't recorded. You can check my pockets, the drawers, anything. Anything you say now will not be used against you in a court of law. So go ahead, speak freely.'

Ashraf still had the stupor-like calmness on his face. Or perhaps he was trying to phrase his words.

I decided to go on. 'Will you even deny that you manipulated events—even misquoted SHO Sahib—to arrange for Mohan's release from jail and informed your Deen brothers so they could have their way with him? And that you manipulated the police records of your brother's wrongdoings so he would never be arrested for any of his crimes?'

When Ashraf didn't speak, I went on. 'Let's revisit Hasan's last few days. Or more importantly, let's go back even earlier. Why was Mohan targeted? What did he say or do?'

'Do you know what filth he was uttering?' Ashraf finally spoke, raising his eyes from his lap to look at me. 'He talked about the unification of religions, that all religions give the same message. Would any respectable Muslim allow Islam to be placed on the same pedestal as Hinduism? Those liberals who let this happen are dishonourable. If we leave it to them, Islam will be in danger. That's what we're waging a jihad for.'

'So Mohan was killed for voicing thoughts that were contrary to Islam, according to you?'

'What else, sir? Don't you understand?'

'I'm not going to comment on anything. I'm just trying to understand why Mohan was lynched. Any other charges against him?'

'Do you know he wanted to marry a Muslim woman—that boy Hasan's sister? And the whole family was asleep. Only the boy had the scruples to do something about it.'

'Did Hasan talk to you guys about it? Or did you put it in his head?'

'We had to. We informed him about what was going on in the Hindu man's classroom. Hasan wouldn't have grasped what was going to happen if we hadn't done something.'

'So you and your party decided to do *something* about it. And you were sure—despite being a policeman yourself—that the police and the judicial system wouldn't mete out justice. So you took it upon yourself to adjudicate on the matter. Am I right? You who say that the system must be allowed to run smoothly? By the way, Mohan never said he wanted to marry her, right?'

For a while, a shadow of doubt lingered on his face.

Outside, the clouds' muffled rumbling had changed to thunder, and the winds began to blow, slamming the doors and windows open and shut. Expectedly, the electricity went off, leaving me and Ashraf in complete darkness. I switched on the torch in my mobile phone, and in its soft glow, I rose and lit the gas lamp.

Returning to my chair, I said, 'Seeing clearly is the most important thing. We can sit without the fan for a while, especially in this windy weather, but light is particularly

important, isn't it? It's when we're completely in the dark that
we realize how important seeing is. Even the mosquitoes can be
tackled.' I clapped my hands to trap a mosquito between them,
but it buzzed away. 'But sometimes people don't even realize
they're in the dark. Worse, sometimes they don't realize that
others might not see something as they see it.'

Ashraf was quiet. I continued, 'Did you know that a non-
Muslim can't be killed as a punishment for blasphemy? That's
what Imam Abu Hanifa, the founder of one of the most
respected schools of thought, said.'

Ashraf was silent, but I could see he was seething inside. I
continued, 'In fact, *Mukhtasar al Tahawi* . . . hmm . . . which
was written by the founder of another school, Imam Abu
Ja'afer—I'm sure you know about all these better than I do—
prescribes a verbal warning as an appropriate punishment for a
non-Muslim offender. Nothing more than that.'

I opened my table drawer and took a printout from it. *"If a
non-Muslim commits blasphemy, he will be given a verbal warning.
If he repeats the offense, he will be punished but not killed."* I'm
reading from an article by Mr Arshad Karim, who did a good
bit of research on the blasphemy issue. Did I tell you this article
helped me in another way: in detecting that your copy of the
autopsy report was fake? This might be a sign of the veracity
of this article: something that leads to the truth must itself be
true.'

I paused and added, 'I don't believe in superstitious stuff,
but I thought you might be impressed. Did you know I
thought Shakir was the mole, but then I realized he knew shit
about computers. Only you could've tampered with computer
documents in this thana, right? *Wasn't it obvious*, I asked myself
when I realized it was you.'

'Sir, one or two articles don't make you a scholar of Islam. To understand Islam, you have to do years of hard work.'

'I thought it was quite simple. Maybe someone's interested in making it obscure.'

'Sir, do you have any idea where Islam is headed these days? It's in danger. If we don't come forward to protect it, its enemies will defile it. They will obliterate it! They're out to destroy it. The whole world—Hindus, Jews, Christians and atheists—have united against Islam. They're hatching conspiracies against it. Do you think you can argue with them and convince them? No, you can't.'

'So the only option is to kill them?'

'Of course. We'll do anything to protect Islam.'

'Okay. Let's talk about Hasan again. Why was he killed? Because he was reading the same article from which I quoted?'

'Yes. Not only that. He began to talk about it. He asked questions about it. Even other students noticed his stupid questions. *Deeni* matters are not for everyone to understand. Don't you see what madness will result if everyone tries to interpret Islam? If we allow that, we will be letting the secular fascists into the citadel of Islam.'

I leaned forward and continued in my patient way, 'But he was an innocent boy. He wanted to understand things. And he had complete trust in you guys. Why else would he have talked about it openly? Because he thought you guys would help him in his search for the truth. And you people killed him? Do you kill people who ask questions?'

'Yes, if stupidity borders on blasphemy, for which the only punishment is death.'

I leaned back again, sighed loudly, and asked, 'Do you also know blasphemy is a pardonable offense? Did you people offer Mohan, and later Hasan, the chance to seek forgiveness?'

'Sir, liberals like you have made a joke of Islam. If we permit what you're saying—letting people debate Islam and offering them chances to apologize—they would be hurling blasphemies at Islam and seeking pardon whenever they're held answerable.'

A murmuring rain had quietly replaced the thunder. With that, a cool breeze began to enter the room. I walked towards the window and opened it wider. Raindrops pattered on the metalware at the blacksmith's behind my office. The cacophony sounded like music for it announced a respite from the heat.

'There's nothing better than fresh, cool air in summer.' I sat down. 'Ashraf, if liberalism would lead to madness, what will your obscurantism lead to? It has already brought us to a world fraught with fear and insecurity. Have you ever considered that? And did you try to help Hasan to understand? Did you try to convince him?'

'We did. Many of us did. But this bug ate away at him. We knew the seeds of doubt had been sown. Doubt is the biggest enemy of faith. Faith is supposed to be blind.'

'So you would prefer to be blind and remain in the dark, right? Anyway, let's come to the things that matter. Do you confess that you perpetrated the crimes I mentioned? Do you have a brother who you've tried to protect from punishment? Did you try to manipulate the events so they would lead to Mohan's lynching? Did you try to fake the autopsy report?'

'You're not going to get anything out of this, sir. You don't know how strong our party is. I suggest you don't meddle in our party's business. Let's close this case. I suggest this for your safety.'

'For your information, Akbar has already been captured. Picked up in Bahawalpur. Guess by whom? The army. He has confessed to killing Hasan and to his role in instigating Mohan's lynching. Try calling him if you don't believe me. I'm sure you have covert numbers for communication. When the army has had enough of him, they'll hand him over—whatever's left of him—to the police. You know how our army brethren operate, don't you?' No harm in exaggerating the army's role in Akbar's capture.

Ashraf's otherwise calm and expressionless face became creased with a few lines. I decided not to relent. 'For once, you need to be honest about what you're going to do. I'm sure Allah has given you no licence to be deceptive. So come clean and let me know what you're going to do and I'll tell you what my plan is. Here are the options: one, if you agree and start recording your statement admitting everything we've talked about, I'll let the law take its course; two, if you refuse to cooperate or play hanky-panky at a later stage, I'll shoot you. And you know how easy it is to fake encounters. *He was trying to run away*, I'll tell my bosses. For now, you're under arrest.'

As the rain settled to a steady rhythm and the winds abated, the electric power returned. I got up and blew out the gaslight. Sitting again, I asked, 'Shall I switch on my voice recorder?'

* * *

'I want to thank you for your cooperation, Furqan,' I said.

Furqan and I sat side by side on a bench in the same park where we had talked a few days ago.

It had been raining on and off for the last few days, suggesting the onset of an early monsoon. The weather was turning humid, but occasional gales of wind left some comfort in their wake. The ground and the little grass growing there were wet from the overnight rain. Families and groups of men were slowly pouring in after their dinner to make the most of what the evening had to offer.

'As I said the other day, I wouldn't have volunteered to help if you weren't in charge of the case. What about the case? What do you think will happen?'

'I can't say what the court's verdict will be, but I consider it a success that we were able to arrest three of the Deen men, although after some behind-the-door deals.'

The clouds gurgled. I looked at the sky and said, 'I prefer the monsoon to summer. It's more humid, which is worse than the heat, but the monsoon gives you hope. A spell of rain is always around the corner.'

'Sometimes the humidity kills. But yes, I agree with you.'

'Akbar has been apprehended and will be tried for murder and for inciting the public to break into rioting that resulted in Mohan's death. Akbar's partner-in-crime, another man from the party who helped him kill Hasan, was also apprehended and will be similarly tried. Ashraf will be tried for obstructing the course of law on several occasions, including the tampering of Hasan's autopsy report, Mohan's arrest and his subsequent release from jail. The least he will get is dismissal from the service but spending a few years in jail is likely. The Deen has agreed to disown the three.'

'That's wonderful.'

'Not really. The legal road is narrow and slippery, and we're not sure where it will lead. Ashraf might change his statement. There will be pressure from other religious parties. Justice is a bridge too far in our country.' The boy looked disappointed. 'But don't worry, we took a step most people wouldn't have taken. Someone might continue this work. Writers will write, people like you will speak out, a good lawyer might uphold the law.'

'*Insha Allah!*'

'There's something more. The Deen wanted something in return for surrendering their men meekly. In return, DSP Sahib and his bosses assured them I would be dismissed from service. He has requested his bosses to change the dismissal to early retirement. He told me it was best for everyone—for me and the police department—that I retire,' I said, laughing.

'You're leaving the police force?' Furqan nearly jumped forward and turned towards me.

'Chill. We've killed two birds with one stone, as they say. I wanted to leave the police force anyway. My wife was not happy either. DSP Sahib knew my plans. He just made it look like he has fired me.' I smiled.

'What are you going to do now?'

'A few friends in my village have recently opened a college, where they need faculty. Remember I told you I have a master's degree in sociology? I guess it qualifies me for a teaching job. My experience with the police will also come in handy. What do you think?'

'Sounds good. Do you think you'll be good at an instructional job? Can't visualize a policeman in the teacher's role.' Furqan sat back and laughed.

'Don't know if I'll be good or not, but I'm sure I'll enjoy it.'

'Mohan used to say that if you're enjoying a job, you'll certainly do well in it. I wish you luck.'

* * *

A few months later, Furqan called me on the phone and said, 'I read an article in *The Breaking News* today and thought I should call. It's full of praises for you—all well deserved.'

'The newspaper correspondent is a friend, so she exaggerated things. By the way, she's the woman whose car you messed up the day you escaped from the Deen prison. She said the smell did not leave the car even after weeks.' I laughed.

'I'm so sorry. I can imagine the filth I carried to the back seat of her car. I was covered with excrement. Can you apologize to her for me?'

'Don't worry about it.'

Amber's article brought a smile to my face. Not only did Fareeha feel proud of me, some of my colleagues at my new workplace said they were impressed. And the best part was when Ms Nida called to congratulate me. The article, if I read the subtext correctly, said I was able to take some pride with me when leaving the police. Should she have mentioned Abba? I wasn't sure. I continued, 'But it's good of you to call. It's been a while.'

Roshni came over and jumped onto my lap. She had quarrelled with her brothers and needed a sanctuary, which Fareeha couldn't provide as she was preparing tea. She had been busy with another move. I promised her this would be our last for some years to come and we could invest in some home décor too. She and the kids were delighted to have a big lawn and a guava tree outside our new home.

'Yes, the college reopened and I suddenly found myself with some workload. Can I ask you something?'

'Sure.'

There was a distinct pause before Furqan spoke, 'The article mentions how you vindicated your father through this case. Was he . . .?'

'I didn't tell you my Abba was also lynched on blasphemy charges—decades ago, when I was still a child.' I told him briefly about it.

There was another long pause at the other end. 'I'm sorry to hear about it.' His voice sounded faint.

'It's okay. How's the college? Has Lubna—Hasan's sister—joined it? The article mentions it.'

'Yes. This is the other news I wanted to break to you. Lubna applied for the post vacated by Mohan, and the college hired her—of course provisionally as she has yet to finish her Master's. The college has tasked her with establishing the Fine Arts department. Isn't this great? Mohan's work will be completed.' Furqan's voice regained some of its initial excitement.

'Yes. I think that's good. Art connects us. We thought Mohan's absence would be felt and there'd be no one to fill the void. But here's Lubna doing the brave thing. I wish her luck. I hope she's not taking undue risks.'

'*Insha Allah*, she will be fine.' Furqan spoke with conviction. 'And Waqas Bhai, talking about filling the void, I think you've partly filled the void left by Mohan's death—for me at least. That's what I felt when I met you.'

'That's so generous of you. Thank you.'

'And you know what? Lubna told me she would name the department after Mohan—the Mohan Lal Department of Fine Arts. But she forbade Ram and me from telling anyone just yet.'

'That's great! How's Ram? I hope he's back to life and his studies.'

'Yes, he is. He's good. The two of us visit Lubna's office sometimes—often, in fact—and talk about Mohan.'

I wanted to know how the Talaba reacted to Lubna's hiring. But I decided it was not a good time to talk about fears. Fears would remain, but we had to look forward to an enlightened future. I brushed back Roshni's curls as I spoke.

'Did you know you were my inspiration, Furqan?' I asked.

A pause at the other end. 'No, I didn't. How so?'

'I wanted to help Abba, to absolve him of the stain that was on him—to make people acknowledge that he didn't do anything wrong. But my own family opposed it. For my own safety, I know. They told me to keep quiet. Even as I grew up, the fear in me didn't go away. I didn't have the conviction that I could do it. Then you reached out to me. If you had not, we might not have come this far.'

'Thanks. I forgot to tell you that Lubna mentioned you one day.' Furqan bubbled with excitement now. 'She said she never expected any police officer to do all that you did.'

'To be honest, I was also inspired by her and Mohan.'

'How's that?'

'While I was in Shanti Nagar, I went to see Karamat. He showed me a book on Meeraji in which the two—Lubna and Mohan—had exchanged notes—pretty comments on sticky notes. The colours—yellow and green—the innocence, and the thirst for knowledge in Lubna's questions. The erudition in Mohan's replies. All these sounded so inspirational—a world of intellect, understanding, love. Love that's cerebral, emotional and spiritual at the same time. Karamat said—and I agreed—it moved Hasan. He read it a few days before his death—the notes, I mean.'

'Beautiful. But I wish Hasan had realized this earlier. I'll go and look at the book at Karamat Bhai's.'

'The book and the notes worked for me in another way. I recalled my question–answer sessions with Abba—something I had forgotten. He was a busy man, but whenever I asked him questions—about Allah, about good and evil, about the world as I saw it—he would listen with patience, putting aside his work—he used to write for religious magazines. I could see my questions were important for him. I noticed one day that he noted down my questions—he asked me to repeat some of them sometimes.'

'Interesting.'

'Yes. He later showed me a magazine in which he had recorded my questions and their answers. He titled the article *A child's understanding of the world*. I was delighted, of course; it was flattering. But the child that I was, I forgot it soon. Lubna's and Mohan's notes reminded me of that phase of my life. I contacted Bhai Jaan—my elder brother—to ask if he still had the magazine with him. And yes, he still had it in his carton, along with others. He had done well to preserve them against termites and bugs.'

I paused. I didn't tell Furqan, but maybe I should have. Those magazines changed my opinion about Bhai Jaan. Fareeha smiled at me as she entered the veranda and set the evening tea—homemade biscuits and carrot cake. Wasif and Rameez raced to reach the table. Roshni showed them how she had already won the first prize by holding out a biscuit.

I continued, 'When I read those questions and answers again, I went back to my childhood. How beautifully and simply Abba wrote. I felt he was still there with me. He is. Bhai Jaan allowed me to take all of Abba's magazines with me. They will stay with me forever. I'm so thankful to Bhai Jaan for taking care of them.'

There was silence at the other end, but Furqan's breathing told me he was still there. Did he just sniffle away his tears?

'I'll take photos of those pages of the book you mentioned and show them to Lubna. She will treasure them.'

'I'm sure she already has them. I'm a bit worried for her, though. She will face stiff resistance to what she has set out to

do. I think she needs to tread carefully.' Finally, the fear came
out. Too much happiness made one feel insecure. Did Meeraji
fear happiness for the same reason?

'She says she doesn't care. She's past this fear.'

I paused a long time as I ran my fingers through Roshni's
hair, her head resting on my chest. 'I see. I appreciate that. I,
too, am past this fear—nearly. With the Deen party aware of
my role in the investigation, I had some fear in my heart. I was
looking over my shoulder. But Lubna's fearlessness is rubbing
off on me—already. You know, all of us—the people who want
to speak against religious bigotry—are like lonely swimmers
tossing around in an ocean—or a quagmire.'

'A kind of bog that sucks you in.'

'Exactly. Initially, everywhere we look we see no one who
can help us. We think we are too few, too far from anyone like
us. That we will sink or will remain distant and will be eaten
by sharks. We don't know that there are many more like us,
although they are just beneath the surface. Those who are afraid
to be visible. We must reach out to each other and all others,
and soon there'll be more and more of us who'll be willing to
connect. And our connection will be through books and arts
and literature. If we don't, as time passes, there'll be fewer and
fewer of us, increasingly scared to speak out or reach out.'

'So beautifully articulated, Waqas Bhai. You've spoken like
a true teacher.'

Glossary of Urdu and Other Non-English Words and Abbreviations

Abba or Abbu	Father
Ammi, Amma, or Ma	Mother
ASI	Assistant sub-inspector
Assalam-o-alaikum	Muslim words of greeting, meaning 'Peace be upon you'; often shortened to *salam*
Badr	A place in Saudi Arabia where, in AD 624, Muslims led by Prophet Muhammad won a war against the Meccans despite being outnumbered
Bandar	Monkey
Barfi	A white-coloured confection made of milk and sugar, served in the form of thin slices
Behan chod	Sister-fucker
Beta	Son
Bhabhi	Sister-in-law or brother's wife
Bhai	Brother

Bhangi	A drug addict; also a lower caste person usually hired as a sweeper
Chacha	Uncle
Dada	Grandfather
Dadi	Grandmother; also modified to Dadu in this book
Danish	Wise
Deen	Religion
Deeni	Related to religion
Dhoti	A loose garment, like a sarong, which is wrapped around the legs and tied into a knot around the waist
DSP	Deputy superintendent of police
Dua	Prayer of supplication, forgiveness or petition to Allah
Dupatta	A woman's long, flowing scarf, considered a sign of modesty
Eid	Muslim festival in the months of Shawwal and Dhu al Hajj.
Fiqah	Islamic jurisprudence
Gulab jamun	A dark-coloured confection in the form of dough balls
Hadith	A collection of Islamic traditions containing sayings of the Prophet Muhammad
Halwa	One of a wide variety of confections, usually in the form of a thick paste
Hazrat	A title used to honour a person; literally translates to 'presence'
Insha Allah	Arabic words meaning 'If Allah is willing'
Isha	Muslims' night prayer
Jaan	Dear; literally meaning 'life'
Jamadar	A cleaner or sanitary worker

Ji or Jee	A suffix used with someone's name to show respect
Jihad	Holy war
Kada	House
Kameez	A shirt, especially one worn with a shalwar (see below)
Kamil	Perfect
Karahi	A deep, circular metal utensil; also a name for a meat dish
Khaddar	A handspun and woven natural fibre cloth
Khala	Vacuum or void
Khilafat	Islamic leadership/government, after the death of Prophet Muhammad, headed by a khalifa (caliph)
Laddoo	A confection in the form of flour balls
Lassi	A sweet or salty drink made by churning yoghurt
Maulvi or Maulana	A Muslim scholar who is well versed in Islamic knowledge
Mela	Festival or fair
Mithai	Sweets, sweet dishes or desserts
Na'at	A hymn read or sung in the praise of Prophet Muhammad
Nafal	Voluntary namaz of Muslims (see below)
Namanzoor	Not accepted
Namaz	One of the five mandatory, daily prayers of Muslims
Nazim	An elected official in a Muslim religious party
Oye	An informal word for hey or listen
Paan	Betel leaves flavoured with spices, chewed by people
Pooja	Hindi word for worship

Rooh	Soul or spirit
Sahib	Mister; often used to address a man with respect
Samosa	Pastry filled with spiced vegetables, usually potatoes, or meat
Shab-e-Juma	Thursday night (Friday night in the Islamic calendar) when religious groups hold sermons and proselytizing sessions
Shalwar	Loose-fitting trousers worn in combination with a tunic
Shirk	The belief that someone other than Allah is worthy of worship
SHO	Station house officer (of police)
Subhan Allah	Glory to Allah
Surkha	A term often used to refer to a follower of Communism. From *surkh*, meaning red.
Tablighi	One engaged in the proselytizing of Islam
Tafseer	Critical interpretation of the Quran
Talaba	Plural of talib, meaning students
Tauba	Word used to seek forgiveness from Allah; also an expression of shock
Thana	Police station
Wallah	A word used to imply association e.g., chai wallah means one associated with the tea business
Yaar	An informal word to address one's friend
Zuhr	Muslims' noon prayer

Acknowledgements

This is my first novel and its publication was not possible without the help of my family, many friends and the people I came to know while working on it.

Bundles of thanks to Suhail Mathur, my literary agent, and his team, The Book Bakers, for making this dream become a reality. Special thanks to Archana Nathan and Saloni Mital, the editors with Penguin Random House India, for their constructive feedback and meticulous editing of the manuscript.

The people I owe gratitude to include those who critiqued various drafts of the manuscripts. Maahliqa Qureishi read the first two drafts and provided me the much-needed initial guidance; at such a youthful age, she possesses remarkable understanding of the craft of novel writing. Oliwia Walkowicz's professional critiques helped me improve the subsequent two drafts. Debi Goodwin was the first person whose feedback and encouragement made me believe in my novel. Nikita Gupta and Tayyba Maya Kanwal provided useful critique. Abrar Akber not only volunteered to read the manuscript, but also provided pertinent comments and remained a source of motivation throughout the journey of this novel. Wendy Knepper's know-how and guidance helped me immensely at various stages of writing. Joanne Johnston, Anna Evanson, Aamir Naved, Irfan Fazal, Wahab Kashmiri and Mahmood Ahmed read parts of the manuscript and their comments were helpful too. I am thankful to all of them.

Mohammed Hanif's words of advice were invaluable for me. I am grateful to him and to Harris Khalique and Saba Naqvi for their comments on the final draft. I am also grateful to Nasir Abbas Nayyar for his book and the discussions on Meeraji. I owe special gratitude to Arafat Mazhar for his articles in the daily *Dawn*; I have never met him but his invaluable research on blasphemy was one of the sources of inspiration for this novel.

Finally, I am thankful to my wife, Tallat, my son, Saalaar and my daughter, Soha, for always standing by me; Soha's enthusiasm especially inspired me to keep going despite several rejections from literary agents.

Notes on Urdu Poetry and Translations

All translations of Urdu poetry in this novel are my own. Most poetry, and especially that of Meeraji and N M Rashid, two stalwarts of modern Urdu poetry, remains open to interpretation. Therefore, some readers might find my translations debatable or even incorrect, for which I apologize in advance. My understanding of Meeraji's poetry owes a great deal to Nasir Abbas Nayyar's book (*Uss Ko Ik Shakhs Samajhna Tau Munasib Hi Nahi*). I iterate that if I misinterpreted the poetry, the shortcoming is mine and not Nayyar Sahib's.

Scan QR code to access the
Penguin Random House India website